THE GAME CALLED
REVOLUTION

Scott Kinkade

Thanks for your
money! :)

Scott Kinkade

THE GAME CALLED REVOLUTION

Copyright © 2011 by Scott Kinkade.

First published April 2012.

ISBN: 978-1-7374646-1-7

Cover by Ramon Macairap (monmacairap@gmail.com).

For Don Odom, and his appreciation of history.

Thanks also to the guys who shared with me their knowledge of France, its history and language.

PART I
Le début des ennuis
(The Beginning of the Trouble)

Paris, France, July 14, 1789 (Infini Calendar), 9:50 a.m.
Eight ramparts eighty feet tall. A large moat. Steam cannons. The Bastille was a veritable fortress within the city of Paris.

Jacques du Chard, one of only a few prisoners left within the Bastille, lounged on his bed. With his sandy-brown hair, simple shirt and grey leggings, the young man did not stand out at all.

At that moment it was deathly quiet within the chamber occupied only by him and five other empty cells; the few guards who kept watch over the room had left about ten minutes ago to go welcome some visitors. There weren't even any rats scurrying about; contrary to popular belief, the prison was not infested with them.

His thoughts kept going back to that strange message that had appeared on the walls of the adjacent cell the other day. What did it mean? All he knew was that that cell belonged to the Marquis de Sade until just recently. None of the guards would tell him anything; they were keeping their mouths carefully shut.

The whole thing was very interesting.

The door of the chamber opened. Four people entered the room. He couldn't get a good look at them until they arrived in the candle-lit center of the chamber. At the head of the group was the Marquis de Launay, the governor of the Bastille, whom the prisoner was familiar with. Jacques would have recognized his fancy brown suit embroidered in gold, along with his white hair that hung limply off either side of his head, anywhere.

The other three were wearing form-fitting suits of silver armor. Jacques recognized them as members of the Ordre de la Tradition, a special group of knights—along with various other exceptionally talented individuals—who had been recognized by the king of France for outstanding service in the military, and who answered only to him. They embodied the knightly traditions of honor, discipline, and chivalry, which meant they did not use guns—only bladed melee weapons. Knights were very rare nowadays, but these individuals were allowed to wear suits of armor made from *irodium*, a revolutionary metal developed by the English. Irodium was lightweight, easy to move in, and could withstand a large amount of punishment (but was very expensive to manufacture). The two larger knights each carried a sheathed broadsword at his side.

A female voice said, "It's dark in here."

The voice came from the knight in the center who was somewhat shorter and slenderer than the ones flanking her. Rather than the broadsword of her larger counterparts, she carried a rapier with a golden hilt bearing the image of a radiant face, in honor of the Sun King Louis XIV (predecessor of the current monarch of France).

She—along with her two subordinates—stepped forward into the light. She didn't look to be older than thirty years of age; she could have even been the same age as him. Her auburn hair fell to the middle of her back in a braided tail, and Jacques noted the purple eye patch over her left eye, along with the flowing purple skirt which opened around the middle of her irodium leggings. Her radiant skin was especially striking to Jacques.

"Excuse me, mademoiselle," he said. "Might you be the one they call 'Jeanne la Juste'?"

***

She looked at him with indifference for a moment, and then responded, "Yes. My name is Jeanne de Fleur. I'm a knight with the Ordre de la Tradition."

"Ah, I thought so. You are well known among the

Third Estate." The Estates General was composed of nobility, clergy, and commoners, respectively. "Ah, but you're supposed to call them the National Assembly now, yes?" The commoners had recently broken away from the other two Estates—with whom they had long been at odds— and declared themselves the National Assembly (although a few members of the clergy and nobility joined them).

Talkative one, isn't he? she thought to herself. "Actually, last week they became the National Constituent Assembly," Jeanne said. She then turned to de Launay. "Where is this message you spoke of?"

"It is in the cell to the left of the forger's there."

He escorted the three knights into the cell next to Jacques'. It was a spacious cell, easily twice as large as the others and clearly meant for someone of importance. The bed in the cell was also a cut above those normally given to prisoners.

On the wall above the bed there was a series of words carved into the wall: "On July 14 the greatest joke will be told."

"And you believe this was written by Monsieur Donatien Alphonse François, the Marquis de Sade?" Jeanne asked upon examining it.

"No one else has occupied this cell since the Marquis was transferred out ten days ago," de Launay said.

"Didn't you question him about it before he was transferred?" Jeanne said.

The governor shook his head. "It didn't appear until yesterday."

"Well, then it couldn't have been him," said the gruff voice of the knight to the right of Jeanne. He was a good foot taller than she, with a neatly-trimmed beard and almond-colored skin. He obviously wasn't entirely of European ancestry.

"Pierre is right," Jeanne said. "If the message didn't appear until yesterday, what makes you think the Marquis is the one who wrote it?"

"It wasn't carved with a knife. The Marquis wasn't allowed to have sharp objects in here. The message was written with a transparent, slow-acting acid he had smuggled in. Once it reacts with oxygen, the acid will begin dissolving whatever it has been applied to. The process is gradual and can take over a week depending on the concentration of the corrosive."

The knight to Jeanne's left examined the message. He was a young man with long dark hair, slightly smaller than Pierre and less muscular, but still larger than Jeanne. "So, the Marquis applies this to the wall—I'm guessing with a brush since we know he was allowed to write his perverted works in here—and is then transferred out, knowing the acid will soon burn his message into the wall."

"Yes, Victor," Jeanne said. "The question is: Why? Why would he go to the trouble of doing this?

From over in the next cell, Jacques said, "Maybe it's all a joke, no? I hear the Marquis de Sade is a real piece of work. We have all heard the stories. He kidnapped girls and did horrible things to them. They say he is the most twisted man in the world."

Jeanne grit her teeth slightly at being reminded of the Marquis' crimes. "I am not his biggest supporter." She turned her attention from Jacques back to the message on the wall. "However, I think we are missing something important."

Pierre cocked one eyebrow inquisitively. "Such as?"

"The message seems to suggest that something will happen on July 14. That's today."

"So it is," Victor said.

"You don't suppose the Marquis is throwing you a surprise party?" Jacques retorted.

Jeanne gave him a stern glance. "Be quiet, you rogue. This is serious."

Suddenly a guard burst into the room. "My Lord! It's terrible! The people....!" He stopped to catch his breath.

"What are you babbling about?" de Launay demanded.

"There is a mob of people outside! At least a hundred of them, and more keep arriving. They're yelling something about us keeping political prisoners here and abusing them. Their leader is demanding we remove the steam cannons aimed at them and allow a civilian militia to take control of the Bastille."

The color rapidly drained from de Launay's face as he took in the guard's ominous words. "T-Those fools! The cannons aren't aimed at anyone in particular. They're here for the defense of the people! And there aren't any political prisoners here; just the one forger."

"What are your orders, sir?"

The Marquis de Launay paced the room while racking his mind to come up with an answer. Finally, he said, "Remove the cannons. I'll go speak with their leader." He turned to leave with the guard.

Jeanne started after him. "I'll go with you. My knights and I can help defend you."

"Are you really prepared to cut down the people you have sworn to protect?" Jacques said with a slight grin.

Jeanne stopped. "Well, I—"

"And so many of them!"

"You stay here," de Launay said, visibly scared. "If I meet them with armed soldiers, it will just anger them more. Besides, as skilled as you three are, I doubt even *you* could hold off all of them."

"I don't know about that. I could hold off a lot of men," Victor happily declared.

Jeanne ignored her subordinate's inappropriate comment; she was used to his quips by now. "Very well. We'll stay here and continue to investigate the message."

The Marquis de Launay and the panicked guard left the chamber, leaving just Jeanne, Pierre, Victor and Jacques.

Jeanne walked over to the wall next to the door they had entered through. Jutting out from the wall was a rubber tube with a wide handle. She dialed a number on the panel below the tube and began speaking. "de Fleur to *Minuit Solaire*. What's going on outside?" The *Minuit Solaire*, or Solar Midnight, was the airship of the Ordre de la Tradition. It was supposed to be anchored on a telegraph pole outside the prison. However, Jeanne's communiqué was met with silence. "I repeat: This is Commander Jeanne de Fleur. Come in, *Minuit Solaire*. What is your status?"

Again, there was only the crackle of static.

"If the mob turned their attention to our airship, the *Solaire* may have had to retreat," Pierre said.

Jeanne frowned. If the mob was violent enough to threaten their vessel into retreating, that was bad news; her crew wouldn't leave her without a very good reason. She didn't need to say it, though. Pierre and Victor no doubt were thinking the same thing. She just hoped her crew on the airship was all right.

"What more can we do here?" Victor said.

Jeanne went back into the cell and began to feel about the walls. "The Marquis de Sade loves to milk his jokes for all they're worth. Stopping with a cryptic message isn't his style. I bet he hid another piece of the puzzle for us to find."

Pierre and Victor helped her look around the cell. "Did he know the Bastille would be attacked today?" Victor said.

"How could he? That would imply the attack was planned well in advance," Pierre said.

Suddenly Jeanne came upon a loose brick in the wall. She took it out, reached inside and pulled out a small glass vial filled with water. However, there were also countless tiny silver dots in the water.

"Just as I thought," she said. "A message pellet."

A message pellet was a little ball about the size of a kernel of corn. Using a magnifying glass, a person could write a message on it and then drop it into water. Once in the water it separates into a thousand copies of itself. Only by reassembling the ball can the message be read.

"We have to get that back to the airship," Pierre said.

Jeanne sighed. "Until the governor can get the mob to disperse, we're stuck here."

2

The Jacobin Club, July 14, 1789 (Infini Calendar), 10:00 a.m.

The Marquis de Sade was escorted into the undersized hall that was being used for the meeting currently in session. The room was crammed with men in red cloaks who all looked the same to the Marquis. He looked to the right side of the room and saw men in red cloaks. He looked up into the low-hanging balcony and saw men in red cloaks sitting beneath windows letting in rays of sunlight. It should have been called the Jaconformist Club.

To his right, sitting at a table on a dais a few feet off the ground, was their leader (also wearing a red cloak). "Welcome to the Jacobin Club, Lord Marquis de Sade."

The Marquis stepped through the aisle separating the left side of the room from the right, and looked around. All eyes were on him. At least, he thought they were; he actually couldn't see very many eyes under those hoods. He then turned his attention to the club's leader. "Quite a warm reception, Monsieur Robespierre. You're all bundled up nicely here in the middle of summer. Personally, I would have preferred a lot more young girls and a lot less clothing. Possibly a knife or two, although I could make do with my bare hands in a pinch. But I digress: It's good to be out of that prison, and in here, with not quite so many people to tell me what I can and can't do." He let out a light cackle.

"Indeed," said Robespierre. "It was not an easy task getting you released under the guise of an official transfer. But it looks like you have upheld your end of the bargain. My sources tell me knights from the Ordre de la Tradition have been sent to the Bastille to investigate a strange message that appeared on the wall of your former cell."

"Causing chaos and confusion to the country that has oppressed me for so long? I would have done that for free. I just wish I could see the looks on their faces right about now, just realizing the lowly rabble is upon them like rabid wolves!"

Robespierre's voice took on a serious tone. "Need I remind you that we represent the 'lowly rabble' that is presently fighting for their rights? And as the newest member of the Montagnards, you represent them as well."

The Marquis dismissed Robespierre's argument with a frilly wave of his hand. "Classes mean nothing to me. The Estates are each fighting for their own selfish reasons. To them it all comes down to 'Me, Me, Me.' But I, the Marquis de Sade, live only to give back. That's why I've written masterful prose. That's why I've offered to share my body with so many different girls. And that's why I'm helping France by spurring this deadlocked country into action."

"On that last point we can certainly agree," Robespierre said. He stood up to address the entire hall. "No positive change can occur within our nation so long as our impotent king kowtows to nobility and clergy. *They*, at least, are selfish. *They* enjoy tax-exempt status. *They* want to keep us down and make sure commoners like us will continue to be their foot rests.

"And how does our king fight this injustice? He gives in to them. He does whatever they say, no matter how much it hurts France. Between the nobility, clergy and his Austrian wife, he cannot think for himself. We have no use for a powerless monarch. For the good of France, Louis XVI must be removed. The *Ancien Régime* shall fall."

The attendees cheered, while the Marquis gave him a half-hearted clap. "You truly are as eloquent as they say, Monsieur Robespierre. But as you National Assembly people know all too well, words alone cannot change a nation. That's why you needed my genius to help you come up with a plan to assassinate the king."

Robespierre sat back down. "And an excellent plan it is. Once those knights decipher your 'message in a bottle,' they will immediately leave and warn the king. And the king, ever so trusting of his knights, will respond in an appropriate manner. Then he will be vulnerable."

"But how do you know the knights will not be killed by the very mob we are letting loose upon them?"

"Don't underestimate their skills. They are survivors. Besides, I know a great deal about the Bastille itself. Those knights won't be killed so easily."

The Marquis chuckled. "Well, if they have to butcher a few peasants, so be it." Robespierre murmured angrily under his breath, so the Marquis decided to change the subject to something else he was curious about. "By the way, you still haven't told me who you've sent to deal with the impudent king."

"That's 'impotent.' And the one who will do the honor of breaking the pavement for a glorious new France is none other than the Count of Saint-Germaine." At the last part he raised a fist for dramatic effect. The other members in the room voiced their pleasure.

The Marquis de Sade was rarely surprised by anything, but this definitely did it. "The Count of Saint-Germaine! I thought he died five years ago."

Now it was Robespierre's turn to laugh. "That's what we wanted the world to think. But in reality, he has long been one of us, and we faked his death so that he could move about more easily. If no one knows he's still alive, no one will be able to anticipate his involvement in this."

"But the Count must be very old by now. How will he be able to kill the king?"

"The Count has mastered the art of alchemy and used it to turn his body into a deadly weapon. No one will be able to stand against him when he decides to strike. He will use the chaos currently sweeping through France to attack Louis XVI while the royal guards are distracted."

Robespierre then moved on to other business involving the Jacobin Club and the Montagnards in particular, and the Marquis sat down in the empty seat in front of Robespierre's table, which had been reserved for him. While the Marquis was thoroughly enjoying all the havoc that had no doubt started already (with even more to come), he couldn't help but note the irony of Robespierre sending the Count of Saint-Germaine to dispatch the king. After all, was it not the Count who had predicted these events some fifteen years ago? That was how the story went, at least.

Not that it mattered. The Marquis loved irony—the crueler, the better. And if he and Robespierre were correct, things were about to get very *ironic* indeed.

3

Paris, France, July 14, 1789 (Infini Calendar), 10:15 a.m.

The Bastille suddenly shook violently.

"What was that?" Victor said.

"Perhaps the Marquis de Launay was unsuccessful in reasoning with the mob," Pierre said.

Jeanne shot down that idea. "That shot was from a steam cannon. If the governor decided to open fire on the crowd, it would be directed *away* from here. And as far as I know, the Third Estate wouldn't be able to get their hands on one."

"That's a good point," Pierre said. "If a steam cannon went missing, an alert would have gone out immediately."

Suddenly de Launay rushed into the room. Even in the low lighting, they could see the color had completely drained from his face.

"What's going on?" Jeanne said.

The Marquis shook his head. "It's far worse than I feared."

"What do you mean?"

"Things were going reasonably well. I met with the leader of the mob. I allowed him inside and he watched as we removed the cannons that were pointing outside at the mob. Unfortunately, they took this to mean we were loading them in preparation for an attack. Someone got a shot off with a pistol—I'm not sure who—and suddenly the mob panicked. The ones carrying firearms began shooting them at my men in the windows. No one was hit, but that was only the beginning."

"What do you mean?" Pierre said.

"An army regiment sympathizes with the crowd and has joined them. They brought their own steam cannons!"

Things suddenly fell into place for the knights. "So, it was *their* cannons that hit us a moment ago," Jeanne said.

"Obviously this place is quite an eyesore to them," Victor observed.

The Marquis nodded grimly. "They see this fortress as symbol of oppression by the *Ancien Régime*—what they call the government—and they're determined to tear it down, one way or another."

"Isn't the Bastille already scheduled for demolition, seeing as how there are so few prisoners here these days?" Victor said.

"Unfortunately," de Launay said, "they don't know that, and they weren't in any mood to listen. They're dead set on getting in here, freeing the prisoners and then leveling everything."

"We have to get out of here," Jeanne said.

"Fortunately," de Launay said, "I've long been worried that something like this might happen. That's why I had an escape tunnel built under the prison."

"Very good. Take us to it," Jeanne said.

"Right away. I just need to get us some light," de Launay responded. He walked past Jacques' cell to the wall and grabbed a torch off the wall.

Jacques walked over to the bars and addressed the Marquis. "What about me? Surely you will not leave a poor Parisian to be feasted on by the mob?"

"You'll be fine," de Launay said, walking past Jacques with torch in hand. "As I already stated, they want to free you, since they think everyone in here is a political prisoner. Personally, I would prefer to have a forger like you stay in here a few more years." He rejoined the knights and pointed towards the door they had entered through. "It's this way."

***

The Marquis de Launay led them down a flight of stairs into the dark cellar of the Bastille. Boxes full of guns and ammunition, as well as what appeared to be rundown steam cannons, were spread out on the floor in rows. At the far end of the cellar was a man-sized opening that had clearly been cut out of the wall.

When they arrived, they could see large pieces of wood that had been scattered in front of the door. "I instructed my men to open up the tunnel and then make their escape ahead of us," de Launay explained.

"Seems ironic to put an escape tunnel in a prison," Victor laughed.

"Today's attack has been brewing for years," de Launay said. "The taxes, the unequal treatment under the law, even the 'Great Fear'—all of it has pushed the Third Estate into action, albeit misguided and reckless action."

The "Great Fear" de Launay spoke of referred to a rumor that had gone around—no one knew how it had started—that the nobility had employed bands of thugs to go around the countryside destroying the crops of the peasantry. The rumor turned out to be untrue, but that didn't stop a wave of panic from flooding across France, adding fuel to an already growing fire.

The prison suddenly shook again with the reverberation of a steam cannon blast, and Jeanne was about to suggest they hurry through the tunnel when someone charged into her from behind. They both fell to the floor, whereupon she elbowed her unknown attacker in the face. The assailant let go of her and all three knights brought their swords upon him.

"Now, now, it is simply I—Jacques du Chard!"

The Marquis de Launay lowered the torch so they could get a good look at him. Sure enough, it was Jacques the forger. Jeanne motioned for Pierre and Victor to sheathe their swords.

"What are you doing down here?" de Launay demanded to know. "How did you get out of your cell?"

"Let's just say you should not have passed so close to me when you went by my cell up there. Didn't you notice yourself missing the key?"

The Marquis check his pocket. "You filthy thief!"

Victor chuckled. "I thought he was just a forger, but he can get out of a prison cell too. What a multi-talented criminal!" He then said under his breath, "And not a bad looker."

Jacques waved his hand in a tip-of-the-hat gesture. "And you, sir, have an eye for talent." He returned his attention to de Launay. "As for why I am here, well, it is simply the fact that I do not care to be placed in the custody of that mob that is currently pummeling the doors of this prison trying to get in."

"Enough of this banter. Let's keep moving," Jeanne said. She hoped they wouldn't pick up any more comedians today.

***

They trekked through the man-made tunnel underneath the Bastille. The passage was so narrow they had to walk single-file; de Launay brought up the rear, followed by Jeanne, Jacques, Victor and Pierre. The Marquis' torch provided just enough light for them to see a few feet in front of them.

Despite the heat of summer, it was cool in the tunnel. It smelled of mud and rock, two things which can block out warmth. Jeanne was glad for that; her armor was lightweight, but could still be unbearably hot this time of year.

She said, "You're a curious one, forger. Do you really think you'll be better off with us than up above with your fellow commoners?"

"Very much so, Mademoiselle. My fellow peasants are not too fond of me at the moment," Jacques said.

"Why is that?" she asked.

"As you know, I was put in prison for forgery. But what you do not know are the details of that crime. You see, I was hired by a poor family to forge documents showing them to be nobility. They wanted to move up in the world, I suppose. Who does *not*? Anyways, they gave me all the money they had to do the job. Sadly, on the way back to deliver the false documents to that family I was caught with the papers on me." His voice took on a melancholy tone. "Under threat of torture I revealed the names of the commoners who had hired me to forge the documents. I later learned they had been split up and sent to different prisons around France. I couldn't even give them back the money as it was confiscated as evidence. Probably wound up in a judge's pocket."

"That's.... unfortunate," was all Jeanne could say. She made it a point to stay in control of her emotions at all times, and she couldn't be showing too much pity to a common criminal.

"Don't listen to him," de Launay said. "Regardless of his reasons, he still broke the law. His punishment was just."

"'Just'..." Jeanne let the word roll around in her mouth for a moment. As the commander of the Ordre de la Tradition, she was known as "Jeanne la Juste," a moniker she had received because she treated everyone fairly. She did not show more respect to the nobility than the clergy or commoners, and she was always fair in her dealings with criminals. Still, she wasn't sure how to look upon Jacques du Chard; he had admitted his guilt, yet his story was nonetheless a sympathetic one.

An abrupt series of reverberations shaking the tunnel saved her from having to think about it any more at the present time. Unlike the previous explosions, these were clearly the result of more than one cannon blast.

"I think they've gotten serious," Victor said.

"They must have commenced the complete bombarding of the prison," de Launay said.

More explosions rocked the fortress above, and mounds of dirt began falling from the ceiling of the tunnel.

"We need to move," Jeanne insisted.

They began awkwardly running through the passage as fast as they could. Jeanne realized it had been a mistake to let the Marquis take point; he wasn't in nearly as good of shape as the knights, or even Jacques. He was slowing them down too much. In addition, the tunnel was too narrow for them to go around him (Jeanne had no intention of leaving him behind, but she wished the others at least had a chance to get out faster.

As the passage continually shook from the bombardment, the tunnel began to crumble more and more around them. Suddenly de Launay tripped on a rock and fell down, his torch landing in a puddle of muddy water and going out. Now the tunnel was collapsing *and* they were blind.

Jeanne almost tripped over the Marquis herself, but managed to stay upright despite all the commotion going on. She felt for de Launay's torso and pulled him to his feet. She then grabbed his shoulders firmly. "Everyone, hold on to the person in front of you!" she shouted to be heard above the rumblings. She felt someone (she had to assume Jacques) put his arms around her waist in a somewhat too-familiar embrace. Still, she didn't have the luxury to complain. After a moment had passed and she was satisfied everyone had had time to carry out her order, she said, "Let's go!"

They slogged forward as a unit, with the tunnel threatening to collapse at any moment. After a minute, a light appeared up ahead, faint but definitely there. As more and more dirt and debris fell from the ceiling, though, she didn't know if they would make it.

Nevertheless, they pressed on towards the exit, one step at a time.

Twenty feet to the exit.

Fifteen feet.

More debris falling.

Ten feet.

Behind them, the ceiling began collapsing entirely.

Five feet.

***

They barreled out of the tunnel and into the open daylight of Paris. Jeanne choked on the cloud of dust that had been discharged by the collapse of the narrow passage from which they had just escaped. Lying on the ground, she coughed in an involuntary attempt to dispel the dust from her throat.

Once she could breathe again, she looked around to take stock of the situation. They were in a wide street behind the Bastille. Dozens of smokestacks from factories in the distance bellowed steam into the Paris sky as was normal for this time of day. This generated a haze above the city, giving it an unclean look. On the contrary; it was much cleaner than the proposed burning of coal which had been briefly considered as a power source for Paris.

She looked around. The Marquis de Launay lay behind her also trying to get himself together. To her right were Pierre and Victor sitting on the ground, apparently no worse for wear. Their armor was covered with dirt, dust and grime, as was hers.

Another series of explosions drew her attention. Past the wall into which the tunnel had been built, the Bastille came crumbling down. Although the falling structure was a good hundred feet away and separated from them by a twenty-foot wall, it still roared with its last breath and produced a dirty white cloud which managed to shoot over the wall.

They put their arms up in front of their faces to shield their eyes from the cloud which came down upon them. For a moment the world went a shade of sickly grey.

Jeanne went through another bout of coughing, and she could hear the others doing the same. "Is everyone all right?" she asked.

"I think so," Pierre said.

"Same here," Victor replied.

"Things could be worse, no?" Jacques added.

"Oh, will you just shut—" de Launay started. However, his words were cut off by a sharp retort: the unmistakable sound of a gun shot.

The cloud cleared and the Marquis lay facedown in a bright red pool, a hole having been put in his shoulder.

In addition, they were surrounded on three sides by eight members of the Gardes Francaises, an infantry regiment of the Maison du Roi, the King's House. Their role depended on whether they were stationed in Paris or Versailles. In Versailles their duty was to guard the palace, while in Paris they helped to maintain order. What they were doing here pointing rifles at her and her group, she didn't know, but she had a few ideas, none of which she liked.

A man whose uniform identified him as their sergeant addressed them. "Please cooperate with us, Mademoiselle de Fleur. We don't want any more bloodshed than necessary."

"I know you," she said. "You are François Joseph Lefebvre. What is the meaning of this?"

Lefebvre was thirty-three years old (having been in the army since he was eighteen). His prominent features were a strong jaw line and hair which was short and dark. Unlike the rest of his regiment, his uniform consisted of a blue coat with red cuffs, a red collar and a red waistcoat, while the leggings and breeches were white. Jeanne had never seen this uniform before, but Lefebvre's coat was embroidered in silver rather than white, distinguishing his status as an officer.

He spoke calmly and eloquently. "The revolution has begun, and we are siding with the National Constituent Assembly. They have long been oppressed by the *Ancien Régime*, and we were recently ordered to suppress the uprising with violence. Please understand that we cannot in good conscience open fire on the people of France."

Jeanne clenched her fist tightly. "'Cannot in good conscience open fire'? You just *opened fire* on the Marquis de Launay."

Lefebvre furrowed his brow slightly. "We merely shot him in the shoulder. He will live, though not for long, I suspect. It is the people who demand his head as the one who ran the Bastille. Once he is dead, their anger will diminish."

"What nonsense is this?" Jeanne demanded. "You are members of the Maison du Roi. You serve the king's household. And now you would turn against those you have sworn loyalty to?"

"We are loyal to the *people*! Our king has abandoned them in favor of the nobles and clergymen. The Third Estate had more members than the other two; by all rights they should have received more votes. But our monarch acquiesced to the petulant First and Second Estates—not to mention his overbearing wife—and shut them out of the hall in which they were to have met. In effect, he has rejected the majority of France. For a ruler to do that is madness."

"And you think you can change things by shooting innocent people and wreaking havoc in Paris? *That* is my idea of madness," Jeanne said.

"I am under no obligation to justify our actions to you. I was simply hoping you would understand and come with us peacefully, either to join us or allow us to keep you under guard so that you do not interfere with our mission. What is it going to be?"

- 21 -

Jeanne turned to Pierre and Victor. "Cover the forger. Do not allow any harm to come to him."

"Yes, ma'am," they said. They ran over to Jacques (who was still on the ground watching the scene) and proceeded to shield him with their bodies.

Lefebvre said, "So you refuse?"

Jeanne removed her rapier and pointed it at him. "We must return to our airship and then report back to the king. You will not stop us."

Lefebvre looked at her with contempt. "That is a foolish choice. Very well."

He raised his hand and then brought it down like the hammers of the rifles his men were carrying. They immediately opened fire on the knights. Jeanne raised her arm to shield her head but took several bullets in her chest plating, while Pierre and Victor similarly took multiple blows.

Jeanne fell backwards onto the ground. "I know that volley wasn't enough to penetrate your irodium armor," Lefebre said. He pulled out his own sword and Strolled over to Jeanne's fallen and seemingly unconscious form. "But it should have stunned you enough for me to deliver the killing blow."

He gripped his sword with both hands and positioned it over Jeanne's throat (which was not covered by armor). He then dropped it with all his might.

However, Jeanne tilted her head ever so slightly and Lefebvre's blade dug harmlessly into the ground. In one fluid and rapid motion she thrust her rapier—which she had never let go of—into his thigh. Unlike the knights, French infantry wore no armor, so Jeanne's blade entered Lefebvre's body unopposed.

He cried out and staggered back. Jeanne took this opportunity to leap to her feet and kick him in the wound she had just made. Now it was *his* turn to meet the ground.

His seven soldiers scrambled to unsheathe their own swords, but Jeanne ran in and cut down two of them before they could. Fortunately for them, she intentionally avoided their vitals.

She turned around to confront two more who were charging her, only to see a massive pair of hands knock their heads together.

It was Pierre.

Victor grabbed a fallen infantryman's rifle and clubbed one of the others over the head, knocking him out cold. He looked at her and said, "We thought you would prefer the nonlethal approach, if possible."

The last two members of the Gardes Francaises obviously realized they had been thoroughly routed and turned tail to run away.

When they were out of sight, Jeanne addressed her subordinates. "I told you two to guard the forger."

"By that point, they were focused entirely on you, ma'am. They weren't even aware of his existence."

Jacques walked up to them with a grin on his face. "That they were not. Admit it: You forgot about me as well. Ah, 'tis a sad thing when a man is important one moment, and unknown the next. But that is just the way of the world, I suppose."

Jeanne felt like rebuking his devil-may-care attitude, but couldn't bring herself to do it. For all his faults, Jacques du Chard was a hard man to hate.

A pained grunt alerted them to the fact that Lefebvre was still there. They turned to see him getting back to his feet with no small difficulty. "This isn't over," he said venomously.

"It had better be, for your sake," Jeanne retorted.

"Why, you—"

Lefebvre's words were cut off by a suddenly cry from a hundred feet up the road. A mass of people rushed towards them.

"Looks like the mob has found us," Pierre said.

Lefebvre began laughing with a righteous fury, a far cry from his earlier demeanor. "Now you'll pay! You and all the other dogs of the *Ancien Régime.*"

With renewed vigor he scooped up the Marquis de Launay—whom they had all forgotten about in the heat of battle—and sprinted towards the rushing mob.

"Get back here!" Jeanne called after him.

"Should we go after him?" Pierre asked.

She shook her head. Even if they managed to catch up with the manic sergeant, they'd still have to fight off the mob. There was a veritable sea of enraged Parisians coming at them, and she didn't see how they could possibly win against them all. That only left retreat.

She looked around them. They were surrounded on three sides by thick walls, those of the Bastille and the adjacent buildings. The only way out was through the mob. The riotous group momentarily stopped to celebrate the capturing of the Marquis de Launay, but Lefebvre quickly reminded them with a pointing finger that there were still enemies of the people waiting to be seized or worse. The crowd wasted no time continuing their charge.

"Gut the oppressors!" one yelled.

"The king's *chienne* must die!" said another.

"Let's take our time with her!"

Jeanne wasn't flattered by being called a bitch. As the mob got closer she could see they were mostly armed with hoes and other blunt farming tools. She seriously doubted any of them alone could even scratch her, but with sheer numbers they had an overwhelming advantage.

"Is this the end?" Jacques said with mild apathy.

Jeanne was about to reply when a familiar whooshing sound drew her attention. "The end of this farce?" she said. "Yes, it is."

They all watched as a massive wall came down between the mob and the knights. Only it wasn't just a wall; it was an airship. It landed just a few feet in front of the knights, and Jeanne's hair was blown wildly by its appearance.

At fifty feet long, the *Minuit Solaire* was a sleek silver marvel of airship technology. Since the outer hull was made of irodium, the ship could fly faster and higher than if it was composed of any other metal. In addition, twin engines on either side of the stern provided thrust while the elongated balloon moored above the ship helped to achieve buoyancy.

While they were admiring the ship's impeccable timing, a teenage girl wearing glasses and a dirty brown jumpsuit appeared on the deck above them. "Sorry to keep you waiting, milady!" She threw down a rope ladder, and Jeanne instructed Jacques to climb up first, followed by Pierre and Victor. Finally, Jeanne herself started climbing, and she motioned to the girl for them to take off.

As the *Minuit Solaire* began ascending into the air, Jeanne once again marveled at the level of technological achievement France had generated in such a short period. It was just ten years ago that Jean Baptiste Marie Meusnier submitted to L'Académie des Sciences his paper entitled "Memoire on the Equilibrium of Aerostatic Machines." In it, he detailed his design for an elongated airship (as opposed to a round balloon) which called for propulsion via the use of propellers. It was nowhere near as advanced as the *Minuit Solaire* or the king's own airship that would eventually be built, and Louis XVI paid no attention to it.

However, his wife and queen, Marie Antoinette, saw the untold benefits of being able to rule the sky, and she convinced her husband to champion research into the field.

They soon brought in engineers from all over the world and had them work together on the Diu du Ciel [God of the Sky] project. Perhaps most instrumental in the success of the airship project was James Watt who came up with the idea to power the airships with technology derived from his steam engine.

At the behest of Marie Antoinette, Louis XVI decreed that the first airship be christened by the end of 1785.

Working feverishly, the team managed to pull it off, and on December 24, 1785, the king and queen rode in the inaugural flight of the *Minuit Solaire*.

Looking back, Jeanne now wondered if it was all worth it. The Diu du Ciel project required vast amounts of France's resources to be completed on time and now the country was heavily in debt—and only two airships had been built thus far. Inflation was at an all-time high; the cost of bread alone had skyrocketed as of late. She understood why the people were so upset, but their solution of extreme violence was only making things horribly worse. *I am sorry,* Monsieur *de Launay,* she added silently. *Rest assured your sacrifice will not have been for nothing.*

Her train of thought—along with her climb up the ladder—was suddenly disrupted by a heavy jolt. The airship spun thirty-five degrees, and Jeanne had to cling to the ladder to keep from falling off. "Celeste!" She shouted. "What's going on?"

Hugging the railing up above, Celeste adjusted her glasses and called back, "They managed to hit us with a steam cannon shell! Don't worry; it was a glancing blow."

Jeanne climbed up the rope as fast as she could. If just a graze managed to do that to them, she didn't intend to be on a flimsy rope ladder if and when they were hit again.

When she reached the polished wood of the top deck, Pierre lent her a hand to help her up. Although it was unnecessary, she appreciated the gesture and allowed him the assist.

"Are you unhurt, milady?" Celeste asked.

"I'm fine. Get below deck and see to any damage we sustained."

"Right away!"

Celeste nimbly bound down the stairs a few feet away.

"Full of energy, that girl," Jacques said. Like Pierre and Victor, he had remained on the railing as they awaited the ship's captain.

"That she does," Victor replied. "Our little engineer has a taste for adventure and she's right at home up here in the sky. In fact, the only thing she likes more than pure excitement may be our captain here."

"Ah, so you are a role model, eh?"

Jeanne dismissed the high praise. "It's just youthful admiration."

She looked up at the balloon above them. It did not appear to be damaged or leaking gas. She silently thanked the Lord for the one thing that hadn't gone wrong today.

Satisfied that the ship would continue to fly (at least for the moment), she headed down the stairs one flight to the command deck below them. When she reached the command deck, immediately behind her was the bridge, located on the ship's bow. Along the corridor in the opposite direction were crew quarters, the captain's being the closest to the bridge so she could get there quickly in an emergency.

Jeanne turned around and walked into the bridge. The captain's chair sat bolted in the middle of the room, while the two operators had their own seats at bulky consoles in front of the canopy window. Each console had large levers and wheels for them to operate in order to fly the ship. Because of the complexity of the airship, it took two people working together just to fly it. The left operator was in charge of altitude control, while the right operator handled acceleration. Of course, there was also a group of people slaving down in the boiler room to keep the ship powered.

As Jeanne entered, the two operators—Adolphe on the left, Claude on the right—stood up to salute her. They wore jumpsuits with a blue left sleeve and red right sleeve, with the rest of the outfit being white (the colors of the French flag).

"As you were," she said, and they returned to their posts.

Jeanne went over to a panel built into the left wall. She pulled on a latch to reveal an opening about the size of her hand, removed the vial she had retrieved from the Bastille from her pocket, and poured the contents into the opening. The water went down a funnel into the depths of the device, where she knew it would be filtered, separating the liquid from the innumerous dots that had once made up the message pellet.

There were two small glass windows a few feet below the opening she had poured the water into. Behind the left window was a transparent vial similar to the one the water had originally been stored in, while the right window simply held a round indentation. As Jeanne watched, water filled the left vial, while metal dots filled the right indentation.

Once it was obvious that all the pieces of the message pellet had been deposited into the right vial, Jeanne pulled a lever on the panel. There was a hiss and the right window filled with green gas. She didn't remember exactly how it worked, but somehow the gas softened up the dots and made them reform into one solid unit.

Sure enough, a solid metal ball dropped down into a small bin below the windows. Jeanne picked up the message pellet, but the writing was still too small for her to read.

Fortunately, though, a magnifying glass hung from the ceiling at the front of the bridge for just such a situation as this. Jeanne went to it and, using the light from outside, was able to read the words written by the Marquis de Sade.

Congratulations, you found the words I 'scribed
And managed to get out before you fried
Now you should return to Versailles
For your good king is going to die

4

Versailles, July 14, 1789 (Infini Calendar), 12:00 p.m.

"Oh, dear," said King Louis XVI as he stood in the hallway at the Royal Palace. The corridor, like the rest of the Palace, was built for those with more discerning tastes. It featured an ornate wooden floor, gold walls, and man-sized paintings from the greatest artists in France. Even the doors in the hallway were intricately crafted works of art.

But it was not the splendor of the Palace that held his attention at that moment. No, it was the scene he was witnessing as he looked through the twenty-foot-high windows that made him understandably uneasy.

The magnificent garden in front of the Palace, with its grand fountain, expertly-maintained trees and elaborate patterns cut out of the grass, was normally a serene location the king and queen liked to take walks in.

However, on this day the garden was anything but peaceful. Currently occupying its grounds was a sea of people—mostly women—currently shouting angrily at anyone in the Palace who could hear them.

"We can't afford bread!"

"This is all the Austrian Chienne's fault!"

"Her and her damn sky boats have ruined us!"

"Don't forget about the American war they dragged us into!"

Louis XVI turned to his advisor, the Duke of Rochefoucauld-Liancourt, and said, "Is this a revolt?"

The fifty-two-year-old duke ran a hand through his graying hair and straightened his black coat before giving his curt reply. "No, my lord. It is a revolution."

"What is going on?" said Marie Antoinette, entering from a set of exquisite marble doors at the end of the hallway. She wore one of her trademark flowing dresses, each one of them priceless. This one was red.

The king turned to face his wife. "Just a demonstration. Nothing to worry about," he lied.

The queen looked out the window and observed the rage on the faces of the crowd when they spotted her. They began yelling with renewed fury.

"Someone should go talk to them," she said.

"Wait, my love. It is dangerous."

However, he was unable to stop her before she opened the terrace and walked out to face the crowd below.

"There she is!" one shouted.

"She dares face us?" said another.

Several members of the mob threw rocks at her. One connected with her forehead, causing a trickle of blood to flow down her face.

She stood there for what seemed an eternity, taking their verbal, physical and overall emotional abuse. Finally, they seemed to grow tired of the tirade, and the abuse subsided. Satisfied that their anger had been quenched, Marie Antoinette bowed her head and went back inside.

Her husband ran over to wipe the blood off her forehead. "I'm so glad they did not do worse to you. What were you thinking?"

She said, "Some storms cannot be waited out. They must be faced."

"Long live the Queen!" a few of the mob shouted outside.

"It seems to have worked," said the Duke, who had followed them.

However, even more of the crowd continued to voice their anger.

"Don't be fooled by her!"

"Yeah! She's hoarding grain just like the rest of them!"

Marie Antoinette shook her head. "I may have simply bought us some time."

"My lord, you need to consider leaving here immediately. I suggest heading to the Chateau at Rambouillet," the Duke said.

"I think that would be best," the queen said. "We can take the *Majesté Divine*."

The *Majesté Divine*, or Divine Majesty, was the royal airship. The chateau she spoke of lay in the town of Rambouillet, about thirty-three kilometers southwest of Versailles. Louis XVI had acquired the property years ago for the purpose of hunting.

The king rejected the idea. "For over a century, this has been home to the royal family of France. I cannot abandon it so easily. Besides," he said, addressing his wife, "you yourself said we need to weather the storm."

"Yes, but I don't think—"

She was cut off by an explosion, followed by a thunderous crash as a cannon ball barreled through the terrace window and missed her head by mere inches.

The three of them dropped to the floor. The king gaped at the crater in the wall where the iron sphere had lodged. "They've brought cannons!"

"They're just normal cannons," the Duke said. "Heaven help us if they brought steam models."

"*'Just'* normal cannons? I very nearly lost my head!" the queen said. She brushed broken glass out of her hair and dress. "We must leave here at once."

The king, though, still refused. "I have been bullied by the Third Estate long enough. They shall not push me out of my own home."

"But what of our children? Would you have them stay in reach of that bloodthirsty mob?"

"We have plenty of guards here. They'll disperse the crowd."

A courtier rushed into the hallway. "My Lord! Are you all right?"

"We are fine," the king replied. "What is that paper in your hand? Is it a message?"

The courtier, seeing that the three of them were all laying low on the floor, did likewise. He handed the king the paper he was holding. "We have received word from the *Minuit Solaire*. They have reported a riot at the Bastille, and not only that..."

Louis XVI read the paper. "*Mon Dieu!* It is far worse than we thought."

5

Paris, July 14, 1789 (Infini Calendar), 12:55 p.m.

The *Minuit Solaire* was currently anchored at a telegraph pole on the southwest outskirts of Paris. The crew had tethered the airship to the tall wooden pole and hooked a cable into it. This way they could transmit messages to the Palace of Versailles. Only a handful of telegraph poles existed thus far, and they were only used for emergencies. However, Jeanne felt this surely qualified.

She listened to the *tap-tap-tap* of the message as Maurice the telegraph operator repeatedly pushed his index finger down on the copper handle at his console at the wall next to the entrance on the bridge, behind the captain's chair. Like the other two operators on the bridge, he wore a red, white and blue jumpsuit.

"All done, ma'am," he said.

"Very good." Now the king would know there would likely be an attempt on his life some time today. She just prayed they weren't too late.

Everything that had happened so far could not be simply a coincidence. The Marquis de Sade had obviously known there would be an attack on the Bastille, but how? The mob had seemed too angry and their rage too spontaneous to have been a premeditated attack. Was it possible someone had been subtly manipulating the Parisian populace, stoking the fires of their hearts in controlled bursts until they exploded on just the right day?

But if so, who? And why would the Marquis de Sade give the knights a chance to warn the king? The more she thought about it, the more uneasy she became.

She sat down in her captain's chair and took hold of a rubber tube with a wide opening that hung down from the ceiling, next to the seat. She spoke into it. "Celeste, I want the communications cable reeled in immediately. We have to get back to Versailles ASAP."

The engineer's voice came through the tubing, slightly distorted by the process of traveling up from the boiler room, through the walls and ceiling, and back down to Jeanne. *"Milady, we're not finished repairing the damage from earlier. It's not safe to go full speed."*

"Give us as much as you can. If we don't return to the Palace soon, I fear something horrible may happen."

"We'll do what we can, but it'll be a bumpy ride. Also, I can't guarantee chunks of the ship won't begin falling off before long."

"We'll make it. I have faith in your abilities."

Even through the tubing, Celeste's voice was gushing. *"Thank you, ma'am! I'm honored to hear that from you."*

***

Within twenty minutes the *Minuit Solaire* reached the Palace of Versailles. Looking on from above, it was obvious the grounds had been thrashed. Numerous fires big and small spread through the garden, and most of the Palace's windows had been shattered. There were also many guardsmen tending to the damage across the grounds and working to put out the fires.

The ship sat down on its designated landing pad behind the Palace, next to the pad for the royal airship, the *Majesté Divine*. That pad was empty, meaning the airship had left—hopefully with the royal family safely on board.

Jeanne, Pierre and Victor disembarked the airship. A royal aide ran up the landing pad's ramp to meet them.

"What's the situation?" Jeanne said.

The aide, a teenager, had obviously been through the worst experience of his life, judging by his lack of composure and the way he trembled as he spoke. "It was awful, ma'am.

A large mob of women—there must have been thousands of them—attacked the Palace. They demanded lower bread prices—along with the queen's head. Her Majesty tried to calm them down, but it only worked on some of them. The rest of the mob began firing cannons—"

She cut him off. "*Steam* cannons?"

"No, ma'am. Just regular cannons. Her Majesty, along with the Duke of Rochefoucauld-Liancourt, tried to persuade the King to leave, but he wouldn't have it. But then we received your message, and His Majesty relented. The royal family left in the *Majesté Divine* thirty minutes ago."

"Where are they headed?" Jeanne said.

"They talked of going to Rambouillet, but ultimately decided to head for Montmédy."

Montmédy was a fortress in the Lorraine region of northeastern France near the German and Austrian borders. It made sense for the royal family to flee there, since the monarchy had so much support in that area, and it was the most unlikely place in France to experience political unrest.

The aide gave Jeanne the heading the royal airship was taking, and she thanked him. The knights then went back into the *Minuit Solaire* and the airship took off along the heading for Montmédy.

The royal family may have escaped the Palace siege, but that didn't mean they were safe just yet. It was the duty of the Ordre de la Tradition that they make sure no harm came to them, no matter what. In order to do that, they had to first locate the *Majesté Divine*.

6

The skies above France, July 14, 1789 (Infini Calendar), 1:00 p.m.
        The king and queen sat together on the luxurious bed in the royal family's cabin aboard the *Majesté Divine*. The bed featured four tall posts supporting a silk canopy. Furthermore, like the Palace their cabin was decorated with priceless paintings and plush carpeting. Sunlight drifted in from the windows next to their bed while clouds sped by.

        Their son, Louis-Charles, and daughter Marie-Thérèse, currently were asleep on separate beds on the opposite wall of the spacious cabin. It had been no trouble for them to lose themselves in unconsciousness after their harrowing escape from the Palace.

        "Are you sure you can raise enough support in Montmédy?" Marie Antoinette asked softly, not wanting to wake the children.

        "They have always been loyal to us. And with order breaking down across France, we cannot risk going anywhere else."

        "We can always go stay with my brother. He would protect us." Her brother was Leopold II, emperor of Austria.

        But Louis XVI said, "I will not abandon my homeland to those wolves of the Third Estate. You've seen what they do when left to their own devices. Don't worry; we shall be safe once we reach Montmédy."

        There was a knock at the door, and the king bade the visitor to enter. It was the Duke of Rochefoucauld-Liancourt, who had escaped with them on the airship. "Your Majesties, how are you faring?"

        "Well enough, all things considered," the king said, though he was visibly lacking confidence in that statement.

The Duke noticed the children sleeping, and came over to the bed, speaking in a hushed tone. "We shall arrive in Montmédy shortly. From there you can rebuild your power base."

The king's voice began dripping with anger. "I swear upon our Lord and God that I will return to crush those barbaric commoners, along with their noble and clergy accomplices."

Marie Antoinette rose off the bed and began walking over to the door.

"You should stay in your cabin until we reach Montmédy, Your Majesty," the Duke said.

"I'm going to the toilettes. I'll be back shortly."

Oddly, the Duke seemed anxious about her leaving. "Wait, my queen. It's not safe—"

He was too late, however. The queen stepped into the corridor and immediately shrieked.

"What is it? What's wrong?" Louis XVI said.

Marie Antoinette stepped back into the room, her face contorted in horror. With a violently shaking finger she pointed at something down the hall. "Th-The guards! They're...!"

The king jumped off the bed and ran into the hallway. Half a dozen bodies lay slumped against the walls or splayed on the floor, blood soaking wherever they lay. In addition, each guard had a hole going all the way through his neck in the same spot. They must have all been killed before they could even cry out to alert others.

Louis XVI turned to the Duke. "What is this?"

The commotion woke up the children. Louis-Charles said, "Are we there yet?"

"Oh, bother," the Duke said, looking over at them. "I was hoping to kill you while they slept, so they wouldn't have to witness it. I was then going to end them in their sleep, painlessly."

"Have you taken leave of your senses, François?" the king demanded to know.

The Duke actually laughed contemptuously. "I'm not your trustworthy duke. If you were to ever get back to the Palace—which you won't—you would find the body of the real Duke of Rochefoucauld-Liancourt hidden in the cellar."

"An imposter? Then who—"

The king forgot his words as the Duke's entire flesh rippled like a body of water after a stone had been dropped in it. The Duke pulsated and the body underneath his clothes was re-molded as if it were clay.

When finished, he was no longer the Duke of Rochefoucauld-Liancourt. Instead, he was someone completely unexpected. Someone who should have been dead.

The king gasped. "You...!"

The imposter spoke again, and now even his voice was different. "I'm glad to see you still recognize me, even though I'm young again and not the old man you remember."

Louis XVI shook with a combination of rage and terror. "The court was right; you *are* a monster!"

The children sat on their beds, too scared to even blink. They were transfixed entirely on the morphing villain in front of them.

"If you had heeded my warning fifteen years ago, none of this would be necessary. I told you what would happen to France if your policies remained as they were. I told you the country would be torn apart."

The imposter took a step towards the king, who immediately removed a golden revolver from his robe and fired at him. The imposter fell backwards to the floor, a black ichor oozing from the wound in place of blood.

The report from the pistol shook the children out of their paralyzed state, and Louis XVI grabbed them off the beds.

Together they ran to the bridge to notify the ship's captain of the assassin, the king and queen covering the children's eyes as they stepped over the corpses.

Unfortunately, when they arrived they found the bridge crew slaughtered just like the guards in the hallway. The captain and operators were dead in their seats with holes punched through their necks.

"Children, please look away," the queen said.

They quietly did as they were told. No doubt this whole experience had left them too shaken to do anything else.

The murdered crew was facing away from the entrance to the bridge, suggesting they had been taken by surprise. That wasn't surprising, since they—like the royal family—must have believed him to be the real Duke of Rochefoucauld-Liancourt, up until the moment he decided to strike. But what weapon had he used? Neither Louis XVI nor Marie Antoinette had seen him carrying anything in his hands.

"No one's piloting the ship," the queen said.

She managed to refrain from voicing her new fears, but the king knew well enough that without operators the ship would soon crash. The idea of any of them taking the controls was out of the question; they were, after all, royalty and not trained to do the work of commoners.

"We'll have to parachute," Louis XVI said.

He ran over to the lockers on the right wall and rummaged through them until he found what he was looking for.

His spirits were raised as he removed four white bundles, but all hopes were shattered as he looked them over. "They've been shredded," he said, deflated.

Indeed, the parachutes had been torn by someone or something, probably the assassin who had come to kill them. They'd never hold up if anyone tried to open them during a freefall.

However, he found a faint glimmer of hope in the form of a narrow white cylinder on one of the locker shelves. He took it and looked it over.

"Is that a smoke tube?" the queen asked.

"Yes. And it seems to be in one piece. If we can light it on the deck, maybe the *Minuit Solaire* will see it and come for us."

"What are the chances that they are even in the area?"

"The Palace will have told them where we are heading. If I know Jeanne de Fleur, she will no doubt come after us with all due haste. It's a slim hope, but it's all we have."

Suddenly the children began frantically tugging at their parents' clothes. Louis XVI and Marie Antoinette turned around to see a horrifying sight: The assassin was standing in the hallway outside the royal family's cabin grinning at them. Furthermore, the wound in his chest was no longer bleeding.

"It's useless," he grinned. "Without a bridge crew this ship will soon crash. And I destroyed the parachutes, so there's no escape."

Louis XVI shot him again, this time in the stomach. The assassin fell to his knees, and the king quickly ushered his family up the stairs onto the top deck. Behind them the assassin shouted, "Shoot me all you want, my wounds won't last long."

7

The skies above France, July 14, 1789 (Infini Calendar), 1:10 p.m.

Jeanne stared intently through the canopy window on board the bridge of the *Minuit Solaire*. So far, they had yet to see any sign of the *Majesté Divine*, though they were flying the same heading given to them by the aide at the Palace. Fortunately, Celeste and her team of engineers had recently made upgrades to the *Minuit Solaire's* engines, so the ship could fly at a greater top speed than the royal family's vessel. This would hopefully allow them to catch up with the royal family before it was too late.

"We've got something," Adolphe the left operator said.

Up ahead they could see a trail of orange smoke—a signal—ahead of them. At the head of the plume was an airship. Since there were only two airships in the world, it had to be the *Majesté Divine*!

"Take us in," Jeanne said. She grabbed the communications tube hanging next to her chair. "Celeste, we've spotted the *Majesté Divine*, but it looks like they may be having problems. Have Harpoon Control ready some anchors."

"*Ma'am, if they lose thrust, we won't be able to keep them afloat.*"

"I'm aware of that. I'm going to take a team in to hopefully stabilize the ship. Just stay focused on keeping *us* afloat. When we get within range, fire the harpoons."

"*Understood!*"

Jeanne went to go retrieve Pierre and Victor, who were on standby in their quarters in case they were needed. Both of them were trained to operate the *Minuit Solaire* in the event of an emergency, and since the *Majesté Divine*

- 41 -

were of the same design, they should be able to operate it as well.

They proceeded up the stairs to the top deck. The wind battered them as they grabbed hold of the railing. Normally crew members were not authorized to go topside while the airship was in motion, but these were special circumstances.

When the *Minuit Solaire* got closer to the *Majesté Divine*, Jeanne could see that it was none other than the king holding the smoke tube. Louis XVI, along with his wife and children, were huddled together at the stern of their ship.

From the bow of the *Minuit Solaire*, two decks below the bridge, a paneled section of the hull was removed and two enormous metal spears appeared in the rectangular hole.

Jeanne motioned for the royal family to step away from the stern of the *Majesté Divine*. They complied, getting clear of what was obviously coming.

Without any further warning the spears exploded from the small bay they had been stationed in. In a rush of steam and cables the spears penetrated the deck of the *Majesté Divine*. Wood splintered as the two airships became locked together in the sky.

The *Minuit Solaire* shuddered as it struggled to adapt to being tethered to its younger sister hundreds of feet above France. It shuddered even more as a crank system in Harpoon Control tightened the cables attached to the spears and pulled the ships closer together.

Once she was satisfied the two airships wouldn't be leaving each other's company, Jeanne threw the rope ladder overboard and rode it down to the deck of the royal airship. Pierre and Victor followed suit.

When they were safely on deck the royal family rushed over to them. "Jeanne, thank God you are here!" the king said.

"Your Majesty, you and your family need to climb up this ladder and wait—"

Suddenly a trio of black tendrils came out of nowhere and sliced the rope ladder from the hull of the *Minuit Solaire*. They then receded back to their source, the arm of a strange young man standing on the deck near the bow.

"Who is that?" Pierre said.

"An assassin!" Marie Antoinette yelled. "He took on the appearance of the Duke of Rochefoucauld-Liancourt. Not only that, but bullets cannot seem to kill him."

The royal family hid behind Jeanne and the knights. "Well, now that the rope ladder is out, it looks like we'll *have* to kill him," Victor said.

Jeanne shook her head. "No, you two need to get to the bridge and fly the ship."

They were reluctant to leave her alone with the assassin, but they nonetheless said, "Understood."

Pierre and Victor cautiously maneuvered around the mysterious assailant—who seemed to take no notice of them—and headed down the stairs to the bridge.

"You're not going to try and stop them?" Jeanne said.

The assassin said, "My real targets are right in front of me. It doesn't matter if your knights can keep this airship aloft; as long as the royal family dies, my mission will be complete."

"Who are you and why are you doing this?" Jeanne demanded to know.

The assassin laughed. "Ironically, I was once the king's biggest supporter. But he failed to heed my advice and now the country is on the road to ruin."

"He is the Count of Saint-Germaine!" Louis XVI said.

It couldn't be! "The Count of Saint-Germaine died five years ago," Jeanne said. "That can't be him."

"I am far older than anyone realizes. Only I had the genius necessary to create the Philosopher's Stone, the holy grail of alchemy. And I have used it to become ageless."

"Let's say for the sake of argument that I believe you. Do you really think murdering the king will help France?" Jeanne said.

"Of course, I do. Our country's rightful leader is waiting to take his place and lead us into the future, even if he has to do it from behind the scenes."

Jeanne sighed. "If you're that determined to commit regicide, then I'll have to stop you."

She unsheathed her sword and took a step towards him, but he put out his palm and motioned for her to stop. "Just a moment, please. I know who you are; you are the Countess de Fleur. There is no need for us to fight, Countess; you can join us. You may be a noble and a dog of the *Ancien Régime*, but that wasn't always the case. Your family was originally poor farmers. Because of your famous ancestor who fought for France and narrowly escaped being burned alive, the monarchy allowed the House of de Fleur to be established in her honor. You have inherited more than her name. Remember your roots, Jeanne de Fleur; join us and together we can make France great again!"

However, Jeanne simply said, "Is that it?"

"What?"

"I can't speak for everyone in the House of de Fleur, but *I* serve the king. He is the one who believed in me and appointed me to this prestigious post. I will not betray him for anything." She pointed her sword at him. "If that is all you have to say, let us now resolve this conflict."

The Count closed his eyes and sighed. "Very well. The Revolution can do without you, I suppose."

Jeanne charged in, but the Count raised his right arm which morphed into a series of black tendrils and speared her in her chest plating.

The Count's tendrils pinned her to the deck and dented her plating. "Your irodium armor is impressive. Any other material would have been thoroughly pierced. But it doesn't really matter; I can turn any part of my body into anything of any hardness thanks to the Philosopher's Stone."

Jeanne swung her sword and batted the tendrils away, but they didn't break. So, the Count wasn't exaggerating about their hardness.

She jumped to her feet and thrust at him. However, his left arm morphed into a dark bulbous monstrosity resembling a battering ram but fleshy with veins, shredding the sleeve which could no longer contain it. The battering ram easily blocked her strike, and he knocked her aside with it. Her rapier went skittering across the deck and against the railing, rattling mere inches from the edge and falling off the airship altogether.

It didn't make any sense; alchemy was only supposed to change objects into things with equal mass. It shouldn't be able to enlarge body parts to the extent that was now happening with the Count. Perhaps he really did have the Philosopher's Stone.

His tendrils once again shot out and pinned her to the deck. She grabbed them but they wouldn't budge. She didn't have any chance of getting free without her sword.

The Count stood over her with his hideous battering ram arm. "Farewell, mademoiselle." The unholy weapon bore down on her. She closed her eyes.

A moment passed, though, and she wasn't smashed, so she looked up to see what had happened.

"Not a moment too soon, eh?"

It was the forger, Jacques du Chard. He stood over her blocking the Count's attack with a broadsword he had obviously borrowed from the *Minuit Solaire*'s armory. He struggled mightily against the Count's battering ram; Jeanne didn't know how much longer he could hold it off.

"How did you get down here?" she asked. "The Count destroyed the ladder."

"Ah, but that is not the only thing connecting these two ships."

She was astonished. "The harpoons? You came across on the cables?"

"My apologies, Mademoiselle de Fleur. Your crew insisted I not do that, but I cannot redeem myself waiting around, no?"

The Count's patience was wearing thin. "Enough of this banter. If you are on her side, then I'll kill you as well."

Jeanne leaned to talk in Jacques' ear. "Can you hold him off for a minute?"

He looked the Count up and down. "I can try."

"Please do. I have a plan, but it will take a little time to pull off. I'm counting on you, forger."

"Your faith shall be rewarded."

She ran over to the railing and retrieved her sword, leaving Jacques to face the Count by himself. "A lowly criminal?" the Count said, indicating Jacques. "Then you should be on our..." he said, but didn't bother to finish his sentence. "Never mind; if you're with them, you're not likely to listen to reason."

The Count raised tendrils and shot them at Jacques. "I've seen that trick already," the forger said, hitting the deck and rolling out of the way.

Meanwhile, Jeanne closed her eyes and mentally steeled herself for what she was about to do. The God's Eye, passed down from mother to daughter in her family and said to have been given to them by the Lord Himself, was an extremely dangerous tool to use. It required a staggering amount of concentration just to maintain the wielder's sanity; more than one of Jeanne's ancestors had been driven insane using it.

When she was certain that she was as ready as she was going to be, Jeanne removed the patch over her left eye. The world in front of her abruptly exploded with information. She could know even the tiniest details about anything she saw; the exact composition of the *Majesté*

Divine's deck, how many molecules were in it, its precise diameter, how many people had been involved in its construction, how many raindrops had fallen on it since its completion, its age down to the last nanosecond, etc.

Focus! She told herself. The sheer amount of information assailing her was the danger of the God's Eye. If she didn't concentrate on one thing at a time, she could easily lose her mind.

There! She set her sight on her target: the Count himself. He was currently fighting Jacques and trying to skewer the forger with his tendrils.

Concentrate only on the Count. All right, then... his grotesque limbs were composed of... his blood! So that was how he managed to expand his size; he had converted large quantities of his own bodily fluids to a solid form and condensed them so they became hardened against attacks.

But then, if his blood had been converted into weapons, what was keeping him alive? Jeanne focused on the Count's midsection. A black substance ran through his veins. Focusing even further on the substance, she perceived that it was a cheap substitute for blood. It was keeping the Count breathing and moving, but not much else.

That being the case, he shouldn't be able to keep up a strenuous battle for long. His stamina would be depleted quickly. That would explain why he was on the defensive against Jacques and being careful not to move around too much. If Jeanne were to join the fight...

She put her eye patch back on, eternally grateful to still be sane after using it. "Forger! Focus on wearing him down! Hit and move!"

"Will do, Mademoiselle!"

While Jacques came at the Count from the front, Jeanne attacked him from his flank. Jacques dodged the Count's tendrils and swung with his borrowed sword. The Count moved to block with his fleshy battering ram, but that left him open for Jeanne's strike.

The Count noticed her coming and jumped out of the way of her sword swing. She managed to graze him across his chest and draw a little bit of the black substance he was using in place of blood. It may not have been a serious wound, but jumping with his heavy arm weapons must have been taxing for him.

Jacques didn't give him time to catch his breath, as the forger swung at him again. Jacques wasn't a trained soldier, but a simple swing was enough to keep the Count on his toes.

The Count didn't have time to prepare a tendril strike, so he simply blocked with them. Jeanne then thrust under his battering ram towards his legs. Again, the Count had to jump out of the way to avoid serious injury.

This continued for what seemed like ages (but was probably mere minutes), Jeanne and Jacques hitting the Count of Saint-Germaine with attacks emphasizing speed over power, and him struggling to either keep away from them or block their assaults with his arm weapons.

Finally, he began huffing and wheezing from exhaustion. As Jeanne had predicted, his cheap black blood and heavy weapon arms caused him to wear out much faster than Jacques and herself.

He leaned back against the portside rail, wheezing. "I won't... haah... be defeated by you," he said between breaths.

"Surrender now, rogue," Jeanne replied. "Your desecrated body was only good for brief but intense bursts of offense. Believe me; your so-called Philosopher's Stone hasn't done you any favors."

"Ungh... fine, then." He grunted with some kind of great exertion and held up his tendril arm. It was pointless, Jeanne thought; she had already determined the tendrils' maximum speed, and both Jacques and she could dodge them now.

However, two of the tendrils merged into the third, increasing its size and length. With one final howl of physical stress, the Count launched it at Jeanne with double the speed of his previous strikes. Even if it didn't penetrate her irodium armor, the force of the attack would surely knock her off the airship.

"Mademoiselle!" Jacques cried out. He pushed her out of the way and took the fleshy spear in his chest.

"Forger!"

Jeanne rushed at the Count and pierced him through the heart with her rapier. No longer able to support himself on the railing, the Count fell over it and was sucked into the portside engine.

The ship shuddered as the engine exploded and the deck pitched sideways. Jacques, who had been freed of the giant tendril when the Count succumbed to Jeanne's attack, began sliding towards the starboard side of the deck.

Realizing he was in danger of sliding off the ship, Jeanne dove in to grab his arm. After a few moments the *Majesté Divine* stabilized slightly—probably due to the efforts of Pierre and Victor at the controls.

"Talk to me, forger," she said.

He coughed up blood. "Did I... do good?"

"Yes, you did very well."

"I... wonder about that. This is... a revolu... tion by the people, the same ones I... wronged. Should I have... gone against them? Will this... really re-redeem me?" He hacked up more blood.

"Believe me; you did a great service to France today. I will make sure your efforts are not forgotten."

"I... would like... something... from you."

"Anything."

"I have not... seen you smile, even once since... we met. Please... smile for me."

She considered his words. It was true that she rarely showed emotions. Maybe... maybe that was something within herself that she should change. "If that is your wish."

She smiled for him, not too much, but more than enough as she shed a single tear for this petty criminal who had been rejected by his own country.

"*Merveilleux*," he said softly. *Marvelous*. And with that, he closed his eyes forever.

A sudden creaking and groaning from the *Majesté Divine* reminded her that it was not over yet. With only one working engine, the airship was going down, and the *Minuit Solaire* would not be able to hold it up much longer.

Jeanne motioned to the crew working in the *Solaire*'s harpoon bay to release the cables. There was no sense in both ships going down, and without the weight of the *Solaire* bearing down on them the *Majesté Divine* might actually be able to land in one piece.

There was a snap as the cables were cut and the *Majesté Divine* was let loose. Jeanne scooped up the body of Jacques and carried it down to the bridge where the royal family, along with Pierre and Victor, were waiting for her.

"We're going down, Commander," Pierre said. "You and the royal family had better strap yourselves in."

There were more seats on this bridge than on the *Solaire* in order to accommodate their special passengers. Jeanne made sure each member of the royal family was secured in his/her seat before strapping herself into the captain's chair.

The ship pitched forward and they could see the ground coming up at them. Pierre and Victor struggled to control their descent, but it looked like it wasn't going to be enough.

Pierre yelled, "Hang on tight!"

Jeanne braced herself as the *Majesté Divine* hit the ground with thunderous force. She rocketed forward in her seat, but the safety harness held.

After a grueling few moments of the ship skidding against the earth, they came to a complete stop. Jeanne slowly got up from her seat and stepped into a puddle of water. The canopy window had smashed and water was pouring in through some sort of pond. It had probably cushioned the impact just enough for them to survive.

"Is everyone all right?" she said.

The king and queen confirmed that they were. Their children were also unharmed, although perhaps only physically. Everyone seemed to be shaken but otherwise fine.

8

Varennes, France, July 14, 1789 (Infini Calendar), 1:30 p.m.
The knights led the royal family out of the airship and onto the solid ground outside. They were in a village which they recognized as Varennes. They had crashed in a portion of the Aire river which ran through the town.

Before they could celebrate their survival, though, the entire village came out to confront them. Angry voices assailed them as they vented their anger.

"The king is trying to flee France!"

"Just abandoning your people, eh?"

"Take responsibility for the mess our country is in!"

It looked like they were going to get violent, and Jeanne didn't think they could face the entire village in a fight. The *Minuit Solaire* flew overhead, but there was no way it would reach them in time.

She took the only option left to her: She bowed down before them. "I implore you! If you are going to kill anyone, it should be me. Please allow King Louis XVI and his family to live. Do not deprive these innocent children of their parents!"

The villagers talked it over with themselves for a few minutes, and then said, "Very well. We will allow the royal family to live. However, it has become apparent that the king and queen cannot be trusted. Therefore, we insist on accompanying them back to Paris where they will be closely watched."

"Thank you," Jeanne said.

While it was obvious that Louis XVI and Marie Antoinette did not like the idea of being prisoners at all, Jeanne once again silently thanked God that their lives had been spared this day.

As they rode back to France in a wagon supplied by the village, Jeanne couldn't help but wonder who was behind this day's violence. Who set up the Bastille and the Palace of Versailles to be attacked? Who sent the assassin calling himself the Count of Saint-Germaine to murder the king?

And finally: Would this be the only plot set into motion?

9

July 15, 1789 (Infini Calendar), 11:00 a.m.
The meeting of the Montagnards sect of the Jacobin Club was an especially tense one. One of the members, who had the floor, said, "The king is still alive! This is unacceptable!"
The yelling of his fellow club members showed that they shared his sentiment. However, Robespierre waved his hands to quiet them down. "No matter. The king is being put under house arrest in Paris and will be under careful watch from now on. We can strike again at any time.
"I am more concerned about the loss of the Count of Saint-Germaine to those knights. I said not to underestimate them, but it seems that is exactly what I have done. Or perhaps I simply *overestimated* the Count. At any rate, we'll have to be more careful next time. And I can assure you all there *will* be a next time."

PART II
Frères et soeurs
(Brothers and Sisters)

1

Château de Fleur, August 1, 1789 (Infini Calendar), 9:30
a.m.
        Jeanne was in the training hall of her family's estate
in Domrémy-la-Pucelle (a village in northeastern France,
and the home of her legendary ancestor), practicing her
swordsmanship techniques on the training dummies that
occupied the room. Wielding her rapier expertly, she
pierced one lifeless target after another with swift, agile
movements.
        She needed to keep her skills from atrophying; it had
been a full two weeks since she had returned to Paris with
the royal family and since then the Ordre de la Tradition had
been unable to go on any missions for the king. That was
because Louis XVI was no longer the absolute monarch of
France. Instead, the Legislative Assembly (formerly the
National Constituent Assembly; formerly the National
Assembly; formerly the Third Estate; from this point
forward referred to simply as the Assembly) which had just
been formed now kept him a veritable prisoner within the
Tuileries (the royal palace of Paris) and had removed many
of the powers he used to enjoy as king.
        The return to Paris was still fresh within her mind.
The entire city had turned out to silently watch the royal
family escorted to the Tuileries in disgrace, angry and
otherwise unsympathetic faces on each citizen. Although
Jeanne hated having to see them go through that, she—
along with her other knights Pierre and Victor—had
managed to keep them alive. As far as she was concerned,
the knights had successfully carried out their duty.
        Since then, the Ordre's airship the *Minuit Solaire*
had been grounded at the Tuileries, kept under armed guard
twenty-four hours a day. The Assembly had wanted to lock

up the knights—Jeanne included—because they viewed them as dogs of the *Ancien Régime*. Fortunately for the knights, the Parisian public still held a great deal of admiration for them and all they had done for France. They wouldn't allow "Jeanne la Juste" to rot in a dungeon somewhere.

When she was finished, Jeanne grabbed a towel to dry herself off. The one bright spot of being off-duty was not having to wear her irodium armor. It may have been lightweight and very durable, but it became almost unbearably hot in the summer. At the moment she simply wore a white blouse and dark-blue leggings. Her long auburn hair wasn't even in its trademark braid going down her back; she was letting it flow freely for now.

One thing, though, that she could not do away with was her purple eye patch she had to wear at all times. Whenever she took it off, she risked losing her mind to the God's Eye, the powerful but mysterious force which possessed her left eye.

Jeanne would never forget the day she inherited it: the day her mother died. Her mother was the previous bearer of the God's Eye, and at the very moment of her death it transferred over to Jeanne, only a twelve-year-old girl at the time. Jeanne was playing in the garden in front of the château when suddenly an onslaught of information assaulted her senses. She was fortunate to lose consciousness before any further damage was done, but she was bedridden for a week afterwards. That was when her father explained to her about the God's Eye, that it had been passed down from mother to daughter for centuries, and that was why Jeanne's mother had to wear an eye patch for all the time Jeanne had known her. And now, he said, it was Jeanne's turn to put it on.

She railed against this horrible burden that had been forced on her. She asked her father why the God's Eye was only passed down to women. Why couldn't her brother Jean-Paul take it? After all, he was older and much stronger than her. That, according to her father, was probably why God only gave it to women. "*Ma petite*, since the beginning of the world, women have had a much harder time of it," he said. "They have been bullied and abused by us men. I think the Lord wanted to give you something to fight back with. But more than that, perhaps he wanted to give women of each generation a champion, someone to fight for them." But if that was the case, why was the God's Eye so dangerous to its users? "There is no such thing as a safe power. Moving mountains requires great determination and effort. You must work hard if you wish to do great things."

So, Jeanne grew up with the weight of her left eye always upon her until the day of her death. She resolved to become strong so that she would own the God's Eye, and not be owned by *it*. To that end, she joined the military and fought her hardest, winning commendations and eventually being picked by the king himself to lead the Ordre de la Tradition, a select group of talented individuals who answered only to His Majesty.

When she had finished cleaning up, she walked through the corridors of the house and entered her room. As was fitting for a noblewoman, her room contained only the finest furnishings. A luxurious blue rug met her feet as she entered, and tall windows adorned with expensive white curtains let in warm sunlight. In addition, her canopy bed was easily large enough for three of her. It wasn't as if she cared about opulence, though; she had simply been raised to keep up appearances.

She ignored all of these things and went over to the far wall where her oak armoire was. She opened it up and pulled out her most prized possession: the violin she had inherited from her mother. Genevieve de Fleur had been celebrated for her ability to play the instrument, and while Jeanne did not have any musical aspirations, she still enjoyed the harmony she could create with it. It gave her a measure of peace she would otherwise not have.

After opening a window, she took the bow and began playing a sonata by Bach. She admired his work, although she enjoyed other Baroque composers such as Handel and Vivaldi. Feeling the breeze from the open window, she allowed the melody to flow through her, and for a brief period her whole world felt exceedingly serene. At times like this, she felt the strongest connection to her late mother.

Eventually, though, there was a knock at the door. It was Eugène, the family's *Maître d'Hôtel*, an elderly gentleman who had served the House of de Fleur for many years. Since the death of Jeanne's father the previous year, she had taken to leaving Eugène in charge while she was out. "I'm sorry to disturb you, milady, but you have a visitor. A Monsieur Pierre Girard."

"I will see to him at once. Thank you, Eugène."

Jeanne met Pierre in the main hall. Like the rest of the house, it was decorated with impeccable tastes. An ornate wooden floor, fine marble fireplace, expensive burgundy curtains over the front windows, and a priceless crystal chandelier were just a few of the luxuries in the room.

"You are looking well, ma'am," Pierre said. He was wearing simple brown clothes, but even without his armor he was still a large man, easily dwarfing Jeanne's small frame. Furthermore, his almond-colored skin hinted at more than French blood inside him.

"As are you. I am glad to see you have been keeping your beard neatly trimmed during our downtime." She motioned for him to sit down in a plush white chair, and she sat in one across from it. She offered him tea.

"I saw the grave out front. The forger?"

She nodded. "He saved my life. He may even have saved all of us. I felt he deserved a dignified burial."

"I have to agree. If it were up to anyone else, though, he probably would have been tossed in a ditch."

She said, "That's true. But I get the feeling you didn't come all the way out here to talk about Jacques du Chard. Is something bothering you?"

"Our downtime may be ending very soon," he said. "Have you heard about Leopold II?"

"The emperor of Austria? I heard he isn't happy about the imprisonment of his sister and our queen."

He shook his head. "It's worse than that. Much worse. He's organized a coalition of neighboring countries. Reliable sources tell me they're planning an invasion to free Her Majesty."

This was news to Jeanne; she hadn't heard anything about a possible invasion. But, then again, lately she had only been concerned with matters at home, most notably the welfare of Louis XVI and the royal family. "An invasion? What countries are allied with him?"

"Supposedly Frederick William II, the king of Prussia, is his main ally. I also hear *émigré* French nobles are on their side. I'm not sure who else."

Jeanne wasn't surprised that the nobles who fled France following the violence on July fourteenth would be involved. Fearful that the revolutionaries would succeed in overthrowing the government and take away their privileges as nobility (or kill them), they left their own country and were currently living in exile. They'd surely jump at the chance to take back control of France from the Assembly which now ran the country. "What does the Assembly plan to do about it?" she asked.

"The power to declare war still rests with the king, and they're urging him to use it. Are you familiar with Jacques-Pierre Brissot de Warville?"

"I've heard of him," Jeanne said casually. "He's the voice of that leftist group within the Assembly, the Girondists, isn't he?"

"That's right; more specifically, the Girondists are a splinter group of the Jacobins. Brissot's also the editor of the *Patriote Français*. He's been speaking out on the dangers of being attacked from both internal and outside forces simultaneously. He believes that in order to prevent France's complete collapse, we should strike Leopold II before he strikes *us*. In his mind, we need to unite against a common enemy."

Jeanne finished drinking her tea and put down the cup. "What are the chances of his succeeding in persuading the king?"

Pierre frowned. "Very good, I'm afraid. The Girondists hold a lot of power in the Assembly. The one most strongly opposing Brissot is the leader of the right-wing faction of the Jacobins, the Montagnards: Maximilien Robespierre. He says a war on two fronts could destroy France. Unfortunately, he doesn't have as much pull as Brissot. His Majesty is expected to declare war any day now."

She looked at the empty tea cup in front of her. "May God help us all."

2

The Jacobin monastery, Paris, August 2, 1789 (Infini Calendar), 2:00 p.m.

Maximilien Robespierre sat quietly in the library of the monastery which the Jacobin Club had recently begun renting. Prior to their move to Paris, the Jacobins had been based in Versailles in order to keep an eye on the activities of the king and queen. Since the royal family had been forced to relocate to Paris, the Jacobins opted to follow suit.

Outside of Montagnard meetings, the thirty-one-year-old Jacobin did not wear his red cloak. Rather, today he wore a brown suit with a puffy white cravat around his neck, as well as a flat white wig which currently was in style for French politicians. Many people who saw him in public immediately noticed his strong chin and confident eyes that marked him as a natural leader.

The current headquarters of the group was a monastery located on the street Rue Saint-Honoré, next door to the building which housed the Assembly. This made it an ideal location to set up operations, as the Jacobin Club was heavily involved with the Assembly (since prominent Jacobins were also members of the Assembly).

The library of the monastery was small, only housing half a dozen book cases. Nevertheless, Robespierre enjoyed sequestering himself in here and reading at the wooden table in the center of the room.

His solitude was interrupted by the opening of the door in front of the table. Robespierre looked up to see the Marquis de Sade enter the room. "You can be a hard man to find, Monsieur Robespierre, tucked away back here."

"It's not a large building," Robespierre said, not wanting to engage the Marquis' tired wit.

Undeterred, the Marquis said, "So it is. I just came by to give you the news."

Without looking up from his book, Robespierre replied dryly, "The king has declared war?"

The Marquis's face contorted into a twisted smile. "Correct! Oh, you must be so sad, having lost the fight to that garish Brissot."

Robespierre dismissed the Marquis' attempt to goad him. "Brissot is a fool. We are sunk beyond our necks in debt, and any further spending on a war budget will only bring further strife. This could well be what breaks our beloved country."

The Marquis said in his most overly dramatic tone, "Oh, whatever will we do?"

This time it was Robespierre's turn to give a wry smile. "All is not lost. This could be just the opportunity we've been looking for. If we survive this crisis, we'll have everything we need to overthrow the king and seize complete control of the country."

"A man after my own heart!" the Marquis laughed. "Even faced with war within and without, you still remain focused on eliminating your enemies in some ruthless way. Of course, I don't have any enemies—I'm a people person, you know—but human suffering is universal, something to which we can all relate."

Robespierre knew that wasn't true at all; de Sade didn't have a moral bone in his body. "Need I remind you this isn't a game? Everything we do is for the good of France. Quit licking your chops; I'm going to need your intellect focused entirely on achieving our goals. We're going to have more than hurt pride if we lose this 'game.'"

"Of course, of course. I have been known to go off on tangents from time to time. From now on, I shall concentrate on using our resources for the revolution." The Marquis turned to leave, then stopped and said, "Perhaps those knights can be put to good use."

***

The Austrian Netherlands, September 9, 1789 (Infini Calendar), dawn.

Colonel Jean-Paul de Fleur marched through the forest that morning, along with a few hundred of his men. They had moved under cover of night and the sun was just now cresting over the horizon. King Louis XVI, having declared war on Austria only a month before, had General Charles-François du Périer Dumouriez hastily assemble a force to invade the Austrian Netherlands in an attempt to gain the advantage against Leopold II early. At least, that was how the Assembly told it.

In actuality, the bull-headed Brissot—along with his Girondists—strong-armed the puppet monarch into declaring war against Louis XVI's brother-in-law, Leopold II. Jean-Paul was no fool; he knew the king would never have gone to war against his wife's brother on his own. There wouldn't have even been any problems with Austria if the Assembly hadn't made Marie Antoinette into a virtual prisoner. This whole thing was unnecessary.

Still, Jean-Paul couldn't afford to voice his concerns openly. The man riding the horse directly in front of him, General Dumouriez, had recently been accepted into the Jacobin club, meaning he was involved with the Assembly.

They soon came to the edge of the forest. About a kilometer up ahead was a field with a modest-looking fort. Their orders were to capture the fort to use as a staging ground for their campaign against Austria, since the structure was the closest to France's border.

One of their scouts popped out from behind a tree and saluted the General. "Welcome, sir. We have been reconnoitering the fort for two days in anticipation of your arrival."

Dumouriez nodded. "And what have you found?"

"We have observed no activity, sir. The place appears to be abandoned."

Dumouriez stared at the fort and its walls. There were two ramparts facing them, and a central building behind the walls, but no enemy troops could be seen. "No activity at all?"

"None, sir. Not even a guard doing his business. We have seen no one."

Jean-Paul said yawned. "Perhaps they moved their troops in anticipation of this attack."

Dumouriez didn't buy it. "If they knew we were coming, the smart thing to do would have been to set up an ambush in the forest. We're at the end of the forest now, and no attack."

"Or maybe they just don't give a damn about one measly fort," Jean-Paul said idly.

The sun was high enough now that they could see the fort quite clearly. Dumouriez surveyed it with his binoculars. "You're forgetting the number one rule of defense: Never let your enemy get his foot in the door." He put the binoculars back in the leather bag at his side. "All right, we're going in, but we're doing it cautiously. I will lead Division One and come at the fort from the front. Divisions Two, Three and Four will move around to surround it on the north, south and east sides, respectively."

They moved forward in formation at a brisk pace. However, they only got a few yards out of the forest before a familiar sound cut through the morning silence from somewhere overheard: the sound of an airship's engines. "Do you hear that? It's the *Minuit Solaire*. Oh, Jeanne, what are you doing here? You're going to announce our presence to every—"

Jean-Paul stopped as he realized the sound wasn't coming from the southwest as it should have been if it had come from France. Within a few moments it flew in low up ahead of them. The early sun glinted off the vessel, and he immediately knew something was very wrong here.

Dumouriez said it first. "It's black. A black airship!"

Indeed, the vessel heading towards them wasn't silver like the *Minuit Solaire* or the royal family's airship the *Majesté Divine*. Instead, it was a dark, foreboding black. Also, as it got closer Jean-Paul noticed the sound of its engines was different as well. He couldn't describe it in words, but something about the sound sent shivers up his backside.

When it came to about thirty feet overhead, Jean-Paul could see the words "Blitzkrieg Rache" painted on the side of the airship. Based on what little German he knew, that translated to "Lightning War Vengeance." He also noticed long metal spikes jutting out from various points on the hull. He could feel it clearly; this thing was a war machine.

He yelled behind him, "Steam cannons, fire!"

Lumbering out of the forest behind him were two metal cylinders, each one sitting atop a pair of steam-powered carriages. Like airships, the steam-powered carriage was invented by a Frenchman—in this case, Nicolas Joseph Cugnot in 1769. His original design was a three-wheeled tractor with a man-sized boiler in front. It was so cumbersome that it could only go a little over two miles an hour.

However, twenty years had been enough to advance the steam-powered carriage a great deal. Now it travelled on four wheels with a chassis built over them, and it could go up to thirty miles an hour on smooth terrain. Some of them, like the models here accompanying the invading force, had even been fitted with steam cannons on top for military use.

A group of soldiers frantically began prepping the cannons to fire. They had to manually aim them at the black airship and feed the boiler in the rear of the carriage in order to build up the pressure needed to fire the cannons.

While the men were preparing the cannons, the metal spikes along the black airship's hull began to glow and crackle with a strange blue energy. Jean-Paul could hear the zipping of the incandescent energy as it built up along the spikes. Somehow, he knew they wouldn't have time to get off a shot with the steam cannons.

"Fall back!" he yelled.

Dumouriez, angry, said, "I'm in command here! Nobody retreats until—"

His words were cut off as the black airship released its built-up energy at the steam carriages, tendrils of strange blue incandescence enveloping the metal conveyances. Their boilers exploded and metal debris went flying in all directions, skewering and otherwise maiming anyone nearby unlucky enough to be in the way. Other soldiers were knocked off their feet and horribly burned by the strange power that now assailed them.

The remaining men panicked and ran back into the forest. Jean-Paul ran over to Dumouriez, who stood dumbstruck in front of him. "General, we have to get out of here!"

Dumouriez simply stood there gaping at the horror of the black airship. Seeing no other choice, Jean-Paul belted him in the stomach. Dumouriez groaned. "The insolence! What did you do that for?"

"We—have—to—go!"

Getting back to his senses, the General began running back into the forest. Jean-Paul took one last look at the black airship. It was building up energy for another attack. He ran as fast as he could back into the forest. He almost made it when an explosion behind him sent him flying forwards. *Damn General; he just had to mention an ambush. Knocking on wood and all that.*

His world went dark even before he hit the ground.

3

The Tuileries, September 14, 1789 (Infini Calendar), 3:05 p.m.

Jeanne entered the war room, wearing her armor and accompanied by her Ordre de la Tradition subordinates Pierre and Victor. True to its name, the war room had a very spartan atmosphere; the walls were covered with maps and other intelligence documents and battle plans, and there were very few comforts to speak of within the room.

Already seated at the table was Louis XVI, his wife Marie Antoinette, and the three representatives from the Assembly, Maximilien Robespierre, Jacques-Pierre Brissot de Warville and Manon Roland.

The daughter of an engraver, Roland was a thirty-five-year-old member of the Girondist faction with Brissot, and an admirer of philosophers like Voltaire. She had a rather immodest opinion of her own beauty, and was known to brag about her silky brown hair, long slender fingers, white teeth and glowing complexion. On this day she wore a lime-green dress and white bonnet on her head.

The knights bowed to the king and queen, and, upon receiving permission, sat down opposite them. Normally, not even knights were allowed to sit with the monarchy as equals. However, the king and queen had been longtime supporters of the Ordre, and the knights' role in saving them from the Count of Saint-Germaine had greatly increased the trust that already existed.

"I appreciate you knights coming today," Louis XVI said. "You're probably wondering what this is all about."

"I assume it has something to do with our recent incursion into Austria, Your Majesty," Jeanne said.

Robespierre's manner was less diplomatic. "*Invasion* is more like it."

"It was necessary," Brissot retorted. "This war will unify France against the rest of Europe."

"All it's doing is unifying the rest of Europe against *us*," Marie Antoinette said.

Manon Roland gave the queen a venomous glance. For years Roland had been a vocal opponent of Antoinette's policies, many of which had been implemented by the king. However, rather than taking this opportunity to once again attack the queen, Roland simply said, "This arguing is not productive. We should focus on the topic at hand."

Pierre said, "Which is...?"

The king explained. "Recently an army regiment under General Dumouriez attempted to gain a foothold in Austria by capturing a fort near Neerwinden in the Austrian Netherlands. Unfortunately, they were soundly defeated."

To Jeanne, that was indeed unfortunate, though not surprising. "If I may speak freely, Your Majesty..."

"Go ahead, Jeanne. I value your opinion very highly."

Jeanne took a deep breath to prepare herself for what she had to say. "With all due respect, it is my understanding that the soldiers weren't given enough time to prepare for the campaign. They were quickly assembled and marched into the Netherlands without proper reconnaissance being done beforehand."

Robespierre said, "I don't think any amount of reconnaissance could have prepared them."

"Why do you say that?" Victor asked.

"Because it wasn't simply another military regiment that routed them. It was an airship."

Jeanne was astonished. "But only France has airships. And even now, we only have one working vessel."

"It would seem that is no longer the case," Roland said. There were a number of survivors—including General Dumouriez—and they all tell the same story, that they were attacked by a black airship which hurled strange blue lightning at them."

"A black airship?" Victor said. "Blue lightning? What in the world...?"

Jeanne interjected. "France doesn't have technology like that. If this story is true, it means some other country has begun developing airships, possibly with a unique power source."

Pierre shook his head. "I don't see how it can be done. Creating just two airships plunged our country into debt. It should logically do the same to anyone else who tries it. The resources required is simply too much."

"Not necessarily," Robespierre said. "While it is true that one country alone cannot effectively handle the cost of building an airship, a number of countries working to together could conceivably do it, in less time and without draining any one nation's budget to crippling levels."

Jeanne stroked her chin with her hand, something she did while deep in thought. "So, Leopold II and his alliance of European countries work together to build their own airship, with each country taking on their share of the burden. If they have been successful..."

Pierre picked up on where she was going with this. "They could build their own fleet of airships and gain complete control of the skies within a decade. Mon Diu!"

"We have to stop them," Brissot said. "We need to find out where they are building their airships and destroy the place. Blow the whole area to bits."

Robespierre gave Brissot a cold smile. "The wisdom of the Girondists: Every problem can be solved with a bang."

"At least I'm not a weakling like you!"

Marie Antoinette said, "Wouldn't it be more prudent to destroy the enemy airship that already exists, then go after the source?"

"For once I agree with Her Majesty," Roland said. "It would be much easier to find where they are building their fleet if we don't have to worry about the black airship which could attack us at any time."

"First we need to find it," Pierre said.

"We may have a chance very soon," Roland said. "The Austrians captured Dumouriez's second-in-command, and they've contacted us about a prisoner exchange."

"Which regiments was Dumouriez commanding?" Jeanne asked.

Brissot said, "The Fifth though Tenth Infantry Units, and the Twenty-Third Artillery Unit."

Jeanne let out a barely audible gasp. "My brother Jean-Paul is the commander of the Fifth Infantry Unit."

The king sighed. "I am sorry to tell you this, Jeanne, but he is the prisoner."

She fought to control the lump in her throat. "I... I understand. Please tell me we are going to rescue him."

"That is our intention," Roland said. "As I stated, the Austrians want to exchange prisoners. You can probably guess who they want to trade your brother for."

Jeanne looked at the queen. "Her Majesty."

Marie Antoinette held her head up high and said, "I will gladly go with them if it means the safe return of a great patriot such as Jean-Paul de Fleur."

However, Roland gave her another icy glare. "You will stay here. You are too important to hand over for a mere colonel."

Brissot agreed. "As if we would allow you to go free after the trouble you've gotten this country into."

Jeanne said, "Now wait just a moment! You can't—" She wanted to say, *You can't treat your queen this way.* She wanted to say, *Her Majesty loves this country just as much as any of you.* She wanted to say, *Have some decency and stop treating her like a common criminal.*

But the king gave Jeanne a look that said it was useless to fight the Assembly on this. They were in charge now, and nothing she said could change that.

Louis XVI had been chosen by God but rejected by man.

***

Jean-Paul had no idea where he was or how long he had been unconscious. Wherever he was, it was pitch-black and cold. As his senses returned to him he remembered the attempted attack on the fort. The black airship had ambushed the French forces and thoroughly routed them. Was he now imprisoned within the fort? Or did he die and this was simply the dullest afterlife anyone could have imagined? Either way, he wished his brutal headache would go away already.

He tried to move and realized he was tied to a chair with his hands bound behind his back. So, not the afterlife, then. Someone was keeping him here, probably as a prisoner of war. What was it the English said? Oh, right. "Capital." Just capital.

The question remained as to who was keeping him here. However, the sound of approaching footsteps and the turning of a lock somewhere in front of him suggested he may have been about to find the answer.

The door opened and he was greeted by a blinding light. It wasn't actually intense, but days spent in total darkness had rendered his eyes totally unprepared for ordinary light. He winced as it assaulted his eyes.

"Finally awake, are we, *dummkopf?*" said a female voice. Jean-Paul cautiously opened his eyes. A shapely silhouette stood in the doorway. He couldn't make out any features because of the light in the room behind her. What was causing it? No lamp could produce illumination that bright.

"I think I need a little more rest," he said. "My memory's a bit hazy, but I seem to recall somebody working me over pretty good recently."

"You should have thought about that before you invaded our country, French worm." Her voice was tinged with malice.

"Heh. Blame the Assembly. They sent us."

"Oh, they'll pay dearly for this. We were looking for an excuse to invade France, and now you've given it to us."

Jean-Paul spit out a bloody tooth (at least, he though it was a tooth). "I aim to please."

"Make all the jokes you want, worm. I will get *meine schwester* back, and then we'll see what kind of mood you're in after you've been subjected to our legendary Austrian torture techniques. We haven't even gotten started yet."

"Fair enough. But if *my* sister comes here, you'll be the one getting tortured."

There was a dark blur, and Jean-Paul felt something collide with his face so hard that he fell backwards in his chair. The last thing he remembered was his head crashing against the wall behind him.

***

The Tuileries, September 15, 1789 (Infini Calendar), 1:00 p.m.

Jeanne approached the *Minuit Solaire* on the docking platform behind the Tuileries palace. The sun was shining and the weather was just perfect that day. A slight breeze ran through her hair. As far as nature was concerned, all was as it should be.

Too bad the same could not be said of the current state of her beloved France. With her brother currently a prisoner of war, and the country heading closer to complete destruction with each passing day, she had definitely seen better days in her life. Hopefully, this operation would bring some much-needed stability to her homeland.

She walked over to the petite engineer in a brown jumpsuit who was supervising maintenance on the airship. The engineer noticed her approach and turned around. "Milady! I haven't seen you in ages!"

Jeanne nodded. "Hello, Celeste. I trust you have been doing well since our last mission?"

The bespectacled engineer gushed at Jeanne's friendly greeting. Celeste's admiration for the commander of the Ordre de la Tradition was the worst-kept secret in France. "The Assembly has mostly kept the crew busy maintaining the ship. It hasn't been difficult; we only suffered minor damage in that last skirmish. I wish I could say the same for the royal airship the *Majesté Divine*; it still hasn't been repaired since crashing in the village of Varennes."

Celeste's words, while factual, caused Jeanne to remember the regret she felt upon the completion of the previous mission. Jeanne was only still alive because the charismatic forger Jacques du Chard had sacrificed himself to save her from the Count of Saint-Germaine, who had transformed his body into a deadly weapon with the use of alchemy. There had been nothing 'minor' about Jacques' heroic loss of life, although Jeanne did not expect Celeste to understand that; the *Minuit Solaire's* engineer was primarily concerned with airships, which she viewed as more like people than most actual people.

"So, the ship will be operating at one hundred percent when we depart tomorrow?" Jeanne asked her.

"Oh, yes, ma'am. For this mission they ordered us to install a steam cannon onboard. One is all we can manage because they're so much heavier than regular cannons. We'd never get off the docking platform with a full complement of them."

"No, we wouldn't," Jeanne replied. "And the recoil from all those steam cannons could tear the ship apart." Normally, the *Minuit Solaire* was armed with ordinary cannons, along with the set of harpoons located on the bow below the bridge. But in the face of their new enemy, the Assembly had authorized one steam model to be loaded on the airship.

Celeste said, "Although, it sounds as if this black airship has found a way around that. Whatever kind of weaponry it uses, it seems to be on par with steam cannons."

"The survivors of the attack said it shot out strange blue energy which was extremely hot."

"Blue energy... very hot... I wonder..."

"Do you have some idea of what it could be?"

"Well... I'm not sure, but within the past few years the Americans have been working on a new source of energy. They call it electricity."

Jeanne had never heard of it. "'Electricity'? What is it?"

Celeste cautioned, "It hasn't been in development very long, but supposedly it allows you to generate energy via the movement of particles such as electrons and protons. Anyway, I don't have nearly enough information to confirm if this is the work of electricity."

Jeanne shook her head. "This is far outside my realm of experience. I don't know nearly as much about these things as you do."

"Oh, there's no need to be ashamed, milady. As I said, the technology of electricity is still in its infancy. There are only a handful of people in the world who have even heard of it. Just think of it as lightning."

"Lightning?"

"Yes, lightning. It's blue energy and it's extremely hot. Essentially what the Americans are trying to do is harness the power of lightning so they don't have to rely on coal, steam or any other conventional power source."

"Lightning," Jeanne said. "Yes, it does fit the description. But I've never heard of anyone being able to control it."

"If the black airship really does possess the power of lightning, it means the study of electricity is much farther along than anyone is willing to admit."

Jeanne frowned. "I suppose tomorrow we'll find out one way or another."

4

The Austrian Netherlands, September 16, 1789 (Infini Calendar), 3:00 p.m.

The *Minuit Solaire* touched down fifty feet from the Austrian fort where Jean-Paul de Fleur was supposedly being held prisoner. There was no sign of the black airship around.

True to Celeste's word, the Ordre's airship had taken them from Paris to the Austrian Netherlands without any problems. It was a very smooth ride.

Jeanne stepped onto the deck of the airship, fully armored and accompanied by Pierre and Victor. She tightly gripped the arm of the prisoner who was to be exchanged for her brother. The prisoner wore a lavish red dress worthy of Marie Antoinette. However, they had placed a burlap sack over her head to make sure things went as smoothly as possible; the Austrians probably believed their native daughter had been horribly mistreated, and while that was not too far from the truth, the knights had decided to indulge this slight misconception. After all, if the Austrians believed the French knights capable of harming Marie Antoinette, that would make them more reluctant to do anything reckless here.

Pierre and Victor lowered the wooden ramp mounted to the *Minuit Solaire's* deck to the ground and they proceeded to follow Jeanne down it. Jeanne kept her hand around the prisoner's arm to keep her from falling off the ramp, as she could not see where she was going with that sack over her head.

"What do you see?" the prisoner asked softly so as not to be heard by any unintended listeners.

"A dozen guards, and what appears to be their leader, are standing in front of the fort," Jeanne said.

"Their leader?"

"A young woman with short black hair—which has dual cowlicks almost resembling horns—and a bladed gauntlet on her right arm. About five-foot-five, seems to be in her early to mid twenties. She's wearing a white corset, under an open brown jacket, with navy blue leggings."

"Hmmm."

"Do you know her?"

"Perhaps, but I can't be sure without seeing her. What are the guards armed with?"

"Each of them has a *windbüchse* pointed at us."

The windbüchse, or "wind rifle," was a weapon employed by the Austrian Army. Rather than gunpowder, it utilized condensed air to propel projectiles. Naturally quiet, the rifle gives off no smoke or muzzle flash, which made it especially useful for sniping. The weapon was known to strike fear in the heart of many an enemy of Austria.

When they were within twenty feet of the Austrians, the leader motioned for them to stop. "That is far enough, French worms. So, you have brought meine schwester?"

Jeanne was taken aback. The enemy leader had used the Austrian word for sister. "Schwester? Who are you?"

The Austrian woman stomped her foot angrily. "Do you dummkopfs know nothing? I am Farahilde Johanna, youngest sister to Maria Antonia Josepha Johanna, whom you call Marie Antoinette—your queen."

"The 'Absolute Darkness of Austria,'" the female prisoner said quietly. "This young woman is a general who answers only to the emperor. She's a member of the Austrian royal family."

Jeanne was unfamiliar with her, so she simply said, "I apologize. Her Majesty has many siblings, and I am unable to remember them all."

Farahilde held up her hand—which was in a black gauntlet with two razor-sharp blades extending outwards—towards the knights in a threatening gesture. "If you worms double-cross me, it will be the last name you ever hear."

"Where is my brother?" Jeanne asked in an acidic tone. Her diplomatic attitude was eroding quickly.

"Your *bruder*?" Farahilde looked surprised. "Ah, now I see what he meant when he spoke of the arrival of his *schwester*." She laughed heartily. "He said you would torture me! What a sense of humor that dummkopf has."

Jeanne clenched her fist. This girl who looked to be at least five years younger than Jeanne herself was getting on her last nerve with her haughty attitude. "Enough of this. Bring him here or we leave."

"Hmph. Very well, then." Farahilde motioned to one of her guards, who stood aside to reveal a prisoner the same height and build as Jean-Paul de Fleur, and who was wearing a French Army uniform which signified that he was a colonel. He, too, had a sack over his head. "March, worm."

The male prisoner began walking forward. Jeanne said to her prisoner, "Walk." The female prisoner began moving forward as well. Both prisoners moved slowly and cautiously, hands bound behind their back, clearly unsure of their position and wondering if they would find themselves betrayed by one side or another. At least, that was how it must have looked to the other side, Jeanne thought.

When both prisoners passed each other in the middle, Jeanne yelled, "Now!" With one fluid motion the female prisoner brought her hands forward (revealing that they had not actually been bound), removed the sack from her head and shuffled the male prisoner over to the knights.

"*Tötet sie!*" Farahilde commanded her troops.

Jeanne, Pierre and Victor huddled over the prisoners as the Austrians fired on them with their air-powered rifles. Although the knights' irodium armor took the brunt of the assault, it wasn't a pleasant experience; Jeanne gritted her teeth as the enemy bullets pounded her body. No doubt she would be bruised tomorrow (assuming they survived whatever else the Austrians threw at them).

When the firing ceased, Jeanne said to the female prisoner, "Mademoiselle Roland, are you all right?"

"Yes, thank you. I'm sorry you had to go through that for me," Roland said.

"With all due respect, I'm doing this for my brother."

Roland smiled. "So you are."

Farahilde, strangely, did not seem terribly upset by this double-cross. "If you worms wanted to get shot up, all you had to do was ask.

Jeanne removed the burlap sack from the male prisoner, only to make an unfortunate discovery. "This is not my brother!"

"Are you certain?" Pierre asked.

Jeanne nodded. This man's hair was a dark brown, rather than the auburn color the de Fleur siblings possessed. His eyes were also blue, rather than Jean-Paul's green.

Jeanne removed the rope gag that had been placed over the man's mouth. "Who are you?"

"I am Private Julian Benoit," He said. "I served under General Dumouriez in the Sixth Infantry Unit, but I was captured when the Austrians attacked."

"I thought the Colonel was the only one captured," Pierre said.

Benoit said, "I think we were the only two. They made me switch uniforms with him to fool you."

"Looks like we had the same idea," Roland said.

Farahilde laughed condescendingly. "Don't you know the most basic rule of war, *fräulein?* Never trust your enemy."

"Chienne," Jeanne swore under her breath. She added aloud, "Where is my brother?"

"If you want him back, you'll have to come get him. You'd better hurry, though; you don't have much time."

Farahilde laughed before turning around and running into the fort. Jeanne said to Pierre and Victor, "Get Manon Roland and the private onto the ship. You must ensure their safety."

"What about you?" Pierre asked.

She unsheathed her rapier. "I believe you know the answer to that."

"It's too dangerous, ma'am," Victor said. "Let one of us go with you."

She shook her head. "You are needed here. Don't forget; the black airship has yet to make its appearance."

They wanted to argue with her, but what was the point? They had their orders; the only thing left for them was to carry them out. So, they simply said, "Understood, ma'am."

With that, Jeanne charged forward to engage the Austrian troops, who had obviously not expected her to be able to move that quickly after the bullets they had just fired into her. She ran through the first several soldiers with cold efficiency; unlike the Parisians she had faced during the storming of the Bastille, she felt no desire to go easy on these men.

The remaining soldiers pulled out their swords and managed to hold her off for a minute, but ultimately her superior training and experience proved more than a match for the greenhorns Farahilde Johanna had brought with her.

With those enemies defeated, she ran into the fort after Farahilde.

***

Back aboard the *Minuit Solaire*, Pierre and Victor took Private Julian Benoit to the airship's medical station. Dr. Aline Rembart, the middle-aged woman with sandy hair tapered up in back, who was in charge of the medical station, told them Private Benoit had not been roughed up by the Austrians—at least, not too badly.

"That's not surprising," Pierre said after they returned to the bridge and he sat down in the captain's chair. "Private Benoit was never of any real importance to them— just a way of screwing us over, if they could."

"That Farahilde seems to think of this as a game. She didn't even really get upset when we double-crossed her," Victor said, standing next to him.

Pierre grimly crossed his large arms over his chest. "She probably wanted to lure the Commander into the fort. And it worked."

Victor patted his tall comrade on the back. "Cheer up! The Commander won't let herself get killed by any Austrian traps. When she catches up with Farahilde Johanna, she'll show that brat what a huge mistake she has made by challenging 'Jeanne la Juste.'"

"I just hope she doesn't have to use her God's Eye. We both know how dangerous that thing is."

"Against that chienne? I doubt it."

Suddenly, Adolphe, the operator in charge of altitude control, announced, "Sir, we've got company. There's an airship coming in from the northeast."

Pierre squinted to see the dark spot that was flying through the sky up ahead. Even though he could only see a small blob, he knew it had to be the black airship coming to challenge them for control of the Austrian sky. They would soon know who had the superior vessel.

Pierre grabbed the rubber tube hanging down from the ceiling beside his chair. "Celeste, the black airship is heading right for us. Make sure the *Minuit Solaire* can give it everything she's got."

"Don't worry, sir; this ship is ready to go," said the engineer's slightly distorted voice from the tube. *"But... where is the Commander?"*

"She went into the fort to rescue her brother. As second-in-command of the Ordre, I'm handling things here."

"Oh... I see." There was certainly no hiding the obvious disappointment in her voice. Here she was, facing her most dangerous mission yet, without her idol to protect her. This could cause a problem with morale. Pierre had to make sure that didn't happen.

"Don't worry; the Commander will be back with us in no time. But meanwhile, she's counting on us to make sure we get through this alive. We're not going to let her down."

There was silence for a moment, then, "*Understood! I will do my best to live up to milady's expectations.*"

"Good girl. All right, let's show our enemy the power of the French spirit."

5

The Austrian Netherlands, September 16, 1789 (Infini
Calendar), 3:15 p.m.
	In the main building of the fort, Jeanne found a set
of stairs leading down into a torch-lit corridor below-
ground. She cautiously descended the steps, wary of any
traps that might be waiting for her. When she arrived at the
bottom, she couldn't tell how far the passage extended, as
only the first twenty feet of it was lit by torches.
	Having no idea what kind of traps Farahilde had set
for her, Jeanne decided to use her God's Eye to scan the
area. She really didn't want to do it; the strain of all the
information that would bombard her senses could damage
her mind. But neither did she want to get killed and leave
her brother in the hands of the enemy.
	With her mind made up, she knelt down to steady
herself, and removed her purple eye patch. She slowly
opened her left eye, and a flood of data rushed at her like
water from a broken dam. When this tunnel was built, the
exact composition of the walls, the name of everyone
involved in building it, whether the dust on the floor was
safe to inhale, the sizes of the footprints recently left in said
dust, the genders of the owners of said footprints; Jeanne
suddenly knew all these things and much more.
	She was beginning to sweat with the strain of all the
information—along with the bruising she had taken from
the Austrians' gunfire a few minutes ago, so she willed
herself to only focus on any traps that might lie ahead. This
wasn't quite as easy as the last time she had used the God's
Eye, though; last time she only had to focus on one
alchemically-twisted man. Today she had to look over an
entire corridor that seemed to drag on forever.

After what seemed like an eternity, she managed to confirm that the corridor held no traps. She put her eye patch back on, grabbed a torch and ran down the passage to confront Farahilde and rescue her brother.

However, at the end of the corridor she discovered another set of stairs leading down to an iron door at the bottom. She cautiously walked down the steps and looked at the door. Splattered on the door in red letters was one word: *Hölle*, the German word for Hell.

Jeanne pressed herself up against the wall adjacent the door, crouched and pushed it open. She was greeted by a flurry of arrows whizzing through the doorway. The arrows hit the stairs with unceremonious thuds.

A malevolent laughing echoed from up ahead. "I hope you aren't hurt, French worm. But that's what you get when you intrude into someone's home."

Did that *chienne* really think of this hellhole as her home? Somehow, Jeanne was not surprised. She needed to save her brother before he became a permanent guest here. And if it turns out he's not here, Jeanne thought to herself, this place really will become Hell for Farahilde Johanna.

She crept through the doorway and found herself in another corridor. She silently cursed her lack of judgment for using the God's Eye earlier in a passageway with no traps. If she used it again so soon after, she had very little doubt she would be overwhelmed by it and possibly lose her mind entirely.

Nevertheless, she continued onwards, constantly on the lookout for traps. Every little sound made her start; as far as she was concerned, there was no such thing as being overly cautious here. Nor did it help that her eye patch gave her a serious blind spot which made it harder to stay vigilant.

Suddenly a block in the floor descended beneath her foot. A whir of gears started up somewhere nearby. She frantically looked around, trying to deduce where the threat would be coming from. No time.

Acting on instinct, Jeanne leaped forward, hoping to avoid whatever was coming. She hit the ground rolling and, a flurry of something sharp whizzing behind her. She looked back; a lethal volley of darts rained down from tiny holes in the ceiling. The darts were so sharp they embedded themselves in the stone floor. Jeanne's irodium armor was quite durable, but there were gaps around her neck and joints (and nothing protecting her head). If the darts had hit her in those areas it would have caused serious injury—and that was assuming they hadn't been coated in poison.

She breathed a sigh of relief and kept going. After about thirty feet she came to a door with iron bars that had been left open by someone (probably Farahilde). Beyond the door she found a series of prison cells on either side of the wall. Most were empty, but a few held rotting corpses. Closer examination revealed them to be wearing French Army uniforms. Were these poor souls captured by the Austrians in the recent ambush? Or had Farahilde played dress-up with other dead bodies like she had with Private Benoit? Ultimately, it didn't matter; Farahilde Johanna would be held accountable for her actions.

Past the dungeon area the corridor continued straight ahead, but also arced off into other areas. The left area seemed to be some sort of dining hall, while the right semi-circle-shaped area was an empty barracks. Both areas curved around and opened back up farther down the corridor.

Beyond that was a large room filled with torture devices. Jeanne felt as if she had somehow travelled back to the Spanish Inquisition while looking at these. An iron maiden, torture racks, a sharp pendulum blade hanging from the ceiling, and other devices she didn't recognize were the gruesome residents of the chamber. Fresh blood painted more than a few of the implements of inhumanity.

However, there was still so sign of Farahilde. Where was she? Jeanne had searched the rest of the underground and as far as she could tell, this was the end.

A muffled, far-off voice suddenly called out to her. "Are you enjoying the tour, fräulein? You'd better hurry up before your bruder experiences a horrible death!"

The voice was definitely coming from beyond the torture chamber, opposite from where Jeanne had entered. That meant there was a secret passageway out of the chamber, and Jeanne had an idea of where it might be. At the far end of the chamber was a bright red curtain hanging over the wall. Jeanne pulled it down to reveal another door.

She opened the door, snapping some sort of wire on the other side. The sound of a spark only gave her an instant's warning, and she quickly jumped to the side as a fireball sailed through the doorway. A cloud of smoke was left in its wake, along with the acrid smell that accompanied it. A cannon had been placed behind the door and rigged to fire if anyone tried to come through.

I tire of that chienne's games, she thought as she went through the doorway towards Farahilde's location.

***

The bridge shook violently as the *Blitzkrieg Rache* hurled another volley of blue energy at the *Minuit Solaire.*

"Return fire!" Pierre ordered from his position in the captain's chair.

"It's no good!" came the voice of Lt. Escoir down in Gunnery Control. Like Celeste in the engine room, he communicated with the captain—or in this case, *acting* captain—through a rubber tube that hung down from the ceiling on the left side of the captain's chair (as opposed to the tube from the boiler room which hung to the right). *"Their hull is obviously made of irodium. Our standard cannons can't penetrate it."*

"Then bring us around so we can use the steam cannon."

Suddenly Celeste's voice came through the communications tube to his right. *"That's not a good idea, sir."*

"What do you mean?" Pierre asked her.

"Based on their attacks so far, I've been able to calculate the maximum effective range of their weapons to be thirty yards. If we come around to use the steam cannon, they'll be able to hit us. Also, their rate of fire is much greater than that of the steam cannon. We'll never win by relying on it. We need to keep our distance from them."

Pierre was losing his patience with the young engineer. "You're suggesting we just run away? We can't abandon the Commander!"

"That's not what I'm suggesting at all. I do have an idea."

He rubbed his temple to dissuade the headache that was coming on. "Pray tell."

"Isn't there a body of water nearby?"

"Yes, there's a lake. I don't think we can beat that vessel by taking a swim, though. That didn't go so well for the royal airship, if you'll recall."

Surprisingly, Celeste replied, *"I think we can. We've got to get them over the water and fire on it."*

The bridge shook again as the *Blitzkrieg Rache* hit them with a glancing blow. "We've *been* firing on them. How will shooting them above water make any difference?"

"No, sir. I mean, fire on the water when they are over it. If I'm right, the splash will short out the electrical systems they're using to generate the energy for their attacks, rendering them powerless. And the splash will need to be large enough to engulf the black airship, so I recommend saving the steam cannon for that."

It sounded like suicide. They might as well fly straight into the ground. Still, Celeste was a pretty sharp kid. She knew what she was talking about (he hoped). "You'd better be right about this." He sighed.

Pierre ordered the operators to reduce altitude, increase speed to maximum and head straight for the lake that was located about a kilometer away. They flew so low that they were almost hugging the ground. The *Blitzkrieg Rache* chased after them, unwilling to let their prey escape, not when they were so close to knocking out Austria's only other rival in the sky.

The *Minuit Solaire* soon arrived at the lake. It was a large one; that meant plenty of room to maneuver, and Pierre was fairly certain they would need it.

"Take us out to the middle of the lake to maximize the effectiveness of our strategy," Celeste advised Pierre through the communications tube. *"If my calculations are correct, they'll have to come within range of the splash radius to attack us with their weapons. As soon as they do, open fire upon the area directly beneath them."*

"All right. I'm trusting you, Celeste, so if this doesn't work and we die, I'm going to pay you a visit in the afterlife, and we're going to have a talk about this," Pierre warned her.

"So, I guess that means you'll be keeping me company, then."

"Count on it."

They flew out to the middle of the lake, nearly skimming the surface of the water, as low as they were flying. As soon as they reached the center, Pierre ordered the operators to stop the airship and turn them around so the starboard (the side with the steam cannon) was facing the approaching enemy—more specifically, the water underneath where the *Blitzkrieg Rache* would soon be.

The enemy was coming in fast, about twenty feet above the surface of the water. Pierre grabbed the tube connected to Gunnery Control. "As soon as I give you the order, fire the steam cannon."

Lt. Escoir replied, "Roger."

Suddenly, the *Blitzkrieg Rache* came to a halt above the lake.

"What are they doing?" Pierre muttered to himself.

The enemy abruptly turned around and began flying back the way they had come. "I think they realized what we're up to," Victor said.

Oh, no, these foes weren't getting away. "After them! Maximum speed!" Pierre ordered.

The *Minuit Solaire* gave chase, but the *Blitzkrieg Rache* would leave the lake within moments. They needed to open fire now.

However, Lt. Escoir informed Pierre that it wasn't likely to work. "Sir, the odds of us hitting the spot directly underneath them while we are both travelling at high speeds are very remote. We need a bigger target.

Like a big, black airship? That gave Pierre an idea. "Shoot the ship itself!"

"But, sir—"

"Do it!"

The *Minuit Solaire* made a sharp turn, pointed its left side at the enemy airship, and opened fire with the steam cannon. A super-heated steel ball four times the size of a standard cannon ball exploded from the ship. The force of the blast rocked the bridge, and the operators struggled to maintain control. Celeste was right, Pierre decided; the *Minuit Solaire* could never have handled multiple steam cannons.

Without time to properly aim the attack, the glowing orange cannonball merely landed a glancing blow on the *Blitzkrieg Rache*. But that was enough; the force of the attack caused the enemy vessel to temporarily lose control, sending them crashing into the lakeshore. A torrent of water crashed over the ship, and sparks danced along the dark metal spikes which had channeled the strange blue energy into a deadly weapon.

The once-menacing airship went careening onto the shore, coming to a halt when it crashed into a cluster of trees. The impact broke several of the black spikes off its hull, though Pierre doubted the protuberances would have remained operational even if they were still attached to the ship. The whole thing was dead in the water. Well, slightly away from the water.

The crew of the enemy airship began pouring out, fleeing in all directions. Not so fast. Pierre wasn't about to let them get away so easily. "Take us in for a landing," he ordered the operators. "We've got some stragglers to round up."

6

The Austrian fort, September 16, 1789 (Infini Calendar), 3:30 p.m.

The giant boulder chased Jeanne down the corridor beneath the fort. This was by far the most annoying trap yet, she thought. Stepping on the wrong part of the floor had dropped this thing to fall from the ceiling after her, and it was taking every ounce of her energy to stay ahead of it. At one point she stumbled and was almost crushed by the boulder. Nevertheless, she managed to keep going.

Up ahead was a doorway too narrow (hopefully) for the boulder to cross through. If she could just get through it before she was flattened, she might just live long enough to set off Farahilde's next trap.

Moving her legs as fast as she possibly could, Jeanne reached the doorway and, almost too late, discovered there was no floor beyond it. There was only some sort of small platform suspended from the ceiling about five feet away from the doorway. With no other options, she charged through the entrance and leaped onto the platform. In actuality, it was more like a three-foot-by-three-foot stone block with a chain in the middle that ran fifteen feet up to the ceiling.

There was a crash behind her. She turned around; the boulder had splintered the doorway before becoming stuck in it. That effectively cut off any chance of escape she might have had; there was no way she could go back with that round hunk of rock blocking the only passage out of there.

"Ah, you finally made it, fräulein. I worried my traps had killed you before your fated reunion."

It was Farahilde, sitting cross-legged on a similar stone block in the center of this... room?

"Room" was hardly an accurate description of the torch-lit chamber Jeanne now found herself in. Twenty feet below her was a pit of spikes, and the only objects in the chamber were nine other stone blocks, each with a sturdy chain rising up to the ceiling. The blocks were arranged in a clockwise pattern and—starting at the top left—numbered one to ten, with the tenth block being the one in the center that Farahilde currently occupied. The blocks were spaced about five feet apart.

Upon closer inspection, though, Jeanne discovered the chamber held one other decoration besides the blocks. "Brother!"

On the far wall, between blocks one and two, was Jean-Paul de Fleur, hanging above the pit and another doorway, his hands manacled in chains that ran up to the ceiling. His face was bloody; obviously Farahilde had subjected him to her particular brand of entertainment.

"So good of you to come, my sister. I do not know how much longer I can listen to this girl's ranting."

Unbelievable. Even in such a perilous situation he could not resist cracking jokes. "Will you be serious for once, Jean-Paul? I've put many people in danger to rescue you."

"You want me to be serious?" he said, suddenly changing his tone. "Fine. You should not have come here. It was foolish of you to charge right into enemy territory just for one insignificant officer."

"You are..." she started. "You are not an insignificant anything. You are a great officer of the French Army, you are a great Frenchman, and... you are a great brother! I've wanted to say that to you for a while now."

Oddly enough, despite the condition he was in, Jean-Paul smiled. "You have changed as of late, Jeanne. I don't know what has made you more open with your feelings, but I'm glad for it."

Farahilde said to Jeanne, "You have certainly proven your resolve. I thought perhaps you were just a dog of the French government, but now I see you actually have heart.

Nevertheless, you failed to give back meine schwester, so you will not be leaving here with your bruder. What I *will* give you is a story. I'm sure you have been wondering why I do this..."

Jeanne, however, was in no mood to listen. "Save your story. I don't care why you're doing this. I simply want my brother back. I'm going to jump over to him on these stone blocks and free him."

She moved to jump to the number seven block—and from there would jump to blocks eight, nine and one in that order, to get to Jean-Paul, but Farahilde held out her gauntleted hand, motioning for her to stop. "I would not be so hasty if I were you, fräulein. You may have noticed that each of these blocks hanging from the ceiling has an iron chain attached to it. Each of those chains runs up through the ceiling to the floor above us, where they are secured to that floor's ceiling. That keeps nine of these blocks in place, and they won't fall to the spikes below from the weight of people jumping around on them.

"How-e-ver, you probably also noticed that your bruder, too, is bound by chains that run up into the ceiling. Those chains are connected to one of these stone blocks in a fragile... how do you say, equilibrium? Each block weighs two hundred pounds—about the weight of a man. And if you were to jump on it, the block will fall, pulling your bruder up to the ceiling. How large do you think the opening in the ceiling that his chains are going through is? Certainly not large enough for him to be pulled through cleanly. Have you ever tried shoving a pig through a hole one foot in diameter? It is not pretty. The same will happen to your bruder if you jump on the wrong block."

Was Farahilde lying? Maybe, but Jeanne didn't have the luxury of putting that to the test. She could use her God's Eye to reveal the secrets of the stone blocks... if only she hadn't used it earlier. Now she was too drained mentally, and she had no doubt that if she used it now, it would overwhelm her and she would fall into the spike pit below.

Jeanne said, "Do you expect me to just sit here all day?"

"It is not so bad. As I said, I shall regale you with a story. And since you have nowhere to go, you *will* listen to it," she said threateningly.

Jean-Paul sighed. "Not this again. She already tortured me with this story."

Farahilde ignored him and began speaking. "It happened twenty years ago during meine first visit to Paris. Meine schwester was in the city on business, and I was so happy to see her for the first time since she had married Louis XVI and become queen of France. We were all so proud of her, our family. And naturally, I assumed the French people were, as well. After all, how could they not be proud to have such a beautiful, strong and elegant woman such as Maria Antonia Josepha Johanna for their queen?

"Oh, how naïve I was! You French worms are a barbarous people, lacking in even the most basic human morals. While in Paris, I witnessed meine schwester being assaulted by every vile word you people could think up. Not only that, but they accused her of every *misdeed* they could think up. Promiscuity; treason; bad fashion sense; haughtiness; these were just a few of the accusations that she had to endure—no, *still* endures to this day. Even a child such as me could see that all of France had gone mad. Here was a country forcing its cruelties onto its queen, whom they should adore with all their heart.

"After that I vowed to one day match their emotional cruelty with physical cruelty. And when I was finally given military authority within the Austrian Army, I had this prison built near the French border in order to punish you French worms whenever you dare invade us. And there has been much punishing to do as of late. It seems your country has grown tired of merely abusing its queen, and now seeks the conquest of meine beloved Austria. Fine by me; it just means more French logs for meine fire!"

Jeanne sympathized with Farahilde... somewhat. "I understand your desire for justice over the wrongs your sister has suffered over the years. I myself have witnessed some of those injustices. Having had a chance to get to know her personally, I can say without reservation that she didn't deserve it.

"But this is not the way to right the wrongs of the past! All you're doing is torturing people needlessly. Do you really think you can change anything by constructing an underground labyrinth of horrors? This makes no sense!"

Farahilde scoffed at her plea for sanity. "Sense? Ha! We have left the world of sense behind, fräulein! As did the French people when they began their torture of meine schwester. All I have done is built an environment to match their hearts. They can only blame themselves for this. Your country abandoned reason and compassion a long time ago."

Jeanne shook her head. "I know your sister personally. And I know she would never approve of this. She's a kind person."

"I can vouch for that," Jean-Paul added.

"Shut up!" Farahilde spat. "You dare claim to know meine schwester better than I do? I don't care what you say! I'm doing this for her!"

She suddenly leaped over to the number six block Jeanne was standing on. The block swung a few feet as it adjusted to the new arrival.

Jeanne held on tight to the block's chain. "What are you—?"

She was unable to finish her sentence as Farahilde jabbed at her with her gauntlet hand, while her other hand was clinging to the chain. Jeanne barely dodged the razor-sharp blades. Farahilde pulled back and thrust at her again, but Jeanne grabbed her wrist in mid-attack. They grappled atop the stone block for several moments without either of them gaining a clear advantage.

"Jeanne, be careful!" Jean-Paul cried out.

Jeanne yelled to Farahilde, "Stop this madness!"

"You want it to end? Very well... just stand still!"

In one impossibly fluid motion, Farahilde spun around, her gauntlet slicing the chain, before leaping back onto the number ten block. Jeanne reacted instinctively, jumping left to the number seven block. In mid-air she realized the mistake she had made: She had jumped without thinking. She could be jumping onto the booby-trapped stone block, sentencing her brother to die a grisly death...

Her mouth opened wide. She wanted to scream, to cry out in anguish for the death of a loved one that may now be inevitable. Instead, however, her cries were entirely inward.

She reached out and grabbed the chain on the number seven block, aware that doing so may kill her brother—but again, it was instinctive. To her surprise and immeasurable relief, though, the stone block held. She steadied herself and waited a moment, but still the block held.

Farahilde gave another twisted laugh from up ahead and to the right on the number ten block. "Why, you were positively wetting yourself there, fräulein. You thought that was the chain connected to your bruder. Don't get too happy, though; there are still plenty more chains to try."

Jeanne took a moment to compose herself. "Jean-Paul, I don't suppose you know which stone block you're connected to?"

"I'm sorry, Jeanne, but I don't. They knocked me out and when I woke up I was in this position."

"Surely, you don't think I would be foolish enough to tell this dummkopf which one it is?" She laughed again.

Jeanne thought about it carefully. She knew the numbers six, seven and ten blocks weren't traps since she and Farahilde had already jumped on them. Unfortunately, that still left seven stone blocks to test. There was a high probability that either Farahilde or herself would jump on the loose block and send Jean-Paul de Fleur crashing up through a hole too small for his body. There was even a chance Farahilde would jump on it intentionally; Jeanne wouldn't put anything past her at this point.

Jeanne said, "No, I guess not."

"You know, fräulein, the look on your face a moment ago was priceless. I want to see it again!"

Farahilde abruptly leaped onto the number eight block in front of Jeanne. Jeanne's heart stopped beating as she watched the unhinged Austrian girl land on the block, not knowing if Farahilde was intentionally jumping to her death in one last attack on Jeanne's psyche or not.

However, the number eight block held as Farahilde's weight was deposited on it. Jeanne remembered to breathe again as she realized that this was yet another of the mad girl's mind games.

"You're insane," she said venomously.

"I am merely living up to meine namesake. Did you know that in Norse mythology, Hilde is queen of Hell? When choosing something to aspire to, one can certainly do worse, don't you think?"

Jeanne didn't answer. She was tired of playing with this lunatic. Instead, she unsheathed her rapier and bounded over to Farahilde's block, grabbing onto its chain. The Austrian was caught off-guard by Jeanne's sudden attack and nearly found herself pierced through the abdomen by the sword. She responded by thrusting her bladed gauntlet towards Jeanne's left eye.

She's going for my blind spot, Jeanne realized as she barely managed to tilt her head just enough to the side to avoid the attack.

"Silly fräulein, your rapier is a poor fit for combat at such close quarters. You need several feet to make an effective thrust with that. With meine gauntlet, however, the space needed is much less."

She was right, Jeanne realized. Farahilde definitely had the advantage in this environment. Although that was hardly surprising; the Austrian girl had had this chamber built for her. Of course she would play to her strengths in here.

After narrowly dodging several more of Farahilde's strikes, Jeanne decided to switch tactics. She sheathed her rapier and decided to go hand-to-hand with her enemy. Farahilde crouched and thrust low at her, but Jeanne grabbed the chain and pulled herself up above the attack before kicking the Austrian in the shoulder.

Farahilde briefly lost her balance, and only managed to avoid falling into the pit by grabbing hold of the chain. Apparently deciding that they had spent enough time on this stone block, she used her gauntlet to cut through part of the chain and turned around to jump on the number nine block. The force of her jump was enough to sever the rest of the chain, and the block fell.

Jeanne held on to what remained of the chain and spent several moments dangling above the pit. Farahilde seemed to find this exceedingly amusing. "Are you having trouble, fräulein? Hang in there!"

However, Jeanne had not lost hope. They were getting closer and closer to Jean-Paul, who had for the most part remained silent so his sister could focus on this battle; only the number one block remained between him and Farahilde, and he was hanging mere feet from that block. Assuming that wasn't booby-trapped, all Jeanne had to do was get past Farahilde, leap on it, and save him. Of course, when was it ever that simple?

Jeanne began swinging her hips back and forth, building momentum and carving a larger and larger arc across the chamber. She got her legs in synch to make the process as efficient as possible.

"You think I don't see what you're planning?" Farahilde said. "You mean to jump over here to me, but," she held up her gauntlet, "I'll knock you into the pit as soon as you try it. Your armor may be formidable, but nothing can survive a fall from this height."

When Jeanne was satisfied she had built up as much momentum as she was going to, she swung towards the number nine block Farahilde was on and let go, but not before giving herself a little twist on the chain. She spiraled through the air above the pit, maneuvering her body in order to make the best landing she could.

"You've done it now, fräulein!"

Farahilde raised her gauntlet and swung it at the incoming Jeanne. To her surprise, though, on Jeanne's last revolution through the air she tucked in her left leg and extended her right one into a kick. Jeanne slammed her right leg into Farahilde's chest, sending her flying backwards. Jeanne grabbed the chain on the stone block and held on until the whole thing stopped moving from the force of her landing.

Farahilde hung on for dear life off the number one block. *It's holding! I can use it to rescue Jean-Paul!* "It looks like you lose, Farahilde Johanna."

Farahilde grunted. "You haven't won yet. Even if you can get over to your bruder, how will you lower him down without dumping him into the pit?"

"Just watch."

Jeanne took out her rapier and leaped onto the number one block where Farahilde was struggling to hang on. The very instant she landed, Jeanne hurled the rapier at Jean-Paul, and, without wasting even a split second, jumped towards him. The rapier hit the chain holding him up, severing it completely. Jean-Paul de Fleur immediately plummeted towards the pit below, but Jeanne tackled him in mid-air, and their momentum carried them both through the doorway beyond.

They landed on solid ground. It wasn't the softest landing, but it was the happiest Jeanne had ever experienced. "Brother! Are you all right?"

He groaned, "Yeah, I'll be fine. Thank you for risking your life to save me."

She smiled. "You are my family. I could do no less."

He gasped. "You're smiling! You really have changed. What happened?"

"Believe it or not, it was a petty criminal that inspired me to change. I'll tell you all about it later. But for now..."

***

Farahilde felt her grip on the stone block loosening. Her gauntlet didn't allow her to get a good hold on it. Damn that French woman! Was it really to end this way, at the hands of a warrior of France?

Suddenly someone jumped onto the block, sending it rocking back and forth. It was her! "Come to finish me off, fräulein?"

Jeanne shook her head. "No, just the opposite."

She grabbed Farahilde's arm and began pulling her up.

"What are you doing? I'm your enemy! I won't be saved by a French worm!"

"Her Majesty would be saddened if I brought back news of the death of a family member," Jeanne grunted. "I couldn't do that to her." Jeanne pulled Farahilde up onto the block. "So, it was the number two block that was booby-trapped. As soon as I cut the chain holding my brother, that block fell. If I had travelled counter-clockwise instead of clockwise, it would have been a disaster."

Farahilde looked away from her. "Gloating over your victory? You have shamed me today."

"You shamed yourself with your actions. Let's get one thing straight: I didn't save you for you. I did it to spare my queen any unnecessary hardships. You tortured my brother and tried to kill us both. I will be very content if I never see you again after this."

"Hmph. Fair enough."

***

Farahilde led Jeanne and Jean-Paul through the emergency escape tunnel she had had built under the fort. After a half kilometer they emerged in the sunlight of the Austrian Netherlands. They were greeted by a beautiful field of green.

"All right, fräulein. I have paid you back for saving meine life. You had better get out of here before long, lest meine troops find you."

"We don't need any further encouragement to do that," Jeanne said while supporting her brother's weight. After his torture sessions with Farahilde, he was too weak to walk.

"I do believe I'm due a commendation after this," he said.

"There you go again, making light of a serious situation," Jeanne said.

Farahilde said, "I'm afraid I have a favor to ask of you. Will you... will you watch out for meine schwester, make sure nothing happens to her?"

Jeanne replied, "Of course I will. But not for you, obviously. It's my duty as a knight of the royal family. Frankly, I couldn't care less about your feelings."

"Do you promise no harm will come to her?"

"Don't worry. I promise," Jeanne said.

"Thank you. Before I go, I'll give you a word of advice: Don't get too confident. You may have defeated me, but meine older bruder Leopold II has more surprises in store for you.

"Such as?" Jeanne asked.

"That, you will have to find out for yourself. *Auf Wiedersehen.*"

Having said goodbye, Farahilde left. Where she was going, they didn't know. Jeanne was just glad to be rid of her.

"Are your subordinates going to be all right?" Jean-Paul asked.

"You just answered your own question. They're *my* subordinates. They'll be fine."

***

Jeanne and Jean-Paul returned to the fort, where they were greeted by Pierre and the crew of the *Minuit Solaire*—along with a host of prisoners from the black airship. Pierre explained that they had captured them after downing the enemy vessel. Jeanne ordered them put in the brig aboard the *Minuit Solaire*.

Afterwards, Jeanne let Pierre command the ship a little longer while she returned to her quarters to rest. Shortly after laying down, she was visited by Manon Roland (still wearing the queen's red dress).

"I am sorry to bother you, Commander, but I wanted to clear up something between us."

"What is that?"

"I understand if you despise me for not allowing Her Majesty to return to her family."

Jeanne sighed. "I'd be lying if I said I was a great admirer of yours as of late, but I'm not petty enough to hate you for that."

"Nor am I Marie Antoinette's biggest admirer. However, please understand that our queen has a great responsibility to her people. Her influence over the king has contributed greatly to the current state of France. Whether anyone likes it or not, she can't just abandon them for the sake of a few soldiers."

Jeanne had to fight to hold her emotions in check. She was tired and felt herself in danger of losing control. "So instead you hold her prisoner like a common criminal."

"If we let her go free, she would abandon the country as she had already tried before."

"You... make a good point, Manon Roland. But I still think there must be a better way to handle the situation."

"If you find it, I'll be happy to listen." She turned to leave, but stopped abruptly. "Oh, there was one other thing. I've always wanted to pay my respects to the descendant of Jeanne d'Arc in private. I think you have done her proud."

Jeanne was taken aback by the sudden compliment from Manon Roland. "Why... thank you."

"I understand that eye patch is passed down from mother to daughter in your family. That seems somewhat of an unusual tradition."

Jeanne honestly couldn't deny it. "I suppose it is."

"Especially since—to my knowledge—Jeanne d'Arc never wore such a thing."

"Well, that's—what?"

"I've seen numerous paintings of her, and she doesn't wear an eye patch in any of them. Also, there is no record of her suffering an eye injury at any time in her life."

Now that she thought of it, Jeanne realized Manon Roland was right. Jeanne d'Arc was never known to have worn an eye patch. But that didn't make sense. The God's Eye was supposed to have originated with her. It was what allowed her to know God's will and helped her defeat the English during that famous war. She would have needed the eye patch to withstand the power of the God's Eye. It was inconceivable that she would have been able to keep her left eye open every day. It would have driven her mad in no time.

What did it mean?

PART III
Il me faut que vous mouriez
(I Need You to Die)

1

Château de Fleur, September 18, 1789 (Infini Calendar), 12:00 a.m.
    Jeanne sat at a fancy marble table within the library of her family's estate in *Domrémy-la-Pucelle*, looking over every document they had relating to her ancestor Jeanne d'Arc.
    She wasn't supposed to be doing this. Ever since the Ordre's return from the Austrian Netherlands the previous day, she had been under doctor's orders to remain in bed. This was because of the injuries she sustained fighting Farahilde Johanna. "Injuries" made it sound a lot more serious than it was, though; really, it was just a lot of bruising on her midsection. Her irodium armor took the brunt of the barrage of bullets from the wind rifles of Farahilde's troops.
    Nevertheless, something had been bothering her ever since the flight home from the Netherlands. Manon Roland's comments about Jeanne d'Arc never having worn an eye patch piqued her curiosity. So here she was, in the library at midnight, after all the servants had gone to bed.
    Jeanne looked through several artists' renditions of her ancestor; drawings of her first talking to God on a hill, leading French armies into battle, clashing with English troops, standing triumphant after battles and, finally, escaping from the English before they burned her alive. True to what Roland had said, Jeanne d'Arc wasn't wearing an eye patch in any of them. Her legendary ancestor was supposed to have passed on the God's Eye to her descendants, but how could that be if she herself did not possess it?
    Jeanne put the pictures back in the trunk between two book cases where she had gotten them. She then looked

through a book about her ancestor written by an historian, trying to find any mention of an eye patch or eye injury. However, there were none to be found. It reported that Jeanne d'Arc suffered numerous injuries throughout her campaign to defeat the English, but none to her eyes. Interestingly, it also didn't say anything about her life after her escape from the English. It was almost as if she ceased to exist at that point.

So instead, Jeanne looked through the book for all references to her ancestor's fabled ability to talk with God. Sure enough, there were passages dedicated to it. According to the book, God spoke directly to Jeanne d'Arc and gave her guidance on how to proceed against the English. It was even reported that Jeanne d'Arc was known to have carried on conversations with thin air. Was this connected to the God's Eye somehow? Did her legendary ancestor simply possess it in a different form? But if that were the case... why?

***

The Tuileries, Paris, September 20, 1789 (Infini Calendar), 9:00 a.m.

Jeanne, Pierre and Victor entered the war room of the Tuileries Palace, the walls of which were adorned with various maps of the surrounding countries. Tables were covered with what appeared to be military intelligence reports. The knights sat down at a round table opposite the king and queen, as well as the representatives from the Assembly, Jacques-Pierre Brissot de Warville and Manon Roland. Roland, as usual, was decked out in a beautiful blue dress that complemented her silky white skin.

"Thank you all for coming today," Louis XVI said. "And my wife especially would like to express her gratitude for your success in your most recent mission."

Marie Antoinette reached over and squeezed the hands of each of the knights. "Thank you so much for sparing the life of my younger sister. I deeply regret the trouble she caused you."

"I will admit it was not easy, Your Majesty," Jeanne replied. "Farahilde Johanna captured my brother, tortured him, and tried to kill the rest of us."

Brissot slammed his fist down on the table. "So why did you spare her? She was an enemy! You should have killed or captured her!"

Jeanne took a moment to collect her thoughts and compose a suitable response for the warmongering Brissot. "There were two reasons for that. One—after the fight was over I didn't have the strength to force her back to our airship. Two—I couldn't bring myself to kill her because it would have been too painful for our queen."

Brissot didn't buy it. "She is a vital member of the enemy's forces! She would have been a powerful bargaining chip against Leopold II and his coalition of ally nations."

Roland said, "Calm down, Monsieur Brissot. Jeanne de Fleur has proven herself a more than capable commander of the Ordre de la Tradition. I trust in her judgment."

The king, perhaps wanting to change the subject, said, "Ahem, where is Monsieur Robespierre? Wasn't he supposed to be here today?"

Brissot gave a *humph!* "I haven't seen him since these knights returned from the Netherlands. Frankly, we're better off without that spineless cur. All he's good for is keeping our heels dragged."

"On that, I think we can all agree," Roland said.

The knights said nothing. They didn't trust either the Girondists or the Montagnards. Both factions had been instrumental in stripping the king of both his power and freedom.

Instead, Jeanne said, "I've been told the war is not going well."

"Unfortunately, you heard correctly," Louis XVI said.

Roland clasped her hands and rested her chin on them. "The coalition has proven better organized than we expected. They have routed our forces in several battles and have gained a solid foothold along our northern borders."

"That doesn't matter," Brissot countered. "We'll push them back soon enough. Our biggest problem is their airship factory. We have to destroy it before they can build any more like that black airship you faced in the Netherlands."

"Have you located the factory?" Victor asked.

Roland said, "We're very close. We should have the location pinned down in a few days. Until then, you knights need to make preparations to move out. Your head engineer has informed us that the *Minuit Solaire*'s crew is working around the clock to make all the necessary repairs. You should be ready to go by the time we find the factory."

"Understood," Jeanne said.

"Know that we have the utmost faith in the Ordre," Louis XVI said. "We know you can do this."

"We won't let you down," Pierre replied.

***

The Jacobin monastery, Paris, September 20, 1789 (Infini Calendar), 9:15 a.m.

Maximilien Robespierre sat in the small library of the monastery which the Jacobin Club had recently begun renting in Paris. He was putting the finishing touches on his speech which he would soon deliver to the Assembly.

There was a knock at the door in front of the table he was sitting at, and the Marquis de Sade entered the room. As usual, the Marquis wore a twisted smile on his face.

Robespierre didn't take his eyes off the paper he had been writing on. "There *are* other people in this place, you know. You don't always have to be bothering *me*."

The Marquis, however, was undeterred. "Oh, but few of them have the country in the palm of their hands like you do. And—I'm sorry to say—they don't care much for me. Maybe it's my reputation for kidnap and rape, hmmm?"

"Probably."

Robespierre was quickly growing tired of his sociopathic partner in crime. Once the king and queen were dead, he would be able to get rid of the deranged Marquis once and for all. The only reason he had bothered arranging de Sade's "release" from the Bastille was to acquire his help in planning the overthrow of the *Ancien Régime*. Unfortunately, their plan to assassinate the royal family back in July had ended in failure thanks to the intervention of the Ordre de la Tradition. Robespierre had underestimated them. That, he vowed, would not happen again.

"I hear those knights are going on another mission soon," the Marquis said.

Robespierre allowed himself a smile. "Yes, the Assembly is sending them on their most important mission yet. And their last."

"Oh, you've decided to go with my latest suggestion?" de Sade laughed. "Won't it be wonderful!"

"Wonderful, indeed. I've been gathering everything I'll need to eliminate the king and queen for good. When the knights leave on their mission, I'll call a special meeting of the Assembly. In addition, I've arranged for a special demonstration of the people's unrest. The royal family's fate shall be sealed."

The Marquis clapped his hands playfully. "And then we shall usher in a glorious new era for France! Of course, I'm just in it for the bloodshed."

You mean I shall usher in a glorious new era for France, Robespierre thought scornfully. *You won't be around to see it, my dear Marquis.*

***

Unknown place, unknown date, unknown time
Everywhere she looked, there was only darkness. It was cold, wherever she was. Cold and empty. No other life existed here. Jeanne had no idea where she was, save that it was someplace she did not want to be. She desperately wanted to be anywhere but here.
Suddenly a bright light shone somewhere above her head. Despite its intensity, it did not illuminate the rest of the void. Perhaps there was nothing else *to* illuminate.
She shouted, "Who's there?"
A voice responded, but she couldn't make it out clearly. Was it male or female? Old or young? Friendly or hostile? She could barely hear it.
Soon... ill come... u must be... eady.
"What do you mean? I don't understand."
Your... ncestor... failed. You... need... make... choice.
"Did you say my ancestor? Are you talking about Jeanne d'Arc? Do you know why she didn't wear an eye patch, even though she was supposed to have passed down the God's Eye to us?"
...rue form... incomplete... lacked faith.
"Who? Who lacked faith? Was it Jeanne d'Arc?"
Time... draws near... show every... ower of... man... spirit.
Jeanne awoke in her bed. It must have been very early in the morning, as she hadn't retired until well after midnight and her room was still completely dark.
She thought back on the dream she had just had. If she had understood the voice correctly, it had said that her ancestor, Jeanne d'Arc, had lacked faith and thus failed in some task. But if that were true, what was the task? And how could the legendary Jeanne d'Arc have lacked faith? According to historical records, she had successfully followed God's instructions and led the French to victory

- 111 -

over the English. She even managed to escape certain death by avoiding being burned alive at the stake. What, then, could she have failed at?

The more the current Jeanne thought about it, the less sense it made. Maybe it was just a dream and didn't mean anything. At any rate, she needed to get back to sleep. There was supposed to be a briefing at the Tuileries in the morning and she wanted to be rested for it.

2

The Tuileries, Paris, September 22, 1789 (Infini Calendar), 9:00 a.m.

Jeanne, Pierre, and Victor entered the war room and sat down once again with the king and queen, along with Brissot and Roland. Jeanne found herself still bothered by the dream the previous night, but she managed to push it out of her mind and focus on the meeting.

Brissot said, "Let's skip the pleasantries and get right down to business. We have found the factory where Leopold II and his coalition are building airships."

"Where?" Jeanne said.

"Inside a volcano in the Austrian Netherlands called Mt. Erfunden," Roland said.

Pierre was visibly surprised. "A volcano? Are you kidding me?"

"Not even close," Brissot replied. "Mt. Erfunden has been dormant for centuries, so that makes it the ideal spot for concealing an airship factory."

"How do you know this is really where the factory is?" Victor said.

Marie Antoinette said, "We sent a number of scouts into the Austrian Netherlands to find it. And one of them reported seeing smoke coming out of Mt. Erfunden. If the volcano is dormant, that shouldn't be."

"Maybe the volcano has become active again," Pierre suggested.

"That is a possibility," Roland replied. "However, there is more. In addition, the scout said he saw a small platoon of Austrian troops entering the volcano. Not enough to get the attention of most people, but suspicious nonetheless. Even if they're not hiding an airship factory in there, there's still something going on inside that we need to know about. Add in the fact that the volcano is located near the Prussian border, and this is a situation we cannot ignore."

"We're sending the Ordre de la Tradition in to investigate. If there really is an airship factory within Mt. Erfunden, shut it down," Brissot said.

Pierre said quizzically, "I figured you'd want us to capture any airships we found there. You know, take them for France."

Brissot explained, "Ordinarily, yes. But the place is too far behind enemy lines; you'd never be able to hold it long enough for us to send in enough people to man the enemy vessels. Besides, their operation could be radically different from the *Minuit Solaire*; we don't even know if there's anyone in France that could fly them, to say nothing of whole crews. Just focus on making sure any operational vessels you find don't stay that way."

"You'll be leaving in two days. Please ensure that all your preparations are complete by then," Roland said.

"Understood," Jeanne said.

***

The Austrian Netherlands, September 24, 1789 (Infini Calendar) 2:04 p.m.

Jean-Paul de Fleur sat in the motorized carriage as it barreled across the green landscape of the Austrian Netherlands. This particular model of steam-powered carriage was outdated, and for good reason. It was bulky, noisy and produced massive plumes of smoke from the boiler attached to its rear. Any enemy would notice it coming from miles away.

However, in an odd twist of fate, that was exactly why it—along with a dozen others of its make—was being used in this mission. They *wanted* to be noticed heading towards Mt. Erfunden. They *wanted* the volcano's defenders to rush out to engage them. And they *wanted* the *Minuit Solaire* to slip in while the enemy was occupied and destroy the airship factory.

The iron carriage hit another bump (going about thirty miles an hour) and Jean-Paul was lifted up a few inches out of his seat. He readjusted the leather strap around his waist and clung to the seat in front of him. Crammed into the carriage with a dozen other soldiers, he couldn't wait until he was able to get out, which hopefully would be soon.

Jean-Paul had, unbeknownst to his sister Jeanne, insisted on joining this mission. He still bore the wounds from his recent treatment at the hands of Farahilde Johanna and he knew his worrisome sibling would have done everything in her power to stop him. Nevertheless, he couldn't just lie in bed while she put herself in danger to save France from its enemies. He needed to do his part. And since he ended up being useless in his last mission (what with getting captured and all), he was determined to do everything he could to make this operation a success.

They soon came within a kilometer of the volcano's base, and that was when the carriage's driver saw it. "Heads up, people! Here they come, right out of the damn volcano!"

So, the enemy had taken the bait. Jean-Paul just hoped he and his fellow troops could keep them busy while the knights of the Ordre smashed their factory. The French forces only numbered around one hundred, so discretion would definitely be the better part of valor in this battle.

***

The Austrian Netherlands, September 24, 1789 (Infini Calendar), 2:10 p.m.

The *Minuit Solaire* flew towards Mt. Erfunden from the east, while the French troops charged the volcano from the southwest. Jeanne hoped the enemy fell for the ruse since she didn't know if the Ordre could handle whatever defenses might await them inside the volcano.

Sitting in the captain's chair on the bridge of the Ordre's airship, she spied the domed form of Mt. Erfunden coming up towards them in the canopy window at the front of the bridge. She was glad they still had the steam cannon aboard. It had proved vital to defeating the *Blitzkrieg Rache* in their previous battle. And if any enemy airships within the volcano turned out to be operational, the steam cannon would likely prove just as vital this time around.

Suddenly, though, the *Minuit Solaire* was rocked by a thunderous blast. The bridge shook violently, and Jeanne had to hold on tight to her chair to keep from being thrown forward, backwards, left and right.

She grabbed the communications tube hanging from the ceiling above her chair (which connected her to the boiler room). "Celeste! Status report!"

Celeste's voice came up through the tube. A horrible cacophony accompanied her. *"We've taken a direct hit, milady! I think it was a steam cannon."*

"Our steam cannon? Did it explode?"

"Negative. Judging by the angle of impact, it had to have come from the ground. There's a gaping hole in the floor! I'm having to hang on to the pipes on the wall to avoid falling out."

"Just hang on!" Jeanne then ordered the operators to bring them in for an emergency landing ASAP. The operators informed her that they probably wouldn't be lucky enough to pull off such a feat, and that she should prepare for a *crash* landing instead.

The ground (and the volcano) raced up towards them at an amazing speed, as if they were old friends who hadn't seen each other in millennia. Jeanne felt a tragic sense of déjà vu; this was too much like the crash landing she had endured on the royal airship, the *Majesté Divine.* This time, however, the situation was even worse. The *Minuit Solaire* was even more heavily damaged than the royal airship, everyone under her command was in mortal danger, and there was no lake below to cushion their fall and no backup airship to see to survivors.

She wasn't even aware of hitting the ground. Did they skip across the landscape like the world's most destructive pebble on the lake, or did they make a single crater in the ground? Jeanne didn't know; everything just went dark in an instant.

3

?????????
　　As awareness returned to her, she found herself riding on a horse into a city surrounded by a high stone wall with forty-four towers. She tried to look around, but found she had no control over her body.
　　What is this? What's going on?
　　Her body turned its head of its own accord, and she saw that she was accompanied on either side by men in full suits of armor. It wasn't armor of the Ordre, though; it looked much older and clearly was made of less advanced metal than her own irodium armor.
　　But when her eyes looked down (also not of her own volition), she saw "herself" wearing the same inferior armor as her companions, except with a red skirt similar to the purple one she typically wore. The question again came to her, much stronger this time: What on earth was going on?
　　The knight to her right, an average-size man with black hair and a left eye shut closed with an impressive scar, said, "I have to hand it to you, girl. When you first came to our lord and said God had commanded you to help us defeat the English, we all thought you had contracted some sort of head fever. But now look at us: marching into Compiègne after a number of victories, and it's all thanks to your brilliant strategies."
　　Compiègne? That's a city in Northern France along the Oise River. But why am I here? Am I here?
　　She replied, but it was not her voice speaking. "You give me too much credit, Philippe. We have gotten this far because the Lord deemed it to be so. And also because His Majesty Charles VII believed in me." The voice was higher-pitched than hers.

Charles VII? He was king during Jeanne d'Arc's time. Is this... no, it can't be.

The knight to her left said, "Don't be afraid to pat yourself on the back, Jeanne. You always charged in to battle without any fear. You practically won victories single-handedly." He was a fair-haired young man, rotund but with a winning smile.

Again she spoke, and again it wasn't her voice. "Who shall be afraid when the Lord is with them? I had faith that we would triumph."

He called me Jeanne, but it seems clear this body is not mine. Is it possible... could I really be... seeing things through her eyes?

They rode through the wall and into the city of Compiègne. Past the wall was a field, and past that were the town's buildings. As they rode along the field's dirt road, they were greeted by crowds of people triumphantly shouting, "*La Pucelle! La Pucelle! La Pucelle!*" They were heralding her as the Maid.

"You certainly are popular," Philippe said. "To think: a nineteen-year-old peasant girl, the hero of France."

She replied, "It is because they have faith. We are showing the people that with faith, anything is possible."

A nineteen-year-old peasant girl? The similarities are becoming hard to ignore.

When they rode into the town square, the girl they called Jeanne stopped to address the masses who had gathered around her. "My dear people of *Compiégne*, you have welcomed me into your town, even though I am no one special, simply a poor girl who carries out the will of the Lord. This is because you have faith, and your faith shall be rewarded. Tomorrow we go to battle with the Burgundians who seek to sack this city and rob you of your freedoms." At this there was a round of boos and heckles from the townspeople directed towards the absent Burgundians.

The Duchy of Burgundy was allied with the English during the Hundred Years' War, which I seem to be experiencing here. If I remember correctly, the Burgundians fought against the French because they blamed them for the assassination of John the Fearless, Duke of Burgundy, in 1419. Compiègne was once controlled by the Burgundians, and Philip the Good, the current Duke of Burgundy—at least in 1430, which it seems to be here— wanted to retake it. Let's see... Jeanne d'Arc found out about his plans and brought a force of at most four hundred soldiers to defend the city. Because of her failure to capture Paris from the English back in the fall, Charles VII would not give her command of a full military force. At least, that's what it says in the history books that are going to be written.

"The Burgundians shall not take Compiègne! They have repeatedly rejected our attempts to make peace with them, so they have only themselves to blame for the defeat they will suffer tomorrow. We shall be victorious!" At this the townspeople switched to cheers and cries of adoration for her.

That night the people of Compiègne put her up in the finest room at the inn. When it came time for bed, she put on a light gown and took a look at herself in the mirror. At that point there could be no doubt.

It is my ancestor, Jeanne d'Arc! I truly am seeing things through her eyes. But why is this happening? Does this have something to do with my dream the other night?

Suddenly there was a flash of light behind her, and she turned around to see a figure hovering mere inches below the ceiling. It was the Archangel Michael, clad in ceremonial armor.

I can't believe it! An angel of the Lord! Not only that, but the angel.

She fell to her knees before him. "I am not worthy."

His voice was deep, yet compassionate. "Arise, my sister." She did so, and he continued. "You have been blessed by the Father. Your task is approaching its completion."

"The war is nearly over?"

"Nay, the war will continue for many years to come. But your part in it is nearly played. Tomorrow you will do battle with the Burgundians who seek to claim this town for themselves."

She made a fist over her breast. "I shall not fail. We shall claim victory in the name of the Lord, and of His Majesty Charles VII, who has been favored by the Lord."

"There is but one condition you must honor from now on."

"What is that?"

"You must not use the God's Body anymore."

She did not understand. "But, why? It has kept me safe through many battles—even saving me from the arrow that pierced my heart back in Septembre—and all but guaranteed victory over the English and Burgundians. I haven't even used its full power."

"That is a command from the Father. But I know that you are strong enough to fight without it. Go forth, Jeanne, and show everyone the triumph of the human spirit."

With that, there was another flash of light, and St. Michael was gone. For several minutes she did not move from that spot. She simply stood there with her head bowed and her eyes closed, softly chanting, "Faith, faith, faith, faith, faith, faith."

She's breathing heavily. I think she's a lot more scared than she lets on. I wish I could help, but for whatever reason, I'm simply an observer here.

***

Margny, France, May 23, 1430 (Pre-Infini Calendar), 9:55 a.m.

Outside Compiègne, Jeanne d'Arc led her troops into battle against the Burgundians. It was a fairly even battle, and the Burgundians were soon on the run. The forces of

Jeanne d'Arc chased them back towards their base. It looked as if it would be an easy victory, but *she* knew better.

If only I could warn her about what's about to happen. But I can't.

As if on cue, Phillipe (who was riding next to her), shouted, "Enemy reinforcements behind us!"

"What?" She looked behind her, and sure enough, hundreds of Burgundian soldiers had appeared. Jeanne d'Arc and her forces had been outflanked. Meanwhile, the Burgundians who had previously been fleeing suddenly turned around and charged back towards them.

"We're outnumbered and outflanked," Phillipe said. "What are your orders?"

Frustrated, she wanted to argue with him, but knew better. He was right; the Burgundians now had an overwhelming advantage. There was virtually no chance of winning this battle.

Perhaps if she had been allowed to use the mysterious power the archangel Michael called the God's Body, she might have been willing to fight it out. But of course, that's mere speculation on my part.

She gave the only order she could. "Retreat! Everyone, fall back to Compiègne. Once inside, close the city gates."

Phillipe sat aghast on his horse. "But what about you, girl? Surely you're retreating with us?"

She shook her head. "Someone has to secure your escape." The look on his face did not betray any optimism. "Don't worry; I have faith this will all work out somehow."

She kicked her horse and rode off towards the oncoming enemies. She took one last look behind her and then charged straight into the heart of the attackers. At first, they were stunned by her reckless assault; they strove to get out of her way, and she used that opportunity to cut down several of them.

She continued to press through the Burgundian ranks, heedless of the extreme danger they posed. Enemy after enemy fell to her sword. It seemed like nothing could stop her.

However, that was a very small percentage compared to their overall numbers. As she dove deeper and deeper into their flank, she faced an increasingly bloated mass of hostility. They shouted their hatred and frustration towards her.

"Grab her!"

"Kill the peasant brat!"

"Show her what *faith* gets you!"

Suddenly she was grabbed by a Burgundian archer. He took hold of her golden doublet and fiercely pulled her off her horse. She fell to the ground with a muted thud, and lay there for several moments.

She was then pulled to her feet by the very same archer who had just dismounted her. "Know your place, wench! I'm going to teach what happens to a woman who thinks herself the equal of a man."

She promptly punched him in the face with her armored hand. Bone cracked as he howled in pain and fell over. Another soldier came at her from the side, but she kneed him in the gut. Two more soldiers tried similar attacks, and both experienced the same amount of success.

It wasn't until they all came at her en masse that she was finally subdued. As she lay struggling in the grass, a towering figure appeared in front of her: an officer with greased-back hair, intense brown eyes and a commanding presence. "That's quite enough, Pucelle. Know when you've lost."

She looked up at him. "Who are you?"

He told her his name.

"Ah," she said, "I've heard of you. The 'Bastard of Vendôme.'"

"That's right. Will you surrender, or do we have to kill you?" He cocked his head menacingly. "Doesn't really matter to me."

She gave what sounded like a light chuckle. "Very well, Monsieur Bastard. I surrender, on the condition that I remain in your custody. I will not give myself over to anyone less than a noble. In other words: an equal."

"All right. Not that it will do you much good, but I accept your terms. Let her up."

The soldiers got off her, and she gingerly stood up. "Lead the way, Monsieur Bastard."

4

Vermandois, France, January 6, 1431 (Pre-Infini Calendar), 9:00 p.m.

The nobleman called the 'Bastard of Vendôme' delivered Jeanne d'Arc to his lord, John II of Luxembourg (also known as the Count of Ligny, who was aligned with Philip III, Duke of Burgundy.

All the while, her tribulations were observed by the silent ghost behind her eyes. The ghost still had no idea why all this was happening, nor was she entirely conscious of the passage of time. How long had she been in this situation? It felt like ages, but she couldn't be sure. Also, she couldn't help but wonder about the fate of her comrades aboard the *Minuit Solaire*. Had they all died, and was this the afterlife for her? Perhaps this was some sort of punishment for the sins she had committed in life. She had ample time to ponder these things while she was trapped behind the eyes of her ancestor.

For the time being, Jeanne d'Arc was imprisoned in a high tower in the town of Vermandois in Northern France. She had made no attempt to escape because she believed this to be God's will. The ghost deduced this from the soft chanting of her mantra, "The Lord is my strength, I shall not waver, thy will be done."

Nevertheless, the ghost knew that for all her brave words, Jeanne d'Arc was ultimately a nineteen-year-old girl, and she was scared. She wanted to follow God's will, but at the moment had no idea what His will actually was, or what it meant for her future. The ghost thought back to her own time as a nineteen-year-old soldier. She had received the proper training, but Jeanne d'Arc had basically winged it. She couldn't help but be scared in this situation.

Her stone cell consisted of a straw mat for bedding and a bucket for... well, *that*. There was also a window on the rear wall above the straw mat. Other than that, the room was empty.

At that moment Jeanne d'Arc knelt praying on the floor, her back to the window. Since her prayers were silent, the ghost didn't know exactly what she wished to communicate to the Lord. But she had a few ideas. Most likely her ancestor was asking for French victory in the war, along with an eventual rescue from captivity.

Suddenly a familiar light enveloped her. She looked up to see the archangel Michael floating in the air above her. "Arise, my sister." She complied. "The Father has heard your prayers. He has sent me to congratulate you on your faith. You fought that battle without using the God's Body, and He is pleased."

"Thank you!" she chimed. "I didn't want to surrender to them, but I had faith the Lord would not abandon me."

"The Father never abandons His children, no matter what happens. Rejoice, for you will be with Him soon."

There was a painful silence, and then she said, "W... What? What do you mean, I will be with him soon?"

"You will be sold to the English, who will find you guilty of heresy." He then added grimly, "You will be burned at the stake."

The ghost's vision (Jeanne d'Arc's vision?) became distorted and cracked, as if the world was splitting in two. This only lasted for a moment, though, before it returned to normal.

Her ancestor's voice became similarly cracked and distorted with stress. "T-There must be some mistake!"

The archangel took on a sterner tone. "The Father does not make mistakes. I promise you will not suffer long. You will then be with Him for all eternity."

She slumped to the ground. "No!" she shouted, though it was a weak, hoarse shout. "I didn't fight my hardest for the Lord just so I could suffer the most horrific of all deaths. That isn't right!"

"It is not for you to determine right and wrong. Only the Father decides that."

She was now in tears. "I know that, but... but..." her voice trailed off. "But why do I have to die? I've done everything He has asked of me, and this is my reward?"

He seemed to sigh. "My sister, one does not do His work for a reward. We do it because we are His faithful children. He has created everything, and it is His right to ask these things of us, no matter how difficult it might be for us."

This did nothing to console her. She was sobbing uncontrollably, and the ghost could see very little through the waterfall in front of her. It was too much.

I have often wondered what she was thinking when she was told she would be burned at the stake. But nothing could have prepared me for this. I would give anything to help her right now, tell her everything will be all right.

The archangel put a hand on her shoulder. "Please be strong, my sister." And with that, he faded from the room.

Jeanne d'Arc sat there on the floor of her cell, bawling with complete abandon. Even when she ran out of tears, the sobbing continued for quite some time. After a while the crying ceased all together, and the cell was totally silent. She simply stared straight ahead for what seemed like an eternity.

Eventually she turned back towards the straw mat, apparently with the intent (the ghost hoped) to get some sleep. That would do her a world of good, the ghost thought; sleep made everything better and helped put things in perspective.

However, her attention became fixed on the window above her "bed." She walked over to it and examined it quite thoroughly. She even stuck her head out and looked down. It had to be at least fifty feet to the ground below. There was no way she could survive a fall from this height, if she actually had the intention to jump.

And yet, on closer inspection, it seemed there was. A dry moat lay below, and it just might be soft enough to break her fall.

That's not a good idea. After all, this was not how Jeanne d'Arc escaped from the English, at least not according to history books.

Nevertheless, that didn't stop her from trying. Discovering the window was large enough for her to fit through, she hesitated a moment while she seemed to contemplate this option.

And then she jumped through it. She fell for what felt like ages (at least to the ghost) before crashing down on the soft earth below.

Although the fall didn't break anything, it still hurt enough for her to grunt in pain. Someone must have heard this, because a voice called out, "Who's there?" An English guard rushed over, torch in hand, and shouted for his compatriots. Several more guards soon arrived. Jeanne d'Arc tried to resist them, but couldn't stand up; her legs were apparently too hurt from the fall. As a result, the guards simply dragged her back to her cell, where she now had to face physical pain on top of her crushing emotional pain.

***

Rouen, France, May 30, 1431 (Pre-Infini Calendar), 9:00 a.m.

Jeanne d'Arc was eventually sold to the English by John II of Luxembourg, a French soldier and member of the nobility. John II had allied with the English during the Hundred Years' War, and led a division of troops in the battle of Compiègne. It was one of his soldiers, the Bastard of Vendôme, who had captured her. The English gave John II ten thousand livres for her.

They subsequently put her on trial as a heretic. The whole thing was a sham, a means of vengeance by the Duke of Bedford, uncle of Henry VI who was heir to the throne of England and would-be king of France. She had greatly assisted in helping give the French crown instead to Charles VII, and Bedford held a serious grudge against her because of this.

During the trial, ecclesiastical law was broken more times than either Jeanne d'Arc or the ghost could count. Legally, there wasn't even enough evidence to go to trial in the first place. Regardless, the trial went ahead and the prisoner's rights were violated at every turn. At one point she was even given a document to sign, despite the fact that she was illiterate. It turned out to be a confession letter. Other violations included the doctoring of the court transcript and the denial of a legal consultant.

In the end, she was convicted of heresy and sentenced to death by burning at the stake, thus ending up at Rouen in Northern France (at this time controlled by the English). She was allowed to wear only a simple white dress for her execution.

She was tied to a wooden column above a pile of logs. The executioner held an unlit torch in his hand and approached her. He looked reluctant to be doing any of this. "Do you have any last words before I carry out my appointed task?"

She was silent for several moments. Surprisingly, her breathing seemed to be calm and measured, at least from what the ghost could tell. The ghost had expected her to be frantic at this point, possibly hysterical.

Finally, she said, "No."

One of the participants lit the torch, and the executioner put it to the logs underneath Jeanne d'Arc. The fire caught on eagerly and began consuming the logs. Smoke then began rising upwards to greet her nose.

She closed her eyes and maintained her composed breathing. The ghost thought she had accepted her fate and was saying a prayer to the Lord.

This wasn't how it was supposed to end. If Jeanne d'Arc died here, then how could the ghost ever be born? Was this all just some fantasy after all?

Suddenly, though, Jeanne d'Arc opened her eyes and began grunting with some sort of physical effort. The ghost then noticed a red aura which looked like it was emanating from all over her body. The participants must have seen it also, because their eyes went wide and they began muttering nervously.

"What is this?" the executioner gasped.

Amazingly, she chuckled lightly. "This is me... taking back my destiny!" Her left arm broke free of the ropes, and a small crack appeared in the ghost's vision, just like she had seen in the tower when Jeanne d'Arc had learned of her fate. "My freedom!" Her right arm broke free, and the crack running down the center of the ghost's vision grew longer. "My life!" Her left leg broke free, and the crack grew again. "You think you can murder me?" The rest of the rope fell from the wooden column, and she was completely free. Not only that, but the crack now completely ran down the middle of the ghost's vision. "I'm going to start a family! I'm going to live my life the way I want!" With that, the ghost's vision split in two, and she could swear she was seeing two images of the executioner—only the one on the right looked sad, as if he had successfully completed the execution. The executioner on the left side of her vision, however, still looked terrified.

The split vision then swiftly disappeared, replaced by the scene that had been on the left side. One of the participants muttered, "This can't be!"

Jeanne d'Arc shouted, "God's Body! Full power!"

Suddenly she leaped what must have been at least twenty feet through the air, past the execution's participants. She landed on the other side of the town square, where a few English guards stood dumbfounded. One of them swung at her with his sword, but he hit only air; she was already leaping again. Before they knew it, she was gone.

***

After she had ran for what seemed like ages, she stopped to rest a moment.

Before she could, though, the left side of her vision began glowing with unbearable luminosity. It was as if her left eye was staring at the sun—up close. Jeanne d'Arc howled in pain and fell to one knee.

"The Father is disappointed in you, my sister," said a voice behind her.

She turned around to see (with her left eye) the archangel Michael hovering ten feet off the ground. "Not... fair!" she gasped.

"All that the Lord does is fair."

The pain subsided enough for her to form a complete sentence. "All I want is to be free to live my life! After all I've done for Him, I deserve at least that much."

He shook his head. "It is not about what we deserve. It is about what the Father commands. He gave you life, and it is within His right to decide how it ends. You were forbidden to use the God's Body, yet you did. And now your punishment has been decided."

"What punishment?"

He said, "Open your left eye."

She reluctantly did so, and she was confronted with exactly what the ghost expected: a crushing sea of information. Jeanne d'Arc, who was completely unprepared for this, once again screamed in mental agony. She began hyperventilating, and a stream of saliva escaped her mouth.

After several excruciating moments, she managed to close her left eye. "W-What is this?"

He looked genuinely saddened to be having to witness her suffering. "Your greatest power has now become a brutal curse. By looking upon something with your left eye, you will know everything about it. Your new God's Eye has the potential to drive you mad, if you let it."

Despite all this, she remained defiant. She even returned to her feet. "Fine, then. I'll just wear an eye patch from now on."

He actually seemed to sigh. "You are free to live out the rest of your life as you choose, but I must tell you that your descendants will each inherit the curse upon the death of her mother."

Her right eye widened greatly at this. "What? You can't punish my descendants for what I've done!"

"This is the Father's decision. Just as Cain carried his mark, so too do you now have yours. But take heart: Each of your descendants will have the ability to break the curse, if they can show the world the power of the human spirit, and there is no one way to do that."

"But... but..."

"Farewell, Jeanne d'Arc. We may yet meet again one day."

The archangel Michael faded away, along with everything else within the ghost's vision.

5

There was a blinding white light. Gradually, though, her eyes adjusted to it and she found herself in a pure white space. Nothing else was in that space besides her. As it turned out, however, that wasn't entirely true. In front of her about ten feet was a figure standing before a large object. When her eyes fully adjusted to the white space, she saw that it was a man in front of a book case. He then turned around to greet her. "Ah, such a good story, don't you agree?"

It was Jacques du Chard, the forger who had saved her life when they fought the Count of Saint-Germaine aboard the royal airship, the *Majesté Divine*. Only now he was wearing a white robe like the characters in Biblical paintings. He was also holding a book entitled *L'histoire de Jeanne d'Arc*, which he promptly returned to the book case.

For a moment she stood silent; she still expected her ancestor to do the talking. Jacques said, "It is all right, now. You are yourself again, Jeanne de Fleur."

She examined her body (now that she again had control of it), and discovered that he was telling the truth. Once again wearing her irodium armor (and having one eye covered by an eye patch), she had no doubt that she was Jeanne de Fleur and Jeanne de Fleur alone. She then returned her attention to the deceased (at least, he was *supposed* to be deceased) Parisian forger. "I am myself again, but what of you? Are you really the same petty criminal to whom I owe my life?"

He held up his hands in a *That's a good question* gesture. "Perhaps, but I have only my word to give you. And the word of a criminal is not very good, no?"

She considered this. "Well, you certainly talk like him. Answer this, then: What did I just experience?"

He gave her a look that suggested she should have already figured it out already, but he simply said, "The answer to your questions."

"So, all of that really happened?"

"Indeed, it did. But I'm sure living it gave you even more questions. Answers have a way of demanding further answers."

She asked the first one that came to mind. "Where am I?"

"This?" His arms gave a sweep of the white space. "Think of it as the walls bordering Compiègne. Right now, you are within the walls, passing through on your way to Heaven, but you are not there yet."

"So, essentially, you're saying I am between worlds."

"That is correct, Mademoiselle."

She pondered this for a moment. "That would suggest, then, that I'm still not back in my real body. Where is it?"

"Back in the wreckage of the *Minuit Solaire*, I think. You see, you crashed—but you probably remember that part. Since you ended up so close to the afterlife, we took the opportunity to show you what ordinarily we could not."

"The vision?"

He gave her a broad smile. "Oui. We wanted you to know the truth about Jeanne d'Arc—what she was asked to do, and how she ultimately responded to the demand put upon her by God."

Jeanne remembered the intense suffering her ancestor was forced to endure in the final year of her life. "Why?" she asked him. "Why did God want her to be burned at the stake? I already know the answer given by the archangel Michael, but I want to hear the truth from you, Jacques du Chard."

His smile persisted. "From me? You must have a lot of trust in me—"

She cut him off. "Enough! Your posturing is unbecoming."

The smile disappeared. "It is not so easy to change your own nature, it seems. For that, I apologize.

"The answer to your question is not a simple one. The Lord did not desire Jeanne d'Arc's suffering, any more than He wished the suffering of His own son all those years ago. It was necessary."

She couldn't believe what she was hearing. "'Necessary'? How can you possibly justify the brutal murder of a nineteen-year-old girl, especially after all she did for Him?"

He sighed. "I told you the answer would not be a simple one. I shall spare you the answer Michael gave about it being the Lord's right to take life, as you've already heard it. You see, it is considerably more involved than that. God never takes life simply because He can."

"Then why?"

"In actuality, it is not so different from when he sacrificed His son. He wanted the world to be reminded of what humankind is truly capable of. Jeanne d'Arc was chosen to show everyone the power of the human spirit, to inspire people, to lift them to new heights. As you can see, she rejected His plan."

"That," she said with a clenched fist, "isn't fair! It should have been her choice."

"It *was* her choice. Why do you think she was allowed to keep the God's Body even after she was forbidden from using it? There is always a choice, Mademoiselle. The Lord insists on everyone keeping their free will, despite the fact that we inevitably let Him down. In another world, she accepted His plan and faced her death with bravery. She inspired not just France, but the human race itself, with her selfless act. In this world, though, she will never be known outside of France. After being cursed with the God's Eye, she ran off to an obscure village on the outskirts of France to quietly live out the rest of her days. She changed her name, and it was only on her death bed that she revealed her true identity. It would be another fifty years before anyone outside of that village learned the fate of Jeanne d'Arc."

She didn't know what he meant about 'another world,' but neither did she care. "So, it was either a horrible death and worldwide fame, or a quiet life and a horrible curse. Either way, she must live with immense suffering. What kind of choice is that?"

He simply shook his head. "When the Lord chooses you for a mission, there is no easy path. That is simply the way it is. Jesus Christ, Noah, the Apostles, King David; none of them had an easy time of it, did they?"

"Well... I suppose you're right. It's just that... it's one thing to read about their trials; it's another thing entirely to live them firsthand."

"You become attached to them, yes? It jeopardizes your objectivity?"

She wasn't sure if he was asking her a question or just being rhetorical. "I would say it puts a human face on their suffering. It makes it hard to simply compartmentalize them as mere characters in a book."

"Perhaps," he said. "But we could debate this until the end of time. I think you're missing the most important question, the one that directly concerns you."

She thought for a moment, and then said, "Why is it so important for me to know all this? Apart from my own curiosity, that is."

He chirped, "Now we get to the heart of the matter. You probably remember Michael telling your ancestor that each of her descendants would have the ability to break the curse of the God's Eye. But, of course, none of them did. They were each missing something, be it opportunity, motivation, strength or resolve. You, Jeanne de Fleur, have all those. All you have to do is remind the world of the power of the human spirit."

"How do I do that?"

"Very soon you will have the opportunity. You will know when it arrives. First, though, you will have to face your own trials. Be strong, and you will get through it. Do not allow yourself to be slain by your despair."

"I still don't—"

"I'm sorry, Mademoiselle, but we are out of time. You must return to your friends and complete your mission. Farewell!"

He waved goodbye as the white space grew brighter and overtook her consciousness.

6

"Commander! Jeanne de Fleur! Wake up!"

Someone was shaking her thoroughly. She opened her eyes; it was Pierre. Not only him, but the bridge crew of the *Minuit Solaire* were standing over her with various expressions of concern on their faces.

She was about to speak, but then realized her head was throbbing. She felt where the pain was concentrated, and when she removed her hand she found a modest amount of blood on it. "What happened?"

Pierre replied, "We were hit by a steam cannon and we crashed. Your seat belt failed and you were thrown to the deck. Thank the Lord you're still with us."

"Heh. I knew she'd make it," Victor grinned.

"We need to get out of here," Pierre said.

With his help, Jeanne managed to stand up. She looked around the shattered remains of the bridge and decided the best exit would be through the jagged hole where the canopy window used to be. She then felt a sense of déjà vu; this was too much like the crash of the royal family's airship, except (sadly) there had been no lake to cushion their landing this time.

***

The Austrian Netherlands, September 24, 1789 (Infini Calendar), 2:30 p.m.

Jeanne, along with the bridge crew, managed to escape the wreckage of the *Minuit Solaire*. Counting the knights, there were only twelve survivors of the crash: Jeanne, Pierre, Victor, the two bridge operators, Celeste and six of her fellow engineers.

"Oh, milady!" Celeste shouted upon seeing her idol alive. "I'm so glad to see you unharmed!"

Jeanne may not have been exactly 'unharmed,' but she could move under her own power, and that was good enough. Even better, they had landed in a dense forest near the base of Mt. Erfunden, which gave them sufficient cover for the now; the enemy wouldn't be able to get any steam cannons in here any time soon.

"What's the plan now?" Pierre asked as they huddled around the wrecked airship.

Jeanne curtly answered, "Same as it always was: get inside the volcano and destroy any airships we find." She turned to the nine noncombatant members of the group. "You all need to stay hidden within this forest. Once we're done in the volcano, we'll return for you."

The engineers and bridge crew started to protest, but she made it clear they would only get in the knights' way if they came along. They reluctantly acquiesced, and the knights headed off towards Mt. Erfunden.

***

National Assembly headquarters, Paris, September 24, 1789 (Infini Calendar), 2:35 p.m.

Maximilien Robespierre took the podium in front of the gathered Assembly. He had called this emergency session in order to make his case against the monarchy.

This was the day for which he had long been waiting; his chance to finally get rid of the royal family and solidify the Assembly's hold over France. The attempt on Louis XVI's life a few months ago had ended in failure and possibly would have meant Robespierre's defeat if not for the king giving into the Girondists and declaring war on Austria only weeks later. A disastrous invasion of the Austrian Netherlands ended up working in Robespierre's favor, assuring this moment would come.

"My brothers and sisters assembled here today, we can wait no longer! We must abolish the monarchy once and for all." The audience responded with hesitant murmurs. They clearly weren't sure if his extreme proposal was necessary, but it *was*. He would convince them of that. "I understand your reluctance to take this admittedly drastic step, but it is necessary.

"Look at what has happened during the reign of Louis XVI. He has—under the guidance of his wife and our queen, Marie Antoinette—undertaken projects which our country could not possibly afford. He involved us in the American war of independence. He had great flying ships built to satisfy his own ego. Do you know what these ventures cost us?"

He went on to list the exact costs of both France's involvement in the American war of independence, as well as the creation of the airships, not just monetarily but in loss of life as well. He made sure to mention the brave French souls who had died needlessly during said ventures.

He then explained how these endeavors had plunged the country into crippling debt and driven inflation to an all-time high. "Our already-downtrodden citizens can barely buy a loaf of bread. They have lost faith in their government, and as a result they were led to storm the Bastille and the Palace of Versailles in a single day back in July." Of course, he neglected to mention that he had had a hand in those incidents; it was better for everyone if they didn't know. "And how did our king respond to that crisis? By attempting to flee the country! To abandon his own people. Is this the action of a trustworthy ruler? Certainly not.

"King Louis XVI was—as you all know—subsequently apprehended in northern France with his loyal subordinates in the Ordre de la Tradition. He had to be brought back to Paris by force, and he has been sequestered here ever since because he cannot be trusted not to attempt flight again if given the chance.

"However, even here he has not been able to stop causing trouble for our country. We mistakenly allowed him to keep his power to declare war. He listened to the Girondists and declared war on Austria, plunging us into yet another endeavor we cannot afford.

"I have heard the people speaking in the streets; they know we cannot survive as a nation with our current rulers, and they are calling for the immediate execution of the king and queen."

This was greeted by members of the Assembly shouting their surprise at this declaration. Surely, they said, it wouldn't have to come to that. Surely the royal family could be spared.

"Regretfully," he continued, "that's impossible. Even if we let them go peacefully, they would still exist as symbols of the *Ancien Régime,* and those loyal to them would still fight for their cause. The only sure way to unite France is to completely destroy the monarchy and establish a new republic with ourselves in control."

This elicited even more vocal objections from the Assembly. They began to question Robespierre's very sanity. *They'll change their tune in a moment, assuming my mob does what I paid them to.*

Suddenly, a messenger burst into the assembly hall. "It's a riot!"

"You must be joking!" Robespierre declared, feigning surprise.

"There is a large group of people storming the Tuilleries! They're demanding the heads of Our Majesties!"

***

The Austrian Netherlands, September 24, 1789 (Infini Calendar), 2:40 p.m.

Jean-Paul de Fleur cut through another couple of enemies with his dual sabers. The Austrians had disabled the steam carriages he and his force had come in on with their cannons; he had just barely managed to get out of his carriage before it exploded and sent him to his maker ahead of schedule. Ever since then he had been dodging Austrian bullets and slashing the Austrians with ruthless efficiency.

There was little doubt the odds were hardly in the French force's favor. After all, they were outnumbered almost two-to-one. However, that could also be seen as an ironic blessing; it meant the enemy definitely had something to hide within Mt. Erfunden, and Jean-Paul de Fleur and his comrades were on the right track.

It wasn't long before the enemy realized who they should be targeting. As Jean-Paul dispatched one after another, more and more began pressing in on him. They fired their wind rifles at him, but his swiftness far exceeded their aim. He found himself very glad that his physicality had not diminished too much during his time with Farahilde Johanna, his sadistic—yet still attractive—captor and member of the Austrian royal family. She had been a real chienne, yet Jean-Paul was glad his sister Jeanne had spared her life. That undoubtedly helped prevent further deterioration of France's relationship with Austria.

Suddenly one of his allies called out, "Sir! Behind you!"

He turned around to see an Austrian soldier lunging at him. This wasn't just any green recruit; Jean-Paul could tell by his speed and the way he held his sword that he was a seasoned fighter. Jean-Paul didn't have time to counter his attack.

The attack, though, never came. A saber abruptly burst through the soldier's chest, and he fell to the ground.

Standing in his place was a French officer. He was short in stature, and didn't strike Jean-Paul as a dangerous man, but based on what he had just done to a veteran soldier, he had to be.

"Are you all right, Colonel?" he asked.

"Uh... fine, I suppose," Jean-Paul said before quickly cutting down another Austrian. "I didn't know we had any soldiers the caliber of yourself in this battle. What is your name?"

The short man swiftly stabbed an enemy before answering. "Napoléon, sir. Second Lieutenant Napoléon Bonaparte."

They continued like this, fighting enemies and conversing at the same time.

Jean-Paul said, "You've got some real skills, Napoléon."

"Thank you, sir. You are not so bad yourself."

Jean-Paul laughed. "Keep this up and you'll make general some day."

"Ha! I have no intention of stopping there."

"What, you want to become king?"

Napoléon said slyly, "Perhaps."

"Best of luck to you," Jean-Paul chuckled. "You're going to need it."

"You insult me, sir. I have no need for luck, as you can plainly see."

"Cutting down garden-variety troops is one thing; displacing the monarchy is something else entirely."

"Nevertheless, a man of my ambition cannot be satisfied until he reaches the heavens."

"No man ever reached such heights without a lot of luck."

"So you say."

"I'm glad you heard me, Monsieur Napoléon. This battle is a noisy affair."

"It should quiet down once we kill all the enemies, Colonel de Fleur."

"That's a sound strategy!"

7

The Austrian Netherlands, September 24, 1789 (Infini Calendar), 2:50 p.m.

In the woods on the other side of Mt. Erfunden, several plumes of orange smoke began to rise in different places on the outskirts. This was because Jeanne had ordered the non-combatant members of her crew to light smoke tubes they had managed to salvage from the *Minuit Solaire*. She told them to light the tubes in different spots and then get away as fast as they could. Meanwhile, the knights lit their own smoke tube at the edge of the forest closest to the base of Mt. Erfunden, which was about half a kilometer away.

As Jeanne, Pierre and Victor stood behind the cloud of orange smoke billowing out of the tube they had placed in the ground, a thunderous explosion erupted on another side of the forest.

"Looks like they fell for it," Victor said.

Pierre concurred. "I'd say you're right. I just hope the others didn't get caught up in it."

Jeanne shared his concern, but didn't express it verbally. Celeste and the others were just as much members of the Ordre de la Tradition as the knights, and they knew the risks when they signed up. Moreover, the knights didn't have time to be worrying about them; they had a job to do (just as the Celeste and the others had done theirs when they set up the decoy smoke tubes to draw the Austrians' fire) and they were going to do it.

The only thing she said was, "Now!"

The three of them charged out of the forest, and through the orange smoke, toward Mt. Erfunden. This wasn't the ideal plan (certainly Jeanne wouldn't have chosen a strategy that involved the destruction of her airship and most of its crew if she had a choice), but this would have to do. Hopefully by the time the Austrians and their steam cannon spotted them, they would be far enough away to avoid an attack.

The smoke masked their presence for a few yards, and then they were out in the open, the base of Mt. Erfunden ahead of them.

Someone shouted to their left. The enemy steam cannon rested on a steam carriage a third of a kilometer away on the edge of the forest. It was gradually shifting position to target them.

"Keep running!" Jeanne shouted. "As fast as you can!" If they could just make it to Mt. Erfunden, there were any number of crags and fissures which could conceal them from the steam cannon's view.

Suddenly the ground exploded behind them. The force of the blast knocked them to the ground. Fortunately, the shot had been off; it hadn't really hit anywhere close to them.

They got back up and kept running. Based on what Jeanne knew about steam cannons, she estimated it would take at least a minute for the Austrians to fire again. The knights had bought themselves a little time, at least.

However, Jeanne stole another look at the enemy and immediately regretted it. The carriage was now driving towards them. Although it was slow starting up, it would soon reach top speed, and at thirty miles an hour, it wouldn't take long to catch up to them.

The knights continued running at full speed, Jeanne's body protesting wildly. It repeatedly shouted at her to stop this madness and let it rest. Nevertheless, she managed to put it out of her mind and kept running.

Now in the shadow of Mt. Erfunden, they were completely dwarfed by its massive round form. It was maybe another thirty seconds to its base. It was beginning to look like they would make it through this.

As if to drag her back to reality, there was another explosion behind them—this time much closer. The three knights went sailing forwards and crashed upon the hard soil of the Austrian Netherlands.

In the following moments, Jeanne's head was like the hazy broth she had sometimes eaten as a child: hot and soupy. She was vaguely aware of trying to move her limbs, but couldn't feel them; she wasn't even sure if they were still attached to her body.

There was a low rumble followed by the hiss of a release of gas. Someone said, "So much for the great Ordre de la Tradition."

"Can you imagine the reward we'll get for capturing them?" Someone else said.

A third voice: "Are these the only survivors of the crash?"

"Who cares? These are the *knights*. They're the only ones we need."

There was laughter all around.

***

Mt. Erfunden, September 24, 1789 (Infini Calendar), 3:30 p.m.

The Austrians tied their arms behind their backs with a thick rope, and marched them through the cavernous tunnels of Mt. Erfunden. These narrow corridors were obviously man-made; Jeanne kept seeing cuts, chips and other evidence of excavation along the walls.

Eventually they arrived in the volcano's cone. It was a massive circular area with open sky one hundred feet above, and an uneven floor. This central chamber had been carved out by lava flows who knew how many years ago. The Austrians had clearly done some more smoothing out of the area, though, judging by how well all the airships fit in here.

The airships. There were a dozen of them in two rows of six on either side of the chamber. Each one appeared to be the same model as the *Blitzkrieg Rache*. Were these airships also capable of harnessing lightning as a weapon? Jeanne wondered.

In addition, each of the airships had what appeared to be a wooden frame built around it to keep it upright. Did that mean they weren't operational yet?

Jeanne didn't have much time to wonder about that, as a burly man with a thick beard and hair as black as midnight strode up to them. He was at least two feet taller than Jeanne and physically comparable to Pierre.

He spoke with a booming voice. "Finally caught the troublemakers, eh?"

One of the Austrians behind Jeanne replied, "Yes, sir. There may be more of them in the forest outside, but we've brought you the high-value targets."

The burly man bellowed, "Good!" He looked down at Jeanne. "Not so tough now without your one airship, are you? Ho-ho!"

"Care to find out?" Jeanne retorted.

"Oh, a feisty chicklet!" He motioned to the twelve airships behind him. "But as you can see, we have a dozen ships primed to invade France. You, on the other hand, no longer have *any*. This is a war of technology, and you have just lost."

Pierre said, "Isn't it customary to introduce yourself before you declare victory in a war?"

"Ho-ho? I suppose you're expecting the clichéd 'Where are my manners?' line. Very well; my name is Commander Danse Thornwood."

"I am also a Commander," Jeanne said.

Thornwood waved off any more exposition from her. "I know exactly who you are, Jeanne de Fleur. You lead the elite branch of the French military called the Ordre de la Tradition—or what's left of it. My spies have enlightened me on your more interesting qualities, such as," he pointed at her eye patch, "your peculiar left eye."

"What about it?"

He gave a big grin. "I hear it is most uncomfortable when opened. Why don't we find out, hmmm?"

Jeanne tensed as she realized what he was planning. Two guards held her tight as Commander Thornwood reached in and ripped the eye patch off her. She struggled fiercely as they pried her left eye open, but couldn't win against their strength. Pierre and Victor yelled at them to release her, but they too were similarly held in place by guards.

Once again, an overwhelming flood of information assaulted her. Only this time, she couldn't stop it by closing her eye or putting the patch back on. She could only stand there helpless as fact after fact pounded her mind into submission.

Focus! Concentrate on one specific thing, she told herself.

There were so many different things in front of her—radiating so much information—that she ended up staring at the floor. But even that was throwing a barrage of data at her.

Focus on one thing!

She looked for a specific aspect of the floor to home in on. But which one?

Wait...

She caught hold of a strange set of facts rising out of the floor, something that didn't make sense to her: the temperature of the rock underneath them had been gradually rising for weeks. It was so slight that most people wouldn't have noticed, but the rate of temperature increase was steadily rising. Did that mean...?

Suddenly Thornwood put the eye patch back on her, and the relief was immediate. "Ho-ho! That's enough for now. That glowing yellow eye really puts the pressure on, doesn't it? I think that's going to be very useful for interrogation purposes."

"Bastard!" Pierre raged.

"Ho? Do you have feelings for your commander? I should warn you: These military romances never work out."

"I think we've put up with this long enough," Victor said.

"Agreed," Jeanne said.

"Ho? You think your stay here is voluntary? You think we're just going to let you waltz on out?" Thornwood gave another hearty laugh.

"Well," Jeanne said, "we don't plan on leaving just yet. But you *are* going to take your hands off us."

Thornwood laughed again. "I think you hit your head in the crash of your airship. My men have you bound quite thoroughly. Do you fancy yourself some kind of magician that can escape any situation?"

Jeanne shrugged. "Something like that. Your men should have examined our armored gauntlets more thoroughly. If they did, they would have noticed the sharp edges."

Suddenly she tore free of the ropes she had been working over for several minutes. She then thrust her head backwards into the head of the guard immediately behind her. She followed this by swinging her arm so that the sharp edge of her gauntlet sliced the throat of the other guard behind her. Blood sprayed her face and armor, reminding her why she didn't like to carry out such crude attacks. Still, she could not afford to be choosy in situations like this.

Pierre and Victor similarly broke free of their restraints. While Victor attacked the guards who had been holding them, Pierre lunged straight for Thornwood. Both men went crashing to the ground and proceeded to rain fists upon each other. It was a titanic clash Jeanne would have enjoyed watching in its entirety, but she had enemies of her own to fight.

The man she had driven her head into swung at her with her own rapier, taken from her when she was captured. He clearly had no rapier training, or else he would know the weapon was for thrusting and not swinging. Jeanne simply ducked underneath it and used her armored palm to smash him in the nose. He howled in pain and dropped the rapier, which she picked up and then ran him through.

She turned around to see that Victor had disposed of the guards he was fighting, but a dozen more assorted personnel were running towards them from the other side of the circular chamber. Not all of them were soldiers—some wore jumpsuits similar to Celeste and the other engineers aboard the *Minuit Solaire*—but all of them were armed.

They raised their rifles to fire at the knights, but Thornwood yelled, "Don't shoot! You'll cause an explosion!"

Jeanne, wondering what he meant by that, looked around the chamber. There were numerous large pieces of equipment and barrels stationed between them and the armed personnel.

Pierre took advantage of Thornwood's momentary lack of concentration to pick up the other big man and hurl him into a large table with multiple sharp instruments on top. Jeanne was amazed; she had seen demonstrations of Pierre's strength before, but they had never been as impressive as this. She secretly hoped one of those instruments was now going through Thornwood's vitals.

"Come on; we need to move quickly," she said.

She hurried past the equipment and the shattered table towards the nearest airship. It was about fifty feet in front of her in front of the left wall of the chamber.

The personnel who had previously been pointing weapons at them were now—perhaps because they had witnessed the dismantling of their leader—running away in the opposite direction, possibly to another exit on the other side of the chamber.

"Looks like the decoys did their work," Pierre said while running behind Jeanne.

Victor—who was running beside him—replied, "Damn right. Most of the enemy soldiers must have left to go fight them, just as we planned."

"But we were going to use the *Solaire's* weapons to take out these airships," Pierre said. "Now how are we going to do it?"

Jeanne reached the airship she had been running toward and began climbing the wooden frame surrounding it. "We have all the weaponry we need right here."

Pierre began climbing right behind her. "Looks like these are all the same model as the ship we took down near that fort. I wonder if their lightning attacks work against each other."

Jeanne reached the top of the frame and dropped down onto the airship's deck. "We're not going to open fire on the other airships. That would take too long."

"Then, how?"

"I have an idea. You'll just have to trust me."

***

Jeanne inspected the bridge of the enemy airship (which, according to the words on the hull outside, was named *Rechtschaffener Dämon*, or "Righteous Demon"). It was similar to that of the French airships, except there was only one operator's chair in front of the captain's chair.

Like the French airships, there was also a communications tube hanging down from the ceiling above the captain's chair. Suddenly, Pierre's voice came from it. Unlike the *Minuit Solaire's* tube, this one had a clean sound. "Commander, are you there?"

She grabbed the tube. "Yes, Pierre. What have you found?"

"We're in what on the *Solaire* would be the boiler room, except there's no boiler. In fact, there doesn't appear to be anything down here that utilizes steam."

"Well, what *is* there?"

"There's a large cylindrical device that stretches up to the ceiling. It has two cranks on either side of it, as well as switches labeled... let's see, my Austrian is a little rusty... *On* and *Off*."

Jeanne thought about this for a moment. "Why don't you and Pierre flip the switches to 'On' and then both of you turn those cranks at the same time. If what Celeste has told me about the generation of electricity is correct, that should start up the ship."

"Aye."

She went over to the operator's chair and examined the console in front of it. There was a black metal stick jutting out from it. Was this used to fly the airship? If so, Jeanne thought, it was a very strange way to do it.

To the left of the stick was a large silver lever about the size and shape of Pierre's knuckles labeled "Fire 1" and to its right was a button labeled "Fire 2." At least, from what Jeanne knew of Austrian military terms, that was what they said.

Suddenly the deck beneath her began to vibrate and hum with energy. It appeared as if Pierre and Victor had been successful in starting the airship. *So, this is what the awakening of an electric beast is like.* It was much subtler than the loud rumbling of the steam-powered airships she was accustomed to.

She returned to the communications tube. "It looks like you did it. Now I'm going to—"

Her words were abruptly cut off by something exploding into the back of her head. She fell to the deck, her vision blurred by bright lights.

"Ho-ho! Did you think you could defeat me that easily?"

Thornwood! They should have made sure he was dead.

He picked Jeanne up and effortlessly threw her into the bridge's canopy window. The glass splintered upon her arrival and—despite her irodium armor—it hurt like hell. He then grabbed her rapier from its sheath at her side and examined it. "This is a very nice sword. It will make a fine gift for my lord Frederick William II, King of Prussia. It's customary to give a *clean* present to one's superiors, but I doubt he'll mind if a little of your blood is on it."

Jeanne sat up straight against the bulkhead. Thornwood gripped her rapier with both hands and thrust it at her head, but her metal gauntlets allowed her to grab the blade. It soon became clear, however, that Thornwood's vastly superior strength would win out in the end and the rapier would pierce her head anyway.

Without thinking, she kicked at his nether region. He stepped back, groaning in pain, but he seemed more enraged than anything else. He allowed his fury to overtake him and charged at Jeanne with the rapier.

She instinctively rolled out of the way, even as her whole body was racked with pain. Thornwood grunted in pain as he became the second person in only a few minutes to collide with the canopy window. It cracked even further under his weight.

Seizing the opportunity, Jeanne locked her fists together and brought them against the back of his head, sending it back into the glass. Again and again she did this until the window was painted with his blood and his face was an unrecognizable mess.

His body slumped unceremoniously to the floor. At almost the same moment, Pierre and Victor rushed in. "Are you all right, ma'am?"

She sat gingerly in the operator's chair in front of the damaged window. "I'll be fine. Right now, I need you two to dispose of Thornwood."

"Understood, Commander," Pierre said with a mix of satisfaction and pride. Clearly, he was going to take pleasure in getting rid of the man who had tried to kill his commander. He turned to Victor. "Let's throw this trash overboard."

Victor grabbed Thornwood's legs. "You really did a number on him, Commander."

Pierre grabbed the arms. "Wish I had been the one to do it."

Jeanne simply said, "Return here once you're done."

They left with Thornwood's body, and then returned a few minutes later. "So, what's the plan now?" Pierre asked.

Jeanne explained. "When Thornwood took off my eye patch, I was able to get information on things going on below this volcano with my God's Eye. There's been a gradual increase in seismic activity over the past few weeks, so gradual that Thornwood and his men probably never even noticed. But," she pointed to her eye patch, "this eye sees everything."

"Are you saying this volcano is active?" Victor said.

"Yes," Jeanne replied. "But at the rate things have been going, the enemy probably would have gotten these airships out of here long before it erupted. With a little coaxing, however, I think we can speed up the process."

Pierre grinned knowingly. "I get it. You want to blow up all that equipment down there, increasing the seismic activity and creating a catalyst to this volcano's eruption."

"Exactly. Those barrels near where we were brought in contain extremely volatile liquids. Destroying them should produce the effect we need."

Jeanne gripped the metal stick at the operator's console and gave it a slight jerk to the right, towards the direction of the barrels. However, the *Rechtschaffener Dämon* banked sharply into the wall of the chamber. The airship shuddered violently under the collision.

Pierre moved swiftly, cupping his right hand over Jeanne's on the stick in an attempt to help stabilize the airship.

"I suppose a lighter touch is needed," she said.

"All right, let's try this again," Pierre said.

Together they gingerly angled the stick until the *Dämon* maneuvered back towards the barrels. Once they were facing their targets, Jeanne pulled back the silver lever labeled "Fire 1." "I hope I understand this correctly," she said. She then pushed the button labeled "Fire 2."

There was a high-pitched whine, followed by a bolt of blue energy erupting from the outer hull of the *Dämon*. It struck the barrels, causing them to explode in a series of massive orange fireballs which quickly merged into one. The gargantuan inferno moved faster than Jeanne's eyes could follow, almost immediately engulfing the *Dämon*.

The three of them instinctively ducked down as the canopy window was blown inward. Without wasting any more time, Jeanne pulled back on the metal stick, which sent the enemy airship climbing upwards and out of range of the explosion.

Now more explosions below them rocked the ship. Jeanne's plan had worked—perhaps too well.

"Maybe we should have gotten higher up *before* firing at the barrels," Victor suggested as wind blew in from the charred hole where the canopy window was.

"It was hard enough getting this ship into position as it was," Pierre retorted.

Jeanne said, "Never mind that. Right now, we have to rescue Celeste and the others before Mt. Erfunden erupts."

8

The Austrian Netherlands, September 24, 1789 (Infini Calendar), 4:10 p.m.

Celeste poked her head out from behind a tree on the outskirts of the forest.

Alphonse, one of the *Minuit Solaire*'s bridge operators, expressed his concern from an adjacent tree. "What are we going to do? The Commander and her group were captured."

As the highest-ranking officer among the group of nine, Celeste was looked to for leadership. "We just have to have faith in them. The Commander won't be beaten easily, you can count on that."

Unfortunately for her, the other members of her group were not as optimistic. They were all facing a dire situation: Even if they survived this day, they would still be stranded behind enemy lines, a long way from France. Their chances of ever seeing home again were dwindling rapidly.

One member of the engineering crew, a twenty-year-old young man, said, "Maybe we could stage a rescue. You know, go in and free them ourselves?"

Celeste shook her head. "We're not soldiers, George. We wouldn't stand a chance in there."

"But—"

George's words were abruptly cut off by an explosion coming from Mt. Erfunden, followed by large plumes of smoke.

"I told you they would do it!" Celeste yelled jubilantly. "Milady is the greatest!"

Alphonse, however, was still reluctant to share her excitement. "It's too soon to celebrate. Even if they *did* succeed in destroying the airship factory, we still don't know if they survived that blast."

Celeste was about to chastise him for his lack of faith when suddenly a dark object arose from the volcano. "It's an airship!" she exclaimed.

"Dammit!" George yelled. "One of those bastards survived!"

Another of the engineers pointed out, "It seems to be damaged. Look how it's moving erratically."

They all observed the airship as it wobbled in circles above the volcano. Celeste could have sworn that whoever was operating it had never done it before.

Wait a minute...!

She burst out into the open, waving her hands frantically at the mysterious airship.

The others cried out in alarm and confusion, pleading for her to return to hiding with them. However, she gave the opposite response. "Everyone, come on! Help me wave to them!"

This went on for a few minutes. They kept trying to convince her to stop, and she in turn kept trying to convince them to join her. Eventually they realized they weren't going to win out on this and cautiously went to her side and waved to the airship.

Within minutes they got the airship's attention, and it flew—albeit erratically—over to them. When it got in close, they could see it had been damaged by the explosion. The canopy window had been blown out, its edges seared by flames. But through the hole they could see who was piloting it.

"It's the Commander!" they shouted.

"Just as I figured," Celeste said. "None of us have ever operated a foreign airship before, so it must have been our knights flying so awkwardly. I mean, the enemy would certainly do a much better job, don't you think?"

They proceeded to berate her for risking their lives on what they considered a flimsy hunch, but she didn't care. The Commander was safe, and the mission was (presumably) accomplished.

Pierre and Victor appeared topside and dropped a rope ladder for them. Celeste waited until everyone else had gone up before she ascended the ladder. While she was climbing, though, there was another explosion from Mt. Erfunden. "What was that?"

"The volcano's erupting!" Pierre shouted.

"What?" she shouted. "I thought it was dormant!"

"Not quite as dormant as we were told," Victor said.

The *Dämon* rose sharply, forcing Celeste to hang on for dear life. She managed to make it up, however, and Pierre and Victor helped her on to the deck. Reddish-orange fountains of lava were hurled into the air from Mt. Erfunden.

"That certainly takes care of the factory," Victor said.

Pierre nodded. "Agreed. Let's just hope that was the only one."

"Are we going back to France now?" Celeste asked.

Pierre put an arm on her shoulder and led her into the *Dämon*. "You're damn right, we are. We've earned it."

They did head back to France, only stopping along the way (very briefly, due to the incoming lava flows) to pick up Jean-Paul de Fleur and the survivors of the battle he had taken part in. Jeanne gave her brother a severe talking to for his participation despite the fact that the injuries he had received at the hands of Farahilde Johanna hadn't yet healed. He simply smiled and lightly brushed aside her concerns.

***

The Tuileries, Paris, September 24, 1789 (Infini Calendar), 4:30 p.m.

King Louis XVI, Marie Antoinette and their two children, Louis-Charles and Marie-Thérèse, were currently hiding in the royal bedroom. They had fled here as soon as the angry mob had rushed the palace gates.

"What do they want this time?" the queen asked, the tension evident in her voice.

"Who knows?" her husband answered. "Let's just wait them out, and hopefully they'll get tired and leave."

Marie-Thérèse, along with her brother, was clinging fiercely to their mother. "Are we going to be all right, mama?"

"Of course, my love. Not even the angriest mob would dare harm innocent children."

"They said bad things about our father," Louis-Charles replied.

"They're just jealous that he's the king," Marie Antoinette said.

Suddenly there was a crash at the door, accompanied by furious voices.

"They're in here!"

"Break the door down!"

"They won't escape this time!"

Louis XVI braced himself against the dresser and oak table he had placed in front of the door as a barricade. The people outside attacked from outside, their voices growing even more bloodthirsty.

The children added their own voices with their terrified bawling. Their mother tried to soothe them, but to no avail.

Gradually the door was torn down piece by piece, and the mob charged into the room, overpowering the king. They seized him and dragged him out of the room. The screams of his family behind him revealed they, too, had been taken.

The mob dragged them outside to the Place de la Révolution, where a scaffold and two guillotines awaited. They forced the king and queen to mount the scaffold where they forced them to their knees to face a large crowd of thousands.

"What is the meaning of this?" Louis XVI shouted.

A voice behind him announced, "That should be perfectly clear." Louis XVI watched as Maximilien Robespierre strode past them and began examining the assembled crowd. "As I've said time and time again, you have driven our once-great country to ruin. The people can take no more, and they now demand your deaths."

Deaths. Plural.

"Please! Do what you will with me, but spare my family. Everything that has happened is my responsibility. I'm the reason for all of this, so I beg of you: Let my wife and children go!"

Robespierre turned to address the crowd. "What say you, people of France? I agree these children are innocent. We should not hold them accountable for the crimes of their parents."

The crowd voiced their assent. After all, many of them shouted, what kind of monsters would put to death blameless children?

Robespierre returned his gaze to the king and queen. "Your last request is granted, *my liege*. Louis-Charles and Marie-Thérèse shall be spared."

Louis XVI gave a fleeting smile, and then turned to look at Marie Antoinette. "What of my wife? She is also innocent."

In response, Robespierre did something that was uncharacteristic for him: He laughed. "Innocent?" He again turned to address the crowd. "Is this woman innocent?"

"Of course not!"

"She gave him all his bad ideas!"

"She was pulling his strings the whole time!"

"If she's innocent, I'm the king of England!"

"And what," Robespierre said, "shall we do with her?"

The crowd gave a single answer. "Off with her head!"

Marie Antoinette struggled in vain against the ruffians holding her down. "Have mercy!"

Robespierre grimly shook his head. "It is too late for that now." He motioned for the members of the mob holding the king and queen down to force them into the guillotines. Someone yelled for the children to be turned away so they wouldn't bear witness to what was about to happen. "Yes, that's for the best. They don't need to see this."

The children yelled, "Mama! Papa!" However, their crying soon devolved into unintelligible wailing.

As the children were led away, Robespierre asked Louis XVI, "Do you have any last words?"

The former king, numb with shock and disbelief, simply said softly, "What has become of my beloved France?"

Robespierre leaned in and whispered, "Only what you have caused it to become." He stood up and raised his voice for all to hear. "Louis XVI and Marie Antoinette, for the crime of high treason, you are hereby sentenced to death! And with your deaths, a new and greater France will be born!"

He motioned to the executioners, who initiated the drop of both deadly blades at once. In the split second before his head was severed from his body, Louis XVI's question echoed in his head. *What has become of my beloved France?*

PART IV
Je vous ai tout pris
(I Took Everything from You)

1

Loire Valley, France, March 20, 1790 (Infini Calendar),
12:01 p.m.
     Robert Westerfield trekked through the southern
edge of Loire Valley, a woodland area in central France. This
was a remote region that very few people inhabited, since it
was quite a ways from big cities such as Paris and Versailles.
Westerfield was smartly dressed in a brown bowler
hat, brown slacks and a vest and tie over his shirt. In
addition, he carried a leather briefcase with him. If anyone
had seen him, they probably would have thought him very
much out of place in this environment.
     He was a reporter from England, and his
publication, *The London Thames*, had sent him to France to
cover the civil unrest that began the previous year. Since
arriving in this country, he had interviewed countless
people, from ordinary citizens to high-ranking government
officials (the latter of which usually preferred the talks to be
off the record).
     He now had most of the story written. It all began
back in July when an angry group of Paris citizens, fed up
with their country's skyrocketing inflation and massive
debt, attacked a prison in the city called the Bastille. The
building was destroyed and its warden killed by that mob.
     On the same day, a completely different group of
people attacked the royal palace at Versailles, while
complaining about the high cost of bread within the country.
The royal family managed to escape on their revolutionary
airship, but it later crashed in a village in the north of France
called Varennes.
     However, no one knew what had gone on aboard the
royal airship while in flight or why it had crashed.

Westerfield only had one clue: An elite branch of the French military called the Order of Tradition was involved. In fact, they had been involved in several pivotal events during the revolution. If he wanted to get the whole story about the country's civil unrest, he needed to find a member of the group and ask them.

Unfortunately, six months ago the king and queen were executed in an uprising. The new regime, called the Legislative Assembly, swiftly issued warrants for the arrests of all members of the Order. The head of the Assembly, Maximilien Robespierre, publicly condemned them as dogs of the king (since they answered only to him) and traitors to France because, as he argued, they had blindly served him despite the damage he was doing to the country. The French people had previously supported the Order, but on September 24, 1789, they turned against them. Robespierre was a very effective public speaker.

The Order of Tradition promptly fled Paris in their airship and disappeared. Despite a thorough search by the new government, none of them had been found.

Fortunately for Westerfield, though, he had recently acquired a lead on the possible location of a woman matching the description of the Order's commander. That is what brought him out to this forest in the middle of nowhere.

After wandering through the woods, he came to a clearing and found what he thought he had been looking for: a simple wooden shack. It was overrun with vegetation and clearly had not been well taken care of, but a well out front with a bucket on top suggested someone was currently living here.

Westerfield walked up to the front door and knocked on it.

There was no answer.

He inquired in his British accent, "Hello? Miss Dufleur? Are you in there?"

No answer.

He tried looking through the windows on the front of the shack, but with all the vegetation growing around them he wasn't able to see much.

He thought to himself, perhaps no one really lives here. Even so, he had travelled too far to give up now. With that in mind, he returned to the door and slowly opened it. He cautiously poked his head inside.

He was suddenly greeted by the sharp end of a rapier pointing at his head. Standing in front of him was a disheveled young woman with reddish-brown hair and a purple eye patch. She was dressed in simple peasant clothing, but the icy look in her eye told him she meant business.

"Who are you?"

He put his hands up. "B-Begging your pardon, ma'am. M-My name is Robert Westerfield. I'm a reporter for *The London Thames.*"

She kept the rapier pointed at him. "You're English? What are you doing all the way out here? Did Robespierre send you?"

He frantically shook his head. "No, ma'am. I was sent here to write a story on the revolution that's been taking place in your country."

She didn't look convinced. "Then go write it. It has nothing to do with me anymore."

He swallowed and summoned the courage he needed. "But I believe it *does.* You are Jeanne Dufleur, are you not?"

"What if I am?"

"You were the leader of the Order of Tradition, isn't that right?"

"So, what?"

"The Order was involved in key events during the beginning of the revolution last year, I've been told. Maximillion Robe Spear said that you were traitors to France, but I want to hear it from you. Please, tell me: What is the truth?"

For the first time since he entered, Jeanne de Fleur lowered her sword. "First of all, Monsieur... Westerfield, was it?"

He carefully put his hands down. "That's right."

"You should work on your French pronunciation."

"M... My apologies, ma'am. I'm still not completely fluent yet."

She sat down at the small table in the center of the room. Now that Westerfield had a chance to look around, it looked like the entire shack was one room. A simple cot accounted for a bed a few inches behind the table, and a dilapidated stove stood a few inches to the right of the cot, against the wall.

"If you're serious about printing my story, I'll tell it to you," she said.

"Much obliged, ma'am. But if I may be so bold... why do you suddenly trust me?"

She let out an exhausted sigh. "It isn't that. It simply occurred to me that whether or not someone kills me is irrelevant. I have nothing left to live for. Right now, I merely exist. That's it."

He didn't know what to say to that, so he said nothing. He scanned the shack for another chair to sit down in, but there were none.

She said, "Sorry, but there's only one chair. You're my first visitor since I came to this place."

"That's all right. I don't mind standing."

There was a flask on the table. Jeanne poured a brown liquid from it into a dirty glass and downed it in short order. She offered him some, but he politely declined. "If it's all the same to you, I'd like to hear your story."

"I neither expected nor desired to tell it to anyone. However, if you're willing to tell the world the truth about the French Revolution, I'll tell you."

He took out a pen and paper from the backpack he had been carrying and began writing. She told him about her beginnings in the French Army, her rise through its ranks and eventual appointment to commander of the Ordre de la Tradition. She told him about the storming of the Bastille and the conspiracy to assassinate the royal family (which she no longer had any doubt was the work of Robespierre), the monstrous transformation of the Count of Saint-Germaine, and the crash of the royal airship. All the while, he grew more and more astonished at the tale.

"Bloody hell," he exclaimed. "That's quite a tale."

She also told him about the Ordre's battles against the Austrian coalition and their electricity-powered airships, and the Ordre's capture of one of them.

"That was our last mission before we were betrayed," she said.

"What happened when you returned to Paris?"

She told him.

***

Six months ago: the outskirts of Paris, September 24, 1789 (Infini Calendar), 7:00 p.m.

The *Rechtschaffener Dämon* docked at a telegraph pole on the northeast edge of Paris. The enemy airship may have been a different design than the *Minuit Solaire*, but it was still equipped with a cable for insertion into the pole. Celeste theorized that this was because the Austrian coalition intended to eventually implement the same telegraph system in their own regions.

Jeanne walked over to the communications console behind the captain's chair on the bridge. "Anything?"

Alphonse, the operator manning the console (because the previous communications officer, Maurice, had been killed in the crash of the *Solaire*), sat idly waiting for a response. Jeanne had ordered him to send an urgent message to the Tuileries Palace notifying them of the crew's situation so that the *Dämon* would not be mistakenly fired on.

He was about to respond that they had not received a response from the Tuileries when there was suddenly a tap-tap-tap from the console. A small paper ticket punched out and Alphonse began to read it. "'Pass code acknowledged. You are ordered to dock at Tuileries Palace for debriefing.'"

Jeanne considered this for a moment. Was it her imagination, or had they accepted the Ordre's pass code a little too easily? She couldn't help but feel they should treat the *Dämon* with more skepticism, considering it *was* an enemy vessel that just arrived on the outskirts of France's greatest city.

She hesitantly ordered the airship to be flown over to the Tuileries, but she couldn't shake the feeling that something was horribly wrong here.

***

The *Dämon* arrived at the landing pad at the Tuileries. Armed guards lined the ramp. Jeanne actually felt relieved by that; under the circumstances, this was how they should be greeted.

The remaining members of the Ordre, along with the two dozen-or-so soldiers they had rescued from Mt. Erfunden, disembarked, thankful to be back home.

However, even when the armed guards on the ramp saw their faces, they did not lower their weapons.

The guard at the front of the column said to them, "Stay where you are."

"I am Commander Jeanne de Fleur of the Ordre de la Tradition."

"I know who you are. But orders are orders."

"Orders?" Jean-Paul shouted. "What orders? From whom?"

A voice behind the guards announced, "From me."

The guards parted and Maximilien Robespierre came through. He made sure to keep his distance from Jeanne and the others, though.

"What is the meaning of this, Monsieur Robespierre?" Jeanne said icily.

"The *Ancien Régime* is dead. The Legislative Assembly now rules France. As such, we have no more use for royalists such as yourselves. The soldiers you rescued from Mt. Erfunden are free to go, but all members of the Ordre de la Tradition are under arrest for treason."

"You can't be serious!" Victor yelled.

Jeanne said, "What have you done with the royal family?"

"The children are unharmed," Robespierre replied. "But I cannot say the same for the king and queen."

"Where are they!?" she roared.

He remained completely calm, almost serene. "You'll find their heads on pikes in front of the Palace."

She froze completely, unable to move except to mutter a single syllable: "No..."

"It's true. You'll soon see for yourself."

She fell to her knees. "You're lying! They can't be dead!"

"And what reason would I have to do that? To torture you? What would be the point? I'm just going to have you executed within a few days."

Lost in her anguish, Jeanne became vaguely aware of an uproar occurring behind her. The soldiers they had rescued from Mt. Erfunden came forward to face Robespierre and his armed guards. Most of the soldiers were only armed with sabers, having expended their rifle ammo during the battle at the volcano.

"For your sake, you had *better* be lying," one of them said to Robespierre.

"We didn't travel all that way and nearly get buried in lava to have scum like you take over France," said another.

- 169 -

Robespierre looked stupefied. "Have you all lost your mind? For one, I said you soldiers could go free. Two—I just saved us all from the road to ruin the monarchy put us on. And three—you are quite out-gunned."

Jean-Paul made his way to the front of the pack. "We have fought hard for the future of France, and we won't let villains like you ruin it. And I *certainly* won't let you stand there and say you're going to kill my sister!"

Napoléon Bonaparte appeared next to Jean-Paul. However, Napoléon suddenly walked over to Robespierre's side. "I'm afraid I can no longer fight by your side, Colonel."

Jean-Paul bared his teeth at Napoléon. "Are you saying you're going to sell out to this piece of garbage, Napoléon?"

"In order to realize my own ambitions, I have to be able to tell which way the wind is blowing. That means I must fight for the side that is sure to win. You and your measly band of soldiers don't stand a chance against the rulers of France, whoever they might be."

A smirk appeared on Robespierre's face as he looked upon Napoléon. "You're a smart man. You'll do well in the new regime. As for the rest of you..." He shifted his attention back to the men who currently stood between him and the remaining members of the Ordre. "You will be blown away by the winds of change."

Jean-Paul, without taking his eyes off Napoléon, said, "Pierre, Victor—can you two hear me?"

"Yes," Pierre said from somewhere in the back.

"I hear you," Victor said.

"Get my sister out of here."

After a moment of silence, Pierre said, "You got it."

"I appreciate it. And Jeanne..." Jean-Paul paused to collect his thoughts. "Thanks for being a great sister."

Jeanne abruptly snapped out of the trance she had been in. "Brother, no!"

She found herself being grabbed by Pierre and Victor. They dragged her back into the *Dämon* while her

- 170 -

brother and the other soldiers charged Robespierre and his guards. The two groups merged into one distorted cluster, and with the sound of gunfire many of them fell.

She lost sight of her older brother, and began to cry because she knew that was the last time she would ever see him.

2

Loire Valley, France, March 20, 1790 (Infini Calendar), 1:00 p.m.

"And that's what happened. We escaped and went into hiding. Some time later Robespierre had my family's estate burned to the ground as punishment for supporting the monarchy. Our staff, which had refused to leave even after I warned them it wasn't safe to stay there, perished trying to put out the fire. They were devoted to the de Fleur family until the very end."

A tear streamed down Jeanne's face as she finished recounting the story.

Westerfield said, "As a journalist, I'm supposed to remain neutral when reporting every story. But let me just say you have my deepest sympathies for what you went through. If you don't mind, though, I do have one more question..."

She downed another shot of her drink. "What is it?"

"Why didn't you try and get vengeance on Robe Spear? As you say, he destroyed your life. He took everything from you. Anyone else would have sought to make him pay for it."

She gave a miserable laugh. "For a while, I wondered that myself. And then I realized: It wasn't him I blamed. It was myself. I couldn't protect anyone, so I have no right to seek revenge. And even if I did, it wouldn't bring them back. What's done is..." She put a hand to her face as fresh tears came forth. "Done."

He finished writing and returned the materials to his backpack. "It will probably be some time before the story appears in *The London Thames*. I plan on waiting around for a while to see how events play out. Thank you for your time."

Westerfield left Jeanne's shack and began walking back through the woods. He hated leaving her in the sorry state she was in; she didn't even say anything when he left. However, he decided that telling her story to the world was the best thing he could do for her.

As he left the clearing, he stole one last look back at the shack...

...and walked straight into another person.

As he was pushed aside to the ground, they said angrily, "Out of the way, dummkopf."

The stranger didn't even slow down as she made her way towards Jeanne de Fleur's shack. As Westerfield studied her, he decided that whoever she was, she wasn't someone to be trifled with.

Are those knives sticking out of her hand? He asked himself incredulously. *And what was that accent she chastised me with? It wasn't French or English.* Was it possible she was a friend of Jeanne? *What if she's an assassin? Should I warn Miss Dufleur?*

He decided that if the mysterious woman was indeed an assassin, attempting to warn Jeanne would only get him killed. And if that were to happen, there would be no one to tell her story. So, he decided, the best thing to do was get out of there as quickly as possible.

***

Jeanne continued to sit at her small table, drinking liquor shots and thinking about the unexpected Englishman who had just paid her a visit. Would he really tell her story, or was he in fact a spy for the Assembly? Either way, it didn't matter. Nothing mattered anymore. Whether she lived or died made no difference whatsoever. She had failed her ultimate duty, so as far as she was concerned, she had no business being alive at this point.

Not for the first time, she thought back to the vision she had when the *Minuit Solaire* was shot down. The forger, Jacques du Chard, had told her she would have a chance to redeem her ancestor Jeanne d'Arc and break the curse of the God's Eye by showing the world the power of the human spirit. As far as she could tell, she must have failed. The curse was still with her and she had lost everything. This must be her punishment.

There's no point in going on. I think pretty soon I'll put an end to everything once and for all. Maybe I'll run myself through with my rapier. Or perhaps I'll drink myself to death. Or I could go out in style by burning this place to the ground.

Only those who have fallen deep into the well of darkness—so deep that they can no longer see any light—know the ultimate despair it takes to even contemplate suicide. There has to be absolutely no hope left, no chance for salvation that can be seen. After having experienced this bottomless desolation, Jeanne had concluded that no one *wanted* to commit suicide. Rather, those who entertain the idea of ending it all have been driven into a corner of madness from which they (seemingly) have no hope of escape, where even the cold unknown of the grave was preferable to remaining alive—the lesser of two evils, in other words. Jeanne de Fleur was now in this corner.

Her self-pity was sharply interrupted by the door of her shack exploding inward. She instinctively covered her face with her hands (momentarily forgetting she really had no reason to do so). When she lowered them, she found she was no longer alone. A figure stood in the doorway in mid kick. The door lay on the floor, shattered into two fragments.

"I finally found you, fräulein!"

Jeanne was dumbstruck. This was the last person she ever expected to pay her a visit. "Farahilde Johanna?"

It was indeed the same young woman Jeanne had fought in order to free her late brother from Austrian imprisonment, complete with the strange dual cowlicks atop her head, and her bladed gauntlet. This time, though, she was wearing a red corset under her brown jacket rather than a white one.

In response to Jeanne's question, Farahilde strode over and punched her in the face with her free hand. Jeanne went sprawling onto the floor.

"This isn't a friendly visit, fräulein! I've come to send you to Hell!"

Jeanne got up to one knee and wiped the blood from her mouth. "I guessed as much as soon as I saw you."

Farahilde grabbed Jeanne and threw her across the table towards the door. "You are not an easy person to find. It took me six months to track you down. After all the trouble I went through, I'm going to take my time killing you."

Jeanne got to her feet but avoided Farahilde's vengeful gaze. "All this time, I've wanted to apologize to you. I wanted to say I'm sorry for letting your sister die. But I'm too weak. Even if I could bring myself to return to civilization and venture to Austria, I knew I couldn't face you. Yes, you tortured my brother and tried to kill us both, but no one deserves to have their family taken away from them."

Farahilde, however, would not be appeased so easily. "You promised me you would protect her! Even though we were enemies, I trusted that you were sincere. That was the biggest mistake of my life. You didn't care about her any more than the rest of the French worms did."

This accusation sparked something within Jeanne. She grabbed her rapier from the wall where she had put it, and pointed it at Farahilde. "How dare you! Few people in France admired Her Majesty as much as I did. You have no idea how much it hurt me to have to sit back and watch while the Assembly branded her a traitor and kept her prisoner in her own home."

"Then why didn't you free her?" Farahilde yelled. "I know how strong you are. You could have done it!"

Jeanne fought back the sobs that were rising in her throat. "It was the king's wish. He felt that any attempt to escape would only make things worse for the royal family. He believed the people's hate would eventually subside if they cooperated with the Assembly."

Now it was Farahilde's turn to release the tears that had been welling up in her for six months. "The man was a fool. He didn't deserve the honor of being married to Maria Antonia Josepha Johanna."

"She was a great woman," Jeanne agreed.

Farahilde lunged at her. "Yet you let her die!"

***

Some time later, Jeanne and Farahilde stood huffing and struggling to catch their respective breaths outside the shack. They had been fighting for a while, and now they had run out of steam.

"I think... you've lost a step... fräulein."

"Oh... really? I thought... you were going to... send me... to Hell. You're certainly taking... your time."

They both fell to their knees, exhausted. Jeanne looked over her clothing. It was riddled with cuts from their fight. She was also bleeding in several places, but Farahilde looked no better. In the end, neither of them had been able to inflict a serious wound on the other.

Suddenly Farahilde said, "Tell me, fräulein: Why are we fighting each other?"

Jeanne was surprised by the question. Surely Farahilde had made her motives quite clear when she arrived. "I let your sister die."

The young Austrian shook her head. "If you had truly accepted your guilt, you would have let me cut you down. But you didn't. You fought me in order to prove your loyalty to meine schwester. Therein lies the blood that keeps your heart pumping; you know deep down inside that it was not you who killed her. And you have convinced me of that as well."

"What does it matter?" Jeanne asked with no shortage of sorrow. "She's gone, and I let it happen."

"Were you the one who killed her?" Farahilde asked rhetorically.

"I just told you—"

She was cut off by Farahilde's sudden roar. "Were you the one who killed her!?"

"I... not directly."

Now, even louder: "Were you the one who killed her!?"

"No."

Farahilde was still not satisfied. "What was that? I can't hear you!"

"No!"

"Then who was it!?"

"Maximilien Robespierre!"

Now Farahilde lowered her voice. "Then should we not punish him for his actions?"

"What good would that do?" Jeanne sighed. "The damage is done."

"Is it? Being all alone out here, you probably don't know what else he's been up to. For instance, I bet you don't know about the Reign of Terror."

"'The Reign of Terror'?"

"That's right, fräulein. He's in control of your country's government, and he's been busily ordering the execution of anyone who disagrees with him. Many of his opponents have been beheaded, and he shows no sign of stopping any time soon."

"That's horrible!"

"He rose to power by claiming his crimes were for the good of France, but things have only gotten worse under his rule. Such a man needs to be stopped, don't you think? I mean, you swore loyalty to the monarchy, but isn't your real duty to your country?"

Jeanne was silent, but after a moment she was forced to agree with Farahilde. "You're right. Things will never get better as long as Robespierre has his way. All this time I've been wallowing in self-pity when I should have been fighting for the betterment of France." She rose to her feet. "Let's go!"

Farahilde also stood up. "Just the two of us, fräulein? You'd better have a good plan. Meine bruder, Leopold II, emperor of Austria, forbade me from even coming here; meine country recently settled on a peace treaty with France, and he does not wish me to jeopardize that by doing anything reckless like trying to assassinate the French leader."

For the first time in ages, Jeanne smiled. "Don't worry about that. I have a team willing and able to take on the world at my command. We just have to find them first."

"Heh. Lead the way, then."

When Jeanne had packed up her few belongings, she followed Farahilde to the edge of the clearing in front of the shack, where the Austrian had a curious silver... thing... waiting for them. "What is this?"

Farahilde beamed with pride. "It is meine country's newest vehicle: the motor bike." She bent down and swiftly turned a metal crank located on the chassis under the handle bars. She then hopped on the bike and repeatedly stomped her foot on the pedal. Within a minute the bike sputtered and began rumbling. Hot steam shot out the rear of the bike. "Hop in the side car, fräulein." Then, seeing Jeanne's apprehension at the prospect of riding this strange new vehicle: "Unless you'd rather walk, of course."

3

Place de la Révolution, Paris, March 21, 1790 (Infini Calendar), 8:15 a.m.
Robespierre watched with great satisfaction as the prisoner was dragged up the scaffold. Since the dissolution of the monarchy six months ago, he had ordered the deaths of more people than even he could remember, but none of the executions so far could compare to the pleasure he was receiving at seeing the utter defeat of this one man.

When the bloody and beaten man was made to kneel at his feet, Robespierre said, "I've waited a long time for this day, Monsieur Brissot."

"Go to Hell, you parasite!"

It was none other than Jacques-Pierre Brissot de Warville, Robespierre's former rival in the Jacobin Club and member of the Girondist faction within the Club that had long been at odds with Robespierre and his Montagnards.

Robespierre beamed magnificently at his triumph. It had taken him months to falsify the evidence against Brissot and his "conspirators" within the Girondist group, and now, on this day, it all paid off.

"You'll pay for this!" Brissot shouted. He spit a gob of fresh blood onto Robespierre's shirt.

Robespierre looked at him with contempt. "A crude man until the end, are you? Well, don't worry; today you will have a companion for your journey to the next life."

There was the sound of footsteps climbing the scaffold, and a second prisoner was deposited next to Brissot. He looked over to see who it was. "Manon!"

Manon Roland, like Brissot, was dressed in simple prisoner clothing. She hadn't been tortured nearly as badly as he had, but her face was a sickly white instead of its usual glossy alabaster. "I'm sorry," she coughed. "It seems solitary confinement does not agree with me."

"Have you lost your mind, Manon? This is no time for jokes!" Brissot said.

Robespierre held up an official-looking piece of paper recently furnished by the Assembly after reviewing the evidence against Brissot, and began reading aloud. "Jacques-Pierre Brissot de Warville and Manon Roland, for the crime of attempting to subvert the sovereignty of France by conspiring with foreign nations to carry out the violent overthrow of the government of this country, you are hereby sentenced to death by beheading."

"Wait!" Brissot shouted. "There aren't any guillotines up here! How do you plan to behead us?"

Robespierre smirked. "I have found a more efficient means of execution." There was now a much softer pattering of footsteps coming up the scaffold behind Brissot. "Meet my own personal executioner."

Brissot craned his neck to see who was standing behind him. "What the Hell is this?"

It was a svelte figure with blond hair and pigtails emerging from either side of her head. She wore a flowing black dress and her face was covered by a harlequin mask with a black smile.

However, none of those things was her most striking feature. No, the thing that grabbed everyone's attention was the massive scythe she effortlessly held with one hand.

"Madame Tussaud is far more cost-effective than any guillotine," Robespierre said.

"You may kill us," Roland said, "but Jeanne de Fleur is still out there somewhere. She will deliver your punishment without fail."

"Hmph. Even if she does, *you* won't be around to see it."

Robespierre signaled to Madame Tussaud, who waited for him to exit the scaffold, and, with one lightning-fast motion, took both their heads with her scythe. Dual geysers of blood spewed out from their open necks as their now-lifeless bodies fell to the floor of the scaffold in a heap.

"Good work, Marie," Robespierre called from the bottom of the steps. "You know what to do next."

Tussaud nodded, and then casually walked over and picked up the severed heads. She may have been a top-notch executioner, but what she would do next was the real reason he had taken her into his employ.

***

Pierrete, France, March 25, 1790 (Infini Calendar), 1: 30 p.m.

Jeanne and Farahilde arrived at the outskirts of the small village located in the French countryside. The village consisted of a dozen houses spread unevenly around a central fountain. All in all, it was a very unremarkable place, though Jeanne believed it held a secret which would prove useful to the two of them.

They left the motor bike (for which Jeanne was thankful; it had not provided the smoothest transportation) and began walking casually towards the fountain in the center of the small community. They wore light-brown cloaks to disguise themselves, as they had no idea what kind of reaction the townspeople would have if they found out the truth. The country had turned against the Ordre de la Tradition six months ago, and according to Farahilde, Robespierre had placed bounties on their heads (and, of course, Jeanne's was the largest).

As they walked along, Farahilde asked, "You think he's just going to be out here in the open waiting for us?"

"He's much more intelligent than that. His bounty is second only to mine, so he's sure to be hiding somewhere."

"And how will you find him? Will you sneak through every house in this place searching for him?"

"With any luck, the villagers will take me to him."

"Oh, it's that easy, is it, fräulein?" Farahilde laughed.

"If I ask them nicely, perhaps."

Jeanne could almost see the smirk under Farahilde's hood. "Well, if that doesn't work, I'm more than willing to interrogate these French worms. I can get his location out of them."

"Don't even think about it," Jeanne warned her sternly. "I won't have any bloodshed here."

"In that case, your silver tongue had better work. We're surrounded, you know."

Indeed, they were. As they had been walking, everyone in the village had gradually come out to confront them. Now they were confronted by peasants wielding hoes and other farming tools and staring at the two of them menacingly.

One of them, a large man with thick arms, stepped forward and pointed his hoe at them. "Why have you come to our village? And why do you hide your faces?"

In response, Jeanne pulled back her hood and revealed her face to them.

One of the villagers, a teenage boy, shouted, "It's her! He said it would be a beautiful woman with reddish-brown hair, tied in a single braid, and a purple eye patch over her left eye."

Another person, a middle-aged woman, chastised the boy. "Quiet, you stupid child! This could be an imposter trying to trick us into giving him up."

"You've been expecting me, I take it," Jeanne said.

The muscular leader, however, wasn't taking the bait. "You certainly match the description of Jeanne de Fleur. But as my wife says, you could be an imposter. It wouldn't be the first time the Assembly has sent people here looking for *him*. How do we know who you really are?"

"Simple. If he's been expecting me—as I believe he has—he must have told you our group's mantra, the creed known only to us and the royal family," Jeanne replied. "'For His Majesty, we defend as the shield. For the country, we strike as the sword. To those who threaten either, we rage as demons.' And right now, there is a certain man I must rage against. He's taken everything from me, and I need the hero of this village to stop him."

The villagers, upon hearing this, suddenly dropped to their knees before Jeanne. "He did tell us your verses. You are indeed 'Jeanne la Juste,' commander of the Ordre de la Tradition, and right now... France's only hope," the leader said.

Jeanne sighed. "If I were as great as you seem to believe I am, the royal family would still be alive."

"Do not blame yourself. It was that fiend Robespierre that killed them. Others in France may have turned their backs on you, but not this village. We still believe in what you stand for. Now come; I will take you to the Pride of Pierret."

Farahilde leaned in to whisper in Jeanne's ear. "Well done, fräulein."

***

The leader of Pierret, who introduced himself as Vincent Reims, led Jeanne and her companion to a nondescript wood house in the middle of the village. There was absolutely nothing to make it stand out from the other dwellings in the community. Vincent's wife, Catherine, accompanied them. The house turned out to be theirs.

Vincent and Catherine opened a hidden door in the floor of the house and took them down into a candle-lit basement. Down there, sitting at a table studying some papers by the light of a lamp, was a man dressed in peasant rags.

"Pierre! She has come, just as you said," Catherine announced.

When they reached the bottom of the stairs, Jeanne was able to get a good look at the man at the table, and it was in fact Pierre Girard, the former second-in-command of the Ordre de la Tradition.

Pierre got up from the table and examined Jeanne closely. After several moments of silence, he smiled and said, "It's good to see you again, Commander. I knew giving you the name of my village before we parted ways was a good idea."

"It's good to see you, too, Pierre. I'm getting the Ordre back together, and only you know where to find the rest of them."

Pierre looked perplexed. "But... it looks like you already found one of them. Isn't that Celeste standing next to you?"

Farahilde pulled back her hood and revealed her face to him. "I hate to disappoint you, but I am not seine engineer."

Pierre was shocked. "You! Commander, what are you doing with this chienne? She tried to kill us! She tortured your brother!"

Jeanne tried to explain. "I'm sorry, Pierre. I know she isn't the most ideal ally, but we need all the help we can get if we're going to take down Robespierre. We have a common enemy."

"Don't misunderstand my intentions, fräulein. I'm only helping you in order to make Robespierre suffer for the murder of meine schwester. I really couldn't care less what happens to the rest of the French worms."

Pierre shook his head in frustration. "Do you see, Commander? Farahilde Johanna can't be trusted. Once an enemy, always an enemy."

"Listen to me," Jeanne said. "We were enemies in a war that none of us started. Politics decided that we fight one another. Now we're in a new war, and I believe Farahilde can be trusted as long as we both seek to bring down Robespierre. Now... are you with us, or not?"

Pierre sighed in resignation. "If that is your order, Commander, I will cooperate with our... new partner."

Farahilde patted him on the shoulder. "That is wise, meine new friend. Now where is the rest of the Ordre?"

He was visibly uncomfortable with this new alliance. Nevertheless, he tried to adhere to his commander's wishes. "Ah, well... all in good time. Tonight, Commander, I insist that you stay for dinner. We have a lot of catching up to do."

***

That night, they were treated to dinner in the house of Vincent and his wife Catherine. Jeanne and Farahilde sat next to each other at the table in the Reims' kitchen, while Pierre sat across from Jeanne. Vincent and Catherine sat at opposite ends of the table.

"So, Pierre, you are not actually from France? I suspected as much, since your skin is much more bronzed than the usual French worm," Farahilde said.

Jeanne nudged her as a reminder to not insult their hosts.

Pierre, however, pretended he hadn't heard that. "No, I am originally from somewhere in the Holy Land, I think. My mother brought me to this village over twenty years ago. She was badly injured from something, though she didn't say what. She just had enough time to ask the people of Pierret to take care of me before she succumbed to her injuries."

"Did you never go home to search for your family?" Farahilde asked.

"*This* is my home. And *this* is my family," he said, indicating the Reims.

"Since his mother didn't tell us the name of the baby she had with her, we ended up naming him after this village," Vincent said.

"He grew up to become the Pride of Pierret," Catherine added.

"I still remember the day he told us he had been invited to join the Ordre de la Tradition," Vincent said.

"It was the proudest day of our lives," Catherine said. "We never had any children of our own, but Pierre has always been like a son to us. And not just us; the entire country held a great deal of respect for him. So, imagine our shock when he suddenly came home six months ago and announced that he had been declared a criminal by the Assembly. We couldn't believe it! If he wasn't such a serious man, we would have sworn he was joking."

"I wish it was a joke. But that's more Victor's style," Pierre said.

"Where is Victor?" Jeanne enquired.

Pierre simply said, "In the last place anyone would expect. Tomorrow I'll take you to see him."

"So, you carried out the Splinter Protocol?" Jeanne asked.

"Of course, Commander. That is standard procedure in case the group has to break up temporarily. That's why the last thing I said to you was 'I'll be in Pierret.'"

The Splinter Protocol mandates that in the event of the *splintering* of the Ordre de la Tradition, the knowledge of each member's location can only be known by the person above him or her. Only the commander knows where to find the second-in-command, who similarly is the only person who can locate the person below him. No one knows the location of the commander (in this case, Jeanne de Fleur), so she is the only one who can initiate the reformation of the group. Although the second-in-command could theoretically reunite the Ordre, they would still be without their leader.

"I wasn't sure if you would actually carry it out," Jeanne admitted solemnly. "If you'll recall, the last words *I* said to *you* were 'Don't look for me. That is the last order I will ever give you.'"

Pierre smiled. "You may have stopped believing in yourself, but I didn't. I kept hoping you would return to put things right. If you don't mind my asking, what changed your mind?"

In response, Jeanne did something she hadn't done in a long time: She chuckled. "You may be surprised to hear this, but it was actually this crazy chienne sitting next to me. She gave me a reason to live again."

"You're going to give me a big head, fräulein. All I did was show you what you weren't smart enough to see for yourself."

It looked as if perhaps Pierre was starting to understand the new relationship between these two women. "Well, then, I suppose I owe you a debt of gratitude for bringing our commander back to us, Farahilde Johanna."

Farahilde simply rolled her eyes and said, "How about we change the subject. Are there any in Paris who would aid us in our battle against Robespierre?"

"I was thinking monsieur Brissot and mademoiselle Roland may be willing to help us. The Girondists were never on very friendly terms with Robespierre and his Montagnard group," Jeanne said.

Pierre, however, shook his head. "I'm afraid that won't be possible, if what I've heard is true."

"What do you mean?" Jeanne asked.

"Yesterday a Parisian man passed through this village. He brought news that those two were recently executed on Robespierre's orders."

Jeanne balled up a fist and squeezed it until her hand went numb. "That rogue! Is there no level of evil he won't fall to?"

"It's really not surprising," Pierre said. "He is a sick, twisted man who nurses grudges and relentlessly pursues greater power. He would probably gouge out his own mother's eyes to get what he wants."

"And that is precisely why he must be punished, the more brutally the better," Farahilde said.

"We *will* stop him," Jeanne assured her.

"I prefer meine wording, fräulein."

***

Later that night, Jeanne and Pierre took a walk through the village. He had invited her to walk with him alone because there were things he wanted to say to her away from prying ears. He especially didn't want Farahilde to hear any of this.

As they passed between the simple houses, the full moon bathed Pierret in an incandescent light. The windows of the various homes were also lit by candles, providing further illumination.

"Do you still remember the first time we met?" he asked her.

"Of course. You had just been accepted into the Ordre, and you reported to my office. You had dark skin and you towered over me—I'd never seen anyone like you."

"Do you remember the first thing I said to you?"

"I'll never forget it. 'This *girl* is our leader? Ridiculous!'"

He laughed. "I may have been a good soldier back then, but I still had a lot to learn, didn't I?"

"And do you remember what I said to *you*?"

"'If you don't like it, get out.' I couldn't believe someone half my size had the nerve to say that to me."

She said slyly, "This *girl* couldn't afford to be nice. If she did, someone might have taken advantage of her."

"You know," he said, "I never told you this, but I vowed long ago to never let that happen."

She smiled proudly at him. "You've always been someone I could trust to support me in any given situation."

He looked away nervously, as if he was suddenly embarrassed to look her in the eye. "This... goes beyond mere duty."

"What do you mean?"

"What that Thornwood man said back at Mt. Erfunden... well, he was right. I may have scoffed at you when I first began serving under you, but it didn't take me long to develop real respect for you. And that respect eventually turned into admiration, which itself ended up turning into... something else."

Jeanne stopped in her tracks and stared into his eyes. "You don't mean..."

He explained, "Everything about you is wonderful, Jeanne."

"You called me by my first name..."

"From your lustrous auburn hair to your unbelievable inner strength, there is nothing about you I don't find perfect. I will dive into the heart of Hell before I allow an enemy to even graze your irodium armor. That is how much I care about you."

So that was the real reason he wanted to go for a walk with her alone. Obviously, he was expecting a response, but...

"I don't know what to say, Pierre. I mean, it goes without saying that I have the utmost respect for you, and it isn't as though I don't find you to be a strong, handsome man. But... I don't think we can do this right now—not as long as you're my subordinate and we are on what could turn out to be a suicide mission."

Pierre looked disappointed, though not necessarily deterred. "So, if we take down Robespierre, we might have a chance to make something of this?"

Shrugging, she said, "I don't know—maybe. I've never really given any thought to having children. If I can't find a way to remove the curse of the God's Eye, any daughter I have will end up inheriting it. There's really no way to describe the suffering it brings. Having to live the majority of your life keeping your left eye covered—knowing that if you ever slip up, you could completely lose your mind—it's like having the Sword of Damocles hanging above your head until the day you die. There is nothing in this world more terrifying than the constant threat of madness."

Pierre was silent for a moment, trying to come up with the words to respond to the revelation of her heavy burden. "You've never spoken of the God's Eye like this before. I had no idea it caused you such pain. You've always carried yourself in such a cool, collected manner that I didn't think it was such a burden."

"I couldn't allow the full extent of the burden to be known. I need my subordinates to have the utmost faith in me; if they can't trust me, I can't trust *them*."

Pierre, however, didn't agree with her. "Pain doesn't mean weakness, Jeanne. We'll follow you to the ends of the earth, God's Eye or not."

She said, with a hint of melancholy, "Can you really speak for the others?"

He gave her a confident grin. "I have a feeling the rest of the Order will prove me right."

Without warning, she suddenly hugged him. "Thank you, Pierre. I needed that."

He enveloped her in his large arms, almost swallowing her with his massive frame. "Any time, Commander."

4

The Tuileries, Paris, March 27, 1790 (Infini Calendar), 2:00 p.m.

Robespierre walked into the building which had been built over the Tuileries garden after the dissolution of the monarchy. Good riddance, thought Robespierre; it was just a large empty space in the middle of the Tuileries before he took over. Now it housed the key to France's domination of the entire European continent.

Flanked by Napoléon and Madame Tussaud (wearing her harlequin mask and carrying her huge scythe as usual), he inspected the hundred-foot object in front of them. It shined a wondrous blue, and its low hum was a symphony to his ears.

"Isn't it the most beautiful thing you've ever seen," he asked, to no one in particular.

Napoléon nodded in approval. "It is a masterwork of engineering."

Tussaud remained characteristically silent.

"With this, no one will ever be able to challenge France again," Robespierre declared emphatically.

"Our future would seem to be secured," Napoléon agreed. "Or, rather, it would be if not for the piece of the puzzle that has gone missing."

Robespierre grunted in annoyance. He knew exactly what his protégé was referring to. "You're worrying about nothing. It doesn't matter what the Marquis de Sade does now. How can he possibly stop us at this point?"

Napoléon said nothing further on the matter.

In truth, Robespierre had intended to have the Marquis de Sade executed immediately upon seizing power; the Marquis had, after all, outlived his usefulness and was a liability because he knew too much about how Robespierre had taken control of France. However, the crafty lunatic somehow got wind of Robespierre's intentions and fled Paris. Now he could be anywhere, doing anything. In front of his lieutenants, Robespierre downplayed the danger de Sade posed. Privately, he wanted him caught and put to death as quickly as possible.

Unfortunately, when Robespierre had de Sade freed from the Bastille, he fabricated documents that showed the Marquis had been transferred to another prison. If Robespierre ordered the manhunt of a supposedly incarcerated prisoner, that would raise uncomfortable questions. That meant that at the moment there was little he could do about the situation.

Robespierre called out to one of his scientists on a platform twenty feet up the glowing, pulsating object in front of them. "How long until it's operational?"

The scientist, probably nervous about being put on the spot, awkwardly spun around to look down at his employer. "N-Not long now, m-my liege. P-Probably another week."

Robespierre frowned in annoyance. "Do I detect uncertainty in your voice?"

"W-Well, sir, it's just that... well, we're working without the project leader. Ever since he was killed by this device in that accident," the scientist pointed to the object. He was referring to the project lead's unfortunate electrocution.

"He died to secure a glorious future for France," Robespierre said, without any real sympathy. "Anyway, he taught you everything you need to know to finish it."

The fearful scientist, however, was not satisfied by Robespierre's hollow assurances. "I'm sorry, sir, but I would be derelict in my duties if I didn't bring up the project lead's concerns about the stability of the system. We're dealing with new technology, and with the massive voltage we're going to be running through the city, we don't know what could go wrong."

"Just get it done," Robespierre ordered. "We've poured far too many resources into this project for it to fail. If it doesn't work, Paris has no future anyway."

"Once the Austrians find out what we're up to here, they will surely attack us," Napoléon added.

Tussaud nodded.

"Exactly. The Alset Project will lead to another war with Austria. Unless, of course, this thing works. Then neither Austria nor anyone else will be able to even touch us. So, get this thing working," Robespierre said. "For France."

***

Grenoble, France, April 1, 1790 (Infini Calendar), 2:05 p.m.

Grenoble was a town in southeastern France at the base of the French Alps where the rivers Drac and Isère intersected. The white peaks of the Alps towered above the town and contributed to its beauty.

Grenoble, having existed for some two millennia, had a rich and interesting history. The most recent event to have occurred in the town at this point in time happened on June 8, 1788 in an event known as the "Day of the Tiles." Some say this is where the Revolution truly began.

Like the storming of the Bastille and the other riots that would occur on July 14, 1789, this event was precipitated by civil unrest due to economic troubles and special privileges shared by the First and Second Estates (namely, the nobility and the church). The government's solution to France's mounting debt was to implement new taxes, and the nobles and clergymen refused to take on their share of the burden. This caused the civil unrest in Grenoble to continually increase.

In response, the government sent in soldiers to put down what it perceived as an uprising. The townspeople got up on their roofs and threw down tiles at the troops, who promptly fled the city.

Although this incident was peaceful compared to latter events of the revolution, it can be argued that it laid the groundwork for everything that was to come.

There was one citizen of Grenoble, though, who at the moment could not possibly have cared less about the Day of the Tiles. After all, the Ordre hadn't been involved in the incident. No, his mind was currently occupied by the boring task of sweeping the vestibule of the Church of Saint-Laurent. Even though this work wasn't stimulating by any means, it kept him out of trouble. And trouble was exactly what he had come here to avoid. No one who knew him would have thought to look for him in a church.

This man was, of course, Victor Mont-Hume of the Ordre de la Tradition. When Pierre decided to implement the Splinter Protocol, Victor needed a place to hide out until the group could get back together. So, he thought to himself, where was the best place for him to hide? A church, naturally; nobody would expect him to hide out in a building full of people known to persecute his kind.

But which church, and where? Victor quickly decided on Grenoble, since he had never been there before and had no family or friends there. All that was left was to ask Celeste where he would be able to find her, since she was directly below him in the Ordre's hierarchy. She told him, and he promptly headed to Grenoble. He became a monk in the Church of Saint-Laurent, and wore the black cassock appropriate for ascetics. He also had his hair cut short, as long hair was not appropriate for men of the cloth.

When he was finished wiping the floor and walls with his grey cloth, he went into the nave to make sure it was clean. As he walked down the aisle between the pews, he happened to glance up at the various images of Christ in the stained-glass windows. Not for the first time, he wondered what the Savior thought of him. Victor's lifestyle was strictly forbidden by the Church, yet he couldn't help the way he felt. Could the Lord truly hate him for something that was beyond his control? This question had been with him since he was a teenager, and had tormented him throughout many of his days. He chose long ago to deal with his pain with humor; he didn't want people to know the depth of his suffering.

In the midst of his thoughts, the vestibule door opened behind him. In walked Sister Marjorie, wearing her black habit, her head covered by her wimple, the traditional apparel of a nun.

"Brother Victor, you have visitors," the elderly nun said.

Thinking it might be Robespierre's dogs looking for him, Victor replied lightheartedly, "Come now, Sister; you know I'm supposed to be cloistered from the outside world."

"But they say they're friends of yours. They even match the descriptions you gave me of them."

Victor sighed. Sister Marjorie had better not have made a mistake. "Fine. Send them in."

"We're already here, actually."

Victor stood stunned as three hooded figures entered the nave behind Sister Marjorie. The one leading the trio pulled back her hood to reveal the visage of Jeanne de Fleur, his commander. It was her voice that had just rendered him speechless.

The much larger person to Jeanne's right removed his hood. It was Pierre. No surprise there, really; who else could it have been? "It is good to see you again, Victor."

The person to Jeanne's left removed her hood and jovially announced, "We've found another dummkopf! *Wundervoll.*"

Victor stared at her for a moment, not sure what to say. Finally, he said the only thing he could. "Who are you?"

The woman with the Austrian accent was shocked. "Are you kidding me? I tried to kill you!"

Sister Marjorie's eyes widened in alarm at the confession.

"M-My friend here has an unsophisticated sense of humor," Jeanne apologized to Sister Marjorie, who forced an uncomfortable laugh.

Pierre just shook his head. "We can't take her anywhere."

"I'm sorry," Victor laughed. "I'm much better with men's faces than women's. Although I do like the cat ears. They're a nice touch."

"I do not have cat ears! My hair is simply... defiant." She let out an exasperated sigh. "I know I say it a lot, but... he really is a dummkopf!"

This time Sister Marjorie chuckled in earnest. "That's just the way Brother Victor is. Well, you're his friends, right? You should know that by now."

The Austrian woman was apparently about to reply in the negative when Jeanne none-too-gently elbowed her.

As if to change the subject, Pierre said to Victor, "I never would have thought to look for you here, what with you being a..." He caught himself before finishing that sentence and ended it with a *harrumph* and a coughing motion from his hand.

"That's all right. Sister Marjorie already knows."

Pierre was astonished. "She does? How did she find out?"

"Well... I told her," Victor replied sheepishly.

"Why would you do that?" Jeanne asked.

In response, he suddenly became very serious. "I've never been what you would call comfortable in holy places. I was brought up to believe that if I even stepped foot in a church, I would burst into flames instantly. I've always been told the Lord hates my kind and can't wait to smite us, and we're abominations that defile this world. So, during my first week here, I couldn't take it—the eyes of Christ up there staring at me, judging me. In my desperation, I went to Sister Marjorie and asked her what I should do."

They turned to the sister to get her side of the story. "I was shocked at first, I admit. I never expected to encounter one of *them* in this sanctuary. I knew I should banish him from here, but as I looked upon the genuine suffering in his eyes, I just couldn't believe that was the Lord's will. Surely there is a place even for ones such as them on His earth. So, I have allowed him to stay."

"I'm sorry. I never wanted any of you to find out what I've gone through my entire adult life," Victor said.

Pierre walked over and patted him on the back. "A friend of mine recently said something similar. But as I told her—or him—suffering is not a sign of weakness. You'll always be our trusted comrade, Victor. Right now, though, there's someone who's in more pain than any of us, and we've got to help her. Are you with us?"

"Who is it?"

"France, Victor. Our country needs us."

Victor smiled at him. "Well, I'd much rather go to the aid of a handsome Frenchman, but what the hell. Let's do it."

They weren't able to enjoy the moment for very long, as a throng of people suddenly burst into the nave. It was yet another mob wielding assorted crude weapons. There must have been two dozen of them, at least.

"Can't we ever have a conversation that doesn't get interrupted by a mob?" Victor said.

"This is the Lord's house! What are you people doing?" Sister Marjorie demanded.

An ordinary-looking man stepped forward. "We've come to claim the bounties on the members of the Ordre de la Tradition. We don't have anything against any of you personally, but things are so bad in town that we need the money to feed our families."

"I sympathize with you, I really do," Jeanne said. "If there were any other way—"

The man suddenly became very nervous, cutting her off. "No—no talking. We have to do this while we have the nerve. Get them!"

The crowd advanced, spreading out to surround them on all sides, and moving among the pews to do so.

"What are you orders, Commander?" Pierre asked.

"I really don't want to fight them, but it looks like we have no choice. Spread out among the pews. At least there we have some semblance of cover."

"Please don't do this," Sister Marjorie pleaded, though Jeanne wasn't sure who she was talking to.

"Fräulein, if these French worms attack me, I *will* butcher them, church or not," Farahilde declared, putting on her bladed gauntlet. She also refused to move from the spot, effectively drawing the line for the mob. Jeanne wanted to yell at her not to harm anyone, but she realized that, realistically, bloodshed may be unavoidable if they wanted to escape from the church. Also, what right did Jeanne de Fleur have to tell another human being not to defend herself if attacked? None, she decided.

Jeanne, then, did the only thing she could. She pointed at Farahilde and told the crowd, "She's not part of the Ordre. There's no bounty on her head." At least, Jeanne didn't think there was.

The nervous man, however, wasn't about to be deterred. "She's obviously with you. The Assembly might pay us extra for her. Everyone, attack! Try to take them alive!"

By this point Jeanne had moved in between pews to the left of the aisle, a few pews away from the mob. Pierre had taken up a position opposite her to the right of the aisle, and Victor was half a dozen rows behind Jeanne. Farahilde, on the other hand, continued to stand her ground in front of the mob and held her gauntlet menacingly, daring them to come at her. Jeanne had counted on the four of them being more coordinated, but Farahilde's stubbornness made that practically impossible. That didn't surprise her, though; at this point, she thought, nothing could surprise her.

She was wrong.

Just as the mob made their move, one of them (who had apparently been running late) suddenly came crashing through the door they had all entered from. He flew through the air and came to a violent stop on the ground next to Farahilde. All eyes fell upon him. "Albert! What on earth...?" the nervous leader said.

Albert, however, was in too much pain to provide much of an answer. All he was able to get out was, "H... Hubert." The single word, though, was enough to resonate with the crowd, and they looked to have been scared to death by the mere uttering of it.

"Oh, dear," Victor said.

"What? What's going on?" Jeanne asked.

To answer her question, in lumbered the biggest man she had ever seen. Easily seven feet tall, with massive arms and legs like tree trunks, he had to have dwarfed even Pierre. His peasant clothing barely fit him, and was ripped in several places. Obviously, it was hard to find clothes for such a colossal figure to wear.

Everyone stood agape at the colossus, except for Victor, who laughed and said simply, "Hubert the Giant."

Jeanne turned to Victor and asked, "You know this... err... man?"

"He is known around here as the 'Human Alps.'"

Hubert shook his dark, unkempt hair out of his eyes and looked around the room until he spied Sister Marjorie. "I saw bad people coming in here," he announced to her in his deep voice. "Worried they were going to do bad things."

"It's not bad! It's for the good of the town!" the nervous man yelled. "Anyway, it's got nothing to do with you."

"No one goes into church with weapons to do good," Hubert argued.

"It's all right, Hubert. I'm sure these men will leave peacefully," Sister Marjorie said.

"Not without our bounties!"

Hubert looked confused. "What's a 'bounty'?"

It seemed Farahilde had already deduced the way the simple giant's mind worked, and where his priorities lay, because she was quick to provide an answer. "It means these dummkopfs have come in here to tear up the place. There's no other reason for them to bring weapons, right? You don't want to see any harm come to Sister Marjorie, do you?"

Hubert balled up his considerable fists. "I won't let them hurt you!"

"Whoa-whoa-whoa-whoa! We're not after her! Just these four!"

Unfortunately for them, the giant didn't believe it. "You're bad men! And bad men lie! Leave here now!"

The mob advanced upon him, though they were careful to maintain a relatively safe distance. There were several tense moments where the mob and the giant stared at one another with the kind of intensity Jeanne knew all too well; it was the intensity of people trying to quickly decide which lines they were willing to cross.

The mob ultimately decided they weren't prepared for a bloody battle with the giant, and reluctantly filed out of the church (though they fired off a few curses and threats at Hubert as they left). Jeanne breathed a considerable sigh of relief at this. They wouldn't have to fight the mob after all— at least, not with Hubert the Giant around.

***

After they finished cleaning up the nave, they gathered in front of the pews and introduced themselves to Hubert.

"Hello, Hubert. My name is Jeanne de Fleur. I'm commander of an elite military unit that answers—or *answered*," she said sadly, "to the royal family."

"And I am Pierre Girard, her second-in-command. It's a pleasure, after what you just did. I take it you already know Victor?"

"He's funny," Hubert replied. "But people in town say the king and queen are dead. 'Lost their heads.'"

"That doesn't change what we have to do," Jeanne said.

"What do you have to do?"

She held up an armored fist. "Crush Robespierre."

The giant got excited at this. "I'll help! He's a bad man. Sister Marjorie said so."

"Now Hubert, what have I told you about keeping our conversations private?" the Sister chided.

"Sorry, Sister Marjorie."

Jeanne shook her head. "I appreciate the offer, Hubert. But our mission is an extremely dangerous one, and there's no guarantee of success. We can't drag civilians into it."

Farahilde whispered in Jeanne's ear. "Perhaps you should reconsider, fräulein. A big, strong dummkopf like him would certainly come in handy."

"Not everyone considers human life as disposable as you," Jeanne replied curtly.

"I don't consider human life disposable. Just *French* lives. And anyway, he wants to help. And we're going to need all the help we can get. Or do you think we can win this without risking people's lives?"

Jeanne hated to admit it, but Farahilde was right... again. They couldn't reasonably expect to win with only the few remaining members of the Ordre. They needed help.

In that moment Jeanne became angry at herself. Here was the renowned Jeanne la Juste in a life-or-death struggle for the very future of France, and she was reluctant to make the hard decisions. In her relatively short career, she had sent many subordinates to their deaths. But she had become uncharacteristically timid after Robespierre's betrayal and the murder of the royal family whom she had sworn to protect. Even after her decision to reunite the Ordre and take down Robespierre, she still wasn't the leader she used to be.

Jeanne couldn't believe it, but she realized she needed to be more like Farahilde. The cold Austrian had no shortage of character flaws, but she also possessed the killer instinct that was needed to win this battle.

Jeanne abruptly reached out and shook Hubert's gargantuan hand. "You are welcome within our ranks, Hubert."

The giant gave her a confused look that said he did not understand her change of heart, but within moments he became giddy. "Yes! Gonna stop the bad men!"

"We're going to go and find the rest of our friends. In the mean time, I have an important mission for you," Jeanne explained.

"A mission?" Hubert said with no small amount of excitement. "What is it?"

"I want you to spread the word around Grenoble that we are looking for volunteers to join us when we attack Paris."

"Attack Paris? Are you seriously planning on doing that?" Sister Marjorie asked.

Jeanne nodded. "We are. We have to if we want to stop Robespierre. He's not just going to let us stroll into the Tuileries and arrest him."

"You can count on me!" Hubert declared.

"Well, I can't let Hubert do this on his own. I'll help him alert the town that you're looking for help. Although, those men earlier weren't exaggerating when they talked about how bad things are. I don't know how many people here will join you," Sister Marjorie said.

"The people of this country want change, and I think they're desperate enough to advance on Paris to get it," Pierre said.

"Yes, but you might want to turn down those 'earlier men' if they volunteer," Victor said playfully to Sister Marjorie.

"I'll be sure to take that under consideration," she said dryly.

Hubert ran out of the church, presumably to carry out the mission Jeanne had given him. When he was out of earshot, she said, "He is certainly a lively one."

"Hubert has a good heart. But because of his size, he's always been an outcast. I've tried to guide him through life for many years now," Sister Marjorie said.

"It sounds like he's lived a long, hard life," Jeanne said.

"I'd like to think he has many more years ahead of him. He's only eighteen, you see."

"Eighteen! He looks and sounds a lot older," Pierre exclaimed.

"His condition makes it seem that way. But truthfully, he only recently reached adulthood."

"I see," she said. Then, "Oh!" She turned to Victor. "Where is Celeste? You can take us to her, right?"

"Ah, I thought we were still talking about me," he said in mock disappointment. "Of course, I can take you to her, whenever you're ready to go."

"Excellent."

5

The Tuileries, Paris, April 2, 1789 (Infini Calendar), 7:00 p.m.
          The new leader of the Alset Project, Adrien, entered the storage room with Madame Tussaud. It was very cold in the room, a necessity for storing the contents of the metal jars they were carrying.
          The young man wore his usual white lab coat, his dark brown hair slicked back over it in a ponytail. His dirty glasses hadn't been cleaned in ages; that simply wasn't a priority with him, although he was clean-shaven.
          They had to make several trips. As usual, Tussaud said absolutely nothing. Adrien found her to be a completely unnerving person, with her constant silence, the creepy smiling mask she never (to his knowledge) took off, and the massive scythe strapped to her back. Yes, she had proven herself an effective killer, but there were plenty of those around already. The real reason Robespierre kept her around was her twisted fascination with death. Every time she killed someone, she made a plaster molding of their face (which were often still contorted in terror); a death mask, in other words. Robespierre displayed these countless masks on the walls outside the Tuileries as a warning to any who would dare oppose him. His enemies could look upon them and instantly know what kind of fate awaited the poor fools.
          And then, of course, there were the contents of the metal jars. Tussaud was reportedly all too eager to fill those jars, and soon they would be needed for the completion of the Alset Project.
          Once again, Adrien found himself wondering if this was really the right path for France. If it worked, their place in the world would be secure. But if it didn't...

He didn't want to think about it and did his best to focus his attention on the task at hand. He and Tussaud finished stacking the jars on the shelves in the room. Once they were done, they locked the door behind them. Tussaud then left without so much as a nod.

All right, he said to himself. *That's one room down. How many are left? One, two, three, four... It's going to be a long night.*

***

Le Junkyard, France, April 5, 1789 (Infini Calendar), 1:17 p.m.

Le Junkyard, just east of Paris, was exactly what it sounded like: a massive dump containing Paris' refuse. It consisted largely of outdated parts for steam-powered machines; boilers and smokestacks, small and large, dominated the filthy landscape. However, Le Junkyard was also filled with all manner of disposed-of building materials such as walls, roofs and floors from Paris' long history. The city had been built up and evolved many times over the centuries, and what was once new and exciting often became old and unnecessary. Thus, Le Junkyard served as the Louvre's ugly counterpart—an unappealing museum tour of Paris' past.

The three (former) knights wandered through the labyrinth of Le Junkyard searching for any sign of the Ordre's head engineer, Celeste. Farahilde had remained behind in Grenoble to help Hubert and Sister Marjorie recruit townspeople for their upcoming assault on Paris (and, as the young Austrian woman put it, she had no interest in wandering through a garbage dump).

The walls of junk were a good thirty feet high. It felt as if they were trudging through a dense forest of rubbish (which, Jeanne realized, they basically were). "Are you sure this is where she said she'd be?" she asked Victor.

"Yes, I made sure we were very clear on that," he replied. "'I'll be in Le Junkyard,' she said. 'So, you're going to be living in piles of crap?' I asked. 'It's the best place to hide the airship,' she explained. 'Okay, good luck with your crap,' I said."

Pierre couldn't help but chuckle lightly. "You could have been nicer to the girl."

"A nice girl like her shouldn't be living in crap," he argued.

"Well, you're right about that. She's saved our lives more times than I can recall. We wouldn't even be here right now if she hadn't kept the *Solaire* in such great shape."

"Let's hope *she's* still alive out here," Jeanne said curtly.

"Just thinking off the top of my head, Commander," Victor said, "But maybe you could use your God's Eye to find some trace of her in here?"

"She wasn't given it for *your* convenience," Pierre chided him. Because of what she had told Pierre in his home village, he was probably being harsher than he would normally have been.

"I might be able to focus on an object around here and see if Celeste has come anywhere near it recently," Jeanne said.

"I'll save you the trouble!"

The three of them looked up at the top of the junk wall to their right. There was the Ordre's chief engineer, smiling down at them in her dirty overalls.

"Celeste!" Jeanne exclaimed happily.

"Look at her up there, like she's Queen of Crap."

"Not that I agree with Victor, but what *are* you doing up there?" Pierre said.

Celeste pointed ahead in the direction they had been walking. "If you turn right at the end of this wall, you'll come across a crude ramp I made. You can use it to get up here."

The three knights followed her directions and walked to where the junk pile Celeste was sitting on abruptly curved right. They followed the curve about ten feet and found a walkway, made out of wooden boards, built into the side of the wall. Celeste had clearly taken a hammer and nails and cobbled the thing together, complete with a railing to hold on to.

Pierre, as the heaviest of them, insisted on trying it first. He slowly made his way up the ramp, and when he was satisfied it was sturdy enough, motioned for Jeanne to follow. She did so, and Victor brought up the rear.

The ramp went up the wall to the other side of the junk pile and then curved around, all the while heading upwards. Soon the ramp led them to the top of the junk pile, and they were face-to-face with Celeste, who gave Jeanne a hearty hug. "It's so good to see you again, milady!"

"It's good to see you, too, Celeste."

"Have you been living out here by yourself all this time?" Pierre asked.

"Yes, but that's okay. I'm used to it."

"'Used to it'? What do you mean?"

The teenage genius, however, didn't seem to hear her. "Let's go downstairs. I have to show you something."

"Yes, let's descend into your house of crap. Wait—what?"

Before anyone could question her further, Celeste bent down and removed a thin metal sheet from the top of the junk pile, revealing a black hatch. She then proceeded to open it.

Jeanne couldn't believe it. "Celeste, don't tell me…"

Celeste promptly smiled and disappeared down the hatch. Pierre followed her in, with Jeanne behind them. Victor again took up the rear. Jeanne found that they were in the dark corridor of the command deck of an airship.

"The *Rechtschaffener Dämon*, just as you remember it," Celeste announced proudly. "Although I took the liberty of changing the name to the *Minuit Solaire II*."

Pierre patted her on the back. "Celeste, you've done it again!"

"You managed to hide a jewel inside this junk," Victor said, impressed.

"How did you do it?" Jeanne asked.

She adjusted her glasses. "It really wasn't that hard; only time-consuming. You see, after we landed here, I had the others help me build a pile of junk around the airship before I sent them on their way. Since then, I've been working to keep the ship operational—as well as repairing the damage to the bridge caused by that volcano. I think you'll find that the *Minuit Solaire II* is good as new and ready to go any time."

They entered the bridge, which was dark because of all the junk which covered almost the entire airship. Celeste pressed a button on the wall and the bridge was suddenly illuminated. She pointed to a spherical glass object—the source of the glow—on the ceiling. "Isn't electricity amazing? We don't even need a lantern in here. I would have had a hard time fixing up the bridge of the original *Minuit Solaire* under these conditions."

The damage caused by the eruption of Mt. Erfunden had been fixed, just as Celeste had said. However, the engineer had clearly used what was available in Le Junkyard. The new canopy window didn't fit exactly right; the areas it failed to cover had been covered with metal sheets. Also, the console in front of it had been repaired with mismatched parts of varying colors and composition.

All in all, though, it was an excellent repair job, all things considered. "Well done, Celeste," Jeanne said.

Celeste gave her classic smile which she radiated whenever she was praised by her idol. "Thank you, milady. That means so much to me!"

"Yes, you definitely chose your friends well."

That had not been spoken by any of them.

They all spun around to see a white-haired man wearing flamboyant (though dirty) nobles' robes standing in the bridge's doorway. Jeanne pulled out her rapier and pointed it at him in one fluid motion, while Pierre and Victor rushed in and grabbed him by his arms.

"Who are you?" Jeanne demanded.

He gave them an innocent smile that implied it was absurd for anyone to think he was up to mischief. "We finally meet, Jeanne de Fleur. To tell the truth, I expected you all to die in one of Robespierre's suicide missions."

Pierre applied pressure to the arm he was holding. The man grunted in pain. "The Commander asked you a question."

"Isn't it obvious? I'm the one who arranged for you all to have some fun at the Bastille."

Jeanne couldn't believe his audacity. "The Marquis de Sade! I don't know what you're doing here, but after what you've done to us, maybe this is a good opportunity to execute you."

The Marquis actually seemed disappointed. "Not my kind of woman. I like them younger and less feisty. If only you were more submissive, we could have such fun." Pierre wrenched his arm even harder, causing him to cry out in pain again, louder this time. "Agh! I was just joking! Come now, there's no need for this."

"How did you find us?" Celeste asked him.

"You aren't the only one who's been hiding out here, my dear engineer," de Sade smirked.

"You're hiding? From whom?" Jeanne said.

"Well, it all has to do the fact that I didn't magically drop dead once I ceased being useful to Robespierre. That was a problem for him, you see, because he really wanted me to die so I couldn't tell people how he came to power. And if I wasn't going to do it on my own, he was going to have it done by his personal executioner. I didn't want that, so I slipped out of Paris. I wasn't sure where to go, so I've just been hiding out here in the one place no one would ever expect a sophisticated nobleman to go."

"Your story sounds plausible—coming from a sadistic madman, that is—but it doesn't explain why you have approached us here," Jeanne said.

The Marquis said, "In my robes I have a document that you will find most useful. No, it's not one of my scintillating texts. It's, well... if one of you would reach in and see..."

Jeanne gave an annoyed exhale. "Pierre, would you do it?"

"Yes, ma'am."

"Carefully," she clarified.

Using his free hand, Pierre pulled one flap of de Sade's robe aside. He reached in and felt around, causing the Marquis to giggle (whether from a tickle or some perverted emotion she did not know or want to know). He then pulled out a rolled-up sheet of paper and tossed it to Jeanne.

Jeanne unrolled it and looked it over. "It's a map of Paris," she said, surprised by how ordinary it appeared. She expected something much more interesting from the Marquis de Sade.

His mouth twisted into a playful grin. "Look closer."

She did so. At first, she didn't see anything out of place. After a few moments, though, she noticed something odd. "What are these symbols at the center of each *arrondisement?*" Paris was divided into districts called arrondisements.

"That is the symbol for electricity, my dear Commander," de Sade explained. "I'm no scientist—my pursuits being more carnal than scientific, you see—but I've had a lot of free time since Robespierre got me out of prison, and I ended up studying his long-term plans out of sheer boredom. That, and I needed something to use against him if he ever tried to slip a metaphorical knife in my back."

"Get to the point, de Sade," Jeanne commanded impatiently.

"Fine, fine. Some people have no appreciation for a good story. Anyway. That map contains the locations of the key components of the Alset Project."

"Alset Project? What's that?" Celeste asked.

"It is what Robespierre foolishly believes will ensure the future of France."

***

They escorted the Marquis to the captain's cabin, which had a table and better lighting. Jeanne laid the map on the table in the center of the room so they could all examine it. Pierre and Victor still held de Sade firmly.

"As you can see," de Sade began explaining, "basically, at the center of each arrondisement in Paris is a tower, built on Robespierre's orders."

"I don't remember there being such landmarks in Paris," Jeanne said.

"Neither do I." Pierre said.

"They seemed to spring up overnight," de Sade said, "right about the time Monsieur Robespierre cut me out of his plans—so I can't tell you how they were built."

"Are the towers used for generating electricity?" Celeste asked.

"Yes, but not for something practical like energy or torturing your unwitting love partner because they have severely misbehaved."

Pierre shot the Marquis a disgusted look. "You really are a sick individual."

"Thank you."

"That wasn't a compliment."

"To me, it was."

"And people call *me* a deviant," Victor said.

"Get on with it, Monsieur de Sade," Jeanne ordered.

"Hmmm? Where was I? Oh, right. As I was saying, at the center of each arrondisement is a tower built to generate electricity. All the electricity generated by each tower will come together at the Tuileries tower, the center of the network."

"And what will happen then?" Jeanne asked.

The Marquis said curtly, "A city will be destroyed."

"Which city?" Pierre asked him.

The Marquis did his best to manage a shrug with the two men holding him tight. "Robespierre hopes it will be Vienna."

Jeanne couldn't possibly have heard that right. "Vienna? Austria?"

"That's right. The central tower will fire an enormous burst of concentrated lightning into Austria. I don't know the details, but supposedly Robespierre's scientists have figured out how to aim it."

Jeanne was glad Farahilde had chosen to stay behind; she didn't know if all of them combined could stop the hot-blooded Austrian if she found out about this monstrous plan. Farahilde could very well have sliced the Marquis into unrecognizable pieces if she were present. And although Jeanne wouldn't have blamed her, they needed to keep de Sade alive, at least until they got more information out of him.

"That's insane," Victor declared. "There's no way such a thing could hit a target hundreds of miles away."

"You may be right. But therein lies the other problem. You see, the man in charge of the Alset Project believes there is a certain danger that the whole thing could go out of control, flooding Paris with deadly electricity."

Jeanne couldn't' believe what she was hearing. "What do you mean, 'go out of control'?"

"I mean, if it doesn't work right. The technology isn't fully understood, you see. If Robespierre's scientists bungle this, it could fry the city's populace."

Celeste shook her head wildly. "Even *he's* not that stupid. Haven't the risks been explained to him?"

"You all should have a firm grasp of his character by now. Once he gets it in his head that some course of action is necessary for the future of France, no amount of explaining can dissuade him," de Sade explained. "Besides, he's invested far too many resources into this project. He can't abandon it now. It's all or nothing."

"Let's put that aside for the moment," Jeanne said. "You said Robespierre is planning to use this thing to attack Austria. Why?"

The Marquis rolled his eyes. "Isn't it painfully obvious?" The looks on their faces told him it wasn't. "All right, look: The reason is twofold. First, he wants to knock out France's greatest enemy once and for all. Second, he's looking to establish our position as the premier superpower of the European continent. He thinks that no one will dare attack this country ever again after he wipes out the Austrian capital from hundreds of miles away."

Pierre looked like he was dying to spill some blood. "After all his complaining about the monarchy's spending, he actually has the audacity to build some monstrosity to commit genocide?"

"He doesn't want to kill *all* the Austrians. Just the ones in Vienna," the Marquis clarified. When he saw the furious look Pierre was giving him, he apparently decided to keep the almond-skinned Frenchman's anger directed away from him. "B-But yes, Robespierre is a sick, twisted man—which admittedly sounds strange coming from me. I believe he has lost sight of his original ideals and is now playing for keeps. If I were to speculate further, I would say he's determined to make up for all that France lost under King

Louis XVI by taking it to spectacular new heights... or destroy it trying."

Jeanne asked, "So, how do we shut down these towers?"

There was another half-shrug from de Sade. "That I do not know. Robespierre keeps them heavily guarded at all times. The same is true of the towers' original schematics. But," he said, "it logically goes that if you were to shut down the main tower at the Tuileries, they wouldn't be able to fire it at Austria."

"But what happens if you shut it down while the other towers are running?" Celeste inquired. "Where would the electricity go?"

"Hmmm. I did overhear one of the scientists mention something about installing insulation in the smaller towers to allow the electricity to dissipate harmlessly if something should happen before it reaches the main tower."

Celeste took a feather pen out of its glass receptacle on the table and began scrawling what looked to Jeanne like mathematical formulas on the edge of the map. "If we shut down the main tower before all the electricity finishes collecting in it, it shouldn't cause an overload. But if we don't, all the insulation in the world won't be enough to contain the sheer amount of deadly energy stored in that tower. Based on what the Marquis has told us, I calculate an eighty-seven-point-nine-nine percent chance of a critical overload which would decimate the surrounding arrondisements. And that's my most optimistic projection."

Jeanne locked a penetrating stare on the Marquis de Sade and asked him, point-blank, "How long until this thing is activated?"

"The project's scientists said they needed at least another month to sort everything out. But who knows if Robespierre will wait that long."

"We've got to shut down the system as soon as possible," Celeste declared. She was being understandably impatient, Jeanne thought. After all, the engineer's very country was at stake and none of them knew how much time they had until Project Alset was operational. However, acting rashly could—and probably would—cost them dearly. "We can't just go charging in blindly," Pierre said. "We need solid information. First thing's first: We need to find out when they plan to carry out their plan."

"Then let's come up with a plan," Jeanne said, and then added to Pierre and Victor, "After you two take the Marquis to the brig."

***

Later that evening, Jeanne found Celeste slaving away in the core of the *Minuit Solaire II*. On a steam-powered airship, that would have been the boiler room. However, their stolen Austrian dirigible was powered by electricity, so there were no boilers or coal or burning fires.

Celeste was using a wrench to tighten a bolt in the bulkhead when she noticed her commander had entered the room. "Oh, milady! Welcome to engine room. Most of the important functions of the ship originate here."

"Is that so?" Jeanne said, looking around the two-story room. A flight of stairs led down to the lower level. There weren't any lights on down there, so Jeanne couldn't see what it housed.

"Yes. The whole thing's actually pretty complex. It's a miracle we've managed to fly this beast with so few people."

"That simply speaks to your abilities as an engineer."

"Thank you, milady."

"You're quite welcome. But actually... I didn't come here to talk about the ship. Or even the mission."

"Oh? Then what did you want to talk about?" Celeste asked, raising an inquisitive eyebrow.

"I wanted to talk about you."

"Me?"

"Yes. Something's been bothering me ever since we arrived here. Earlier when Pierre commented about you living all alone out here, you said you were used to it. What did you mean by that?"

Celeste turned away from her. "I shouldn't have said that. I was hoping you would forget I did."

"Listen, if you don't want to talk about it..."

Shaking her head, Celeste said, "No, now that it's out, I think... I think I need to tell someone. And you're the person I trust most in this world, milady." She turned back around to face Jeanne. "Can you promise you won't tell anyone about this?"

Jeanne nodded and said, "Your secret will be safe with me. That is... if you really feel you're ready to tell me."

Celeste took a deep breath, held it in for a moment, and then let it out. "All right, here it is. You see, I'm not exactly who people think I am. You remember the first time we met, right?"

She nodded. "It was a year and a half ago. Her Majesty brought you to my office. She said you were the most promising engineer in France, having graduated head of your class at L'Académie des Sciences."

"That was only partially true," Celeste said, averting her gaze momentarily. "I'm not who you think I am."

"What do you mean?"

"My real name is Eloise Rose de Versailles-Champlaine."

Once again, Jeanne believed there was positively no way she had heard correctly. "I hope you're joking, Celeste. Either way, it's not funny. The entire Versailles-Champlaine family was brutally murdered twelve years ago." The family they were talking about was a noble house formerly located in Versailles. One cold winter morning, they were all found butchered on their family's estate. Despite an investigation, no clues to the identity of the perpetrator were ever found, and the case was eventually dropped.

"Not all of them. The youngest daughter escaped," Celeste said.

"All bodies were accounted for," Jeanne insisted.

Celeste shook her head firmly. "With all due respect, milady... I was there. I saw the monster that did it. He was covered all in black and had a long tentacle-like arm. My family's guards managed to hold him off long enough for me to escape."

That sounded disturbingly familiar to Jeanne. "A 'long tentacle-like arm'? Wait... you don't mean..."

Celeste gave a macabre confirmation to Jeanne's suspicions. "It had to have been the Count of Saint-Germaine. When I saw him on the royal family's airship, I knew." She wiped a tear from her eye. "I was so happy when you killed him."

Jeanne considered the young girl's story. Celeste's display of emotion was so convincing. If the horrific tale was true, it made sense on a sick level. "The Count of Saint-Germaine was a master of alchemy. If anyone could create a fake corpse to fool people into thinking you were dead, he could."

"But... why would he go to the trouble of making a dummy of me in the first place?"

Jeanne said, "If someone sent him to murder your family—which I believe likely considering he was Robespierre's dog when we met him—he wouldn't want it to look like he didn't finish the job. He probably created the fake corpse to show his boss he had succeeded. Now," she said, continuing on, "as I recall, the Versailles-Champlaine family was heavily critical of the monarchy. For a long time after the murders, suspicion rested on the king and queen. I, for one, never believed they were capable of such barbarism. It is entirely possible someone had the Count kill the Versailles-Champlaine family in order to both eliminate some nobles and damage the monarchy's reputation."

Celeste's expression suggested they were thinking the same thing. "Robespierre?"

Jeanne nodding, saying, "I certainly wouldn't put it past him. He's always had it out for both the nobles and the royal family."

"We have to stop him!" Celeste pleaded. "Otherwise... otherwise..." She abruptly broke down and began sobbing.

Jeanne embraced her with a comforting hug. "We're going to. This I swear."

***

After Celeste calmed down, she accompanied Jeanne to the captain's cabin. They sat at the table and Celeste finished telling her story to Jeanne. "After I fled from the estate, I just kept wandering east. I didn't go to the royal family for help because at the time I believed they were responsible for what happened to my family. So, I just kept walking in a sort of daze. I didn't know who I could trust, so I ran from everyone who approached me.

"Eventually I found myself in Le Junkyard. There were so many hiding places in here; I decided to stay for a while. One day, I found a discarded book on engineering and began reading it. I discovered I had a talent for it, even though I was only six years old. I spent the next few years reading it over and over again, each time understanding it a little more. After a while I became confident enough to try experiments with all the materials lying around in this place. Let's just say... they were not entirely... successful."

"What do you mean?"

Celeste shifted awkwardly in her seat. "I sort of caused an explosion that could be seen from Paris."

"*You* did that?" Jeanne gaped.

"Uh-huh. You'd be surprised how much explosive material is lying around in Le Junkyard. Anyway, I was knocked out for quite a while, during which time the king sent scouts to investigate. They found me lying unconscious out there and brought me to the palace in Versailles. After they treated my wounds the king and queen tried to get me to tell them who I was. Well, I wasn't about to tell them the truth, since I still suspected them of the attack on my family, so I convinced them I was a lowly orphan—a lowly orphan who just happened to have a genius IQ. Her Majesty took pity on me, an orphan with so much potential, and had me enrolled in L'Académie des Sciences. The rest you already know."

"That's amazing," was all Jeanne could say.

"You're the only person I've ever spoken to about my past. Please don't tell the others about this."

Jeanne again assured her, "I promise. If the day comes when you are ready, you can tell them yourself. Until then, we'll keep this just between us."

"Thank you so much for hearing me out, milady. I feel like a great weight has been lifted off me."

"I'm glad I was able to help. You've been carrying that pain around for a long time, as it seems we all have."

Perplexed, Celeste asked, "What do you mean?"

"You're not the only one on this ship who's had to shoulder a heavy burden. But you know, as long as you have friends to support you, I believe you can overcome any problem. Rest assured, we will always be there for you, Celeste... or should I call you Eloise?"

"Celeste works just fine," she said, beaming a radiant smile. "It may not be the name I was born with, but it's the name I chose for myself, and I think... it's who I am now."

"That's good to hear."

"Listen," Celeste said suddenly, "Do you mind if we change the subject now? There's something else I would like to talk to you about, milady."

"I suppose not. What is it?"

"I was wondering what the plan will be when we storm the Tuileries."

"I'm still working on that," Jeanne admitted. "But I do have an idea of how we're going to do reconnaissance of the central tower."

"How?"

"The Marquis mentioned a scientist who is in charge of the thing. I think we need to pay him a visit. Discreetly."

6

Paris, France, April 11, 1789 (Infini Calendar), 8:09 p.m.
Having just got off work at the Tuileries, Adrien sat down at the bench overlooking the Seine to eat his dinner. He did this every night after work. It was part of his routine; he found the fresh air and sound of the lapping waters to be relaxing after a hard day of dealing with Robespierre's ever-increasing demands.

Adrien found himself more and more exhausted after each day, his fatigue rising proportionally with Robespierre's impatience. The leader of the Assembly wanted the Alset Project completed as quickly as (in)humanly possible.

As he ate his baguette, found himself once again dwelling on his mounting fear. His boss had limited patience to begin with, and each sunset brought it closer to snapping. When that happened, Adrien was scared Robespierre would send his terrifying executioner, Madame Tussaud, to punish him for his failure to complete the project. Or maybe he would send his right hand, Napoléon, to do it. Both prospects worried Adrien equally.

And even if the project was completed on time and successfully wiped out Vienna, could he live with the knowledge of what he'd done? Yes, the Austrians had lately been their enemies, but they were just as human as he was.

What was he going to do?

"It's a beautiful night, don't you think?"

Startled, Adrien turned to see a man sitting to his right on the bench. Adrien had been so lost in thought he hadn't even noticed the man sitting down. "Uh... yeah, I guess."

"Just getting off work?" the stranger asked. He had short brown hair and was wearing nondescript Parisian clothing. In short, he looked just like every other Frenchman in his mid-twenties.

"Yeah." If Adrien were any other citizen of Paris, he would probably brag about his important job at the Tuileries. However, given the doubts and fears he had been in the process of dwelling over when this guy showed up, he didn't feel like it.

"You have an important job, don't you?"

"Maybe." What was he getting at?

"In fact, you look like the kind of fellow on whose shoulders the future of an entire country rests."

Adrien was getting annoyed and nervous at the same time. "What do you want?"

"My apologies, handsome sir. My name is Victor. I represent someone who's going to be visiting Paris soon, and who would like to have someone as a guide when she gets here."

"So, hire a guide," Adrien replied dismissively.

"She's going to be visiting the Tuileries," Victor said as if that was a real explanation.

"The Tuileries is off-limits right now. There's construction going on."

A predator's grin crossed Victor's face. "It's not off-limits to *you*, Adrien."

Adrien jumped to his feet and stared down the newcomer. "Dammit! I knew something wasn't right with you. How do you know my name?"

Victor shrugged, and replied, "It was just a matter of finding someone within the Alset Project with the knowledge we need. After that, it was easy. You're a creature of habit, so it wasn't hard to track your movements. And here we are."

"Who do you work for?" Adrien demanded.

"Well, I was told to gain your trust, so I guess I should tell you. I answer to Jeanne de Fleur."

"de Fleur," he said, searching his brain for the name. "Wait—de Fleur? As in, the disgraced former commander of the Ordre de la Tradition?"

Victor suddenly became cross at his inquiry. "Choose your words carefully, Adrien. I may not be head over heels for her like some people I know, but I still have the utmost respect for her, and I won't let you speak ill of her."

"F-Fine. I apologize, I guess. But tell me: Is Jeanne de Fleur really coming here for revenge?"

"If she was willing to wage war for revenge, we wouldn't follow her. No, she's coming here to put a stop to the Reign of Terror."

"She intends to stop Robespierre."

"I'm pretty sure that's what I just said."

Shaking his head, Adrien dismissed the idea. "Forget it; Robespierre's become too powerful. He has the resources of an entire country at his disposal."

"But he doesn't have the hearts of the people, does he?" Victor countered. "Oh, sure—he might be able to convince them to go along with his ideas with his lovely speeches. But how long do think that will last? I'll let you in on a little secret: I've been doing an 'informal' poll of the people of Paris. They're sick to death of his antics, and I don't think it will take much to sway them to our side."

"What do you mean, *our* side? I never said I would help you. What reason could I possibly have to do that?" And with that, he turned to walk away. However, he did it slowly, part of him hoping the knight would be able to stop him.

As if on cue, Victor said behind his back, "It doesn't take a genius to read the expression on your face when I arrived. You're scared to death, my handsome friend. Whether you're scared of failing or succeeding, it's obvious you don't want to finish the Alset Project."

Adrien considered the other man's words, but they still weren't enough to persuade him. "If I quit now, Robespierre will have me executed by that crazy blond woman."

"I know a thing or two about crazy women," Victor laughed. "That's why I don't even bother. Listen—I'm not asking you to quit. I just need a little information. You help us out, and when we storm the city, we'll stop the madness and you won't have to crap your pants whenever anything goes wrong."

Adrien sighed; was he actually going to go along with this? In the end, none of his choices filled him with confidence. "I want a promise of amnesty when this is all over."

"If that is what it takes to gain your trust. Sure," Victor shrugged. "You have my word as a gentleman."

Adrien adjusted his glasses and sat back down. He felt like he was going to be sick, but he also felt this was the right thing to do. After all, the Ordre had always fought for the best interests of France (despite what Robespierre claimed). Siding with them was really the only way to ease his conscience.

***

Le Junkyard, France, April 12, 1789 (Infini Calendar), 4:01 p.m.

Jeanne sat idly in the captain's chair aboard the *Minuit Solaire II*. She knew she could be of more use elsewhere, but she wanted to make sure she was present the very instant Victor returned with his report. Ever since she had sent him to Paris to perform reconnaissance on the Alset Project, she had spent much of her time on the bridge of their stolen airship, either pacing back and forth or sitting in her chair with her head resting on her hand. She couldn't even look out the window since almost the entire airship was covered in garbage. The boredom and tedium were near-overwhelming, but she had a hard time leaving the room, even for important things such as meals (fortunately, the vessel was fully stocked with canned goods when they took it from Mt. Erfunden).

The monotony was suddenly broken by the distinctive sound of the *Minuit Solaire II*'s hatch. She turned around to see Victor descending the stairs in the corridor outside the bridge. He entered the bridge and greeted Jeanne. She then summoned Pierre and Celeste to the bridge where they gathered around Victor to hear him out.

"Report," she said.

"I found the current head of the Alset Project, a young man named Adrien. After following him for a while and learning his patterns, I eventually made contact with him at the spot he always goes to after work. He wasn't hard to convince; turns out he had his own... *reservations*... about what they're doing in Paris. Whether that was out of conscience or fear of failure," he shrugged, "I didn't ask. It was plain as day he didn't want to be involved in it anymore."

Jeanne was skeptical yet hopeful. "And he'll help us?"

"He already has. He told me the date the system will be activated: May third."

"That doesn't give us a lot of time," Pierre said.

"It's enough," Jeanne said. "We're going to take every single day between now and then to prepare. Celeste, you said there's a generous amount of explosive material here in Le Junkyard?"

The engineer nodded. "Yes, milady—although it is mostly discarded rocket canisters."

Jeanne knew what Celeste was talking about. Years ago, before the advent of airships, France experimented with rockets. The idea was to fill iron rods with fuel and launch them at enemy forces. Supposedly the Count of Saint-Germaine was the one who created the liquid fuel, which he called *propellant*.

However, the rockets were very difficult to control; they had a habit of exploding on the very people trying to launch them. Moreover, the Count never shared the secret of the propellant with anyone (as far as Jeanne knew), and upon his death—his *first* death—France lost all means of producing it. Jeanne now suspected that he had created the fuel using alchemy. Perhaps he even manufactured it from his own blood as he did the organic weapons he fought with aboard the royal airship. If that were the case, it was very unlikely the world would ever see such a fuel source again.

At any rate, the iron rockets were eventually dumped in Le Junkyard, where they would be forgotten until a poor orphan stumbled upon them and nearly blew herself up with them.

"Your story about causing an explosion with them gave me an idea. Do you think you could make some bombs from the materials available?"

"Yes, easily. But we'd have to be very careful; you're surely aware how unstable the propellant is."

"What's this story about causing an explosion?" Victor inquired. The look on Celeste's face told Jeanne she'd said too much.

"Ah, well... it's nothing. Just a story Celeste told me about someone she used to know." Jeanne hated to lie, especially to the subordinates who trusted her, but she'd promised Celeste she wouldn't reveal her past. That was for the young engineer herself to do if and when she was ready.

Victor looked as if he didn't entirely believe his commander, but Pierre helped her out by getting them back on track. "You're thinking we can drop bombs on Paris. As a diversion?"

"Y-Yes, exactly, Pierre," Jeanne said. "We'll be carcful not to target the civilian population, of course. We just need to get the military's attention away from our real target: the Tuileries tower."

"Won't Robespierre simply order all troops back to the central tower to defend it?" Victor said.

Jeanne shook her head. "He has no military experience. In all likelihood, he'll either be slow to react, or he'll make the wrong call."

"Milady, I actually have other ideas for tools we can make out of the junk on hand." Celeste shared her ideas, most of which Jeanne approved of. These things could indeed be made quite easily from materials already available in Le Junkyard.

At the end of the briefing, Jeanne said, "In the morning I want the engines fired up. We're going back to Grenoble to share the battle plan with Farahilde."

7

Grenoble, France, April 5, 1789 (Infini Calendar), 10:10 a.m. Farahilde stood next to Hubert outside the Church of Saint-Laurent. The morning sun shone overhead, bathing the town in comforting warmth—one of the few things Farahilde actually liked about France. As of late they had mostly stood in front of the doors to the church soliciting men to join their cause and fight for them when they stormed Paris. So far, they had received around two dozen volunteers. The worms who had barged into the church recently had, unsurprisingly, stayed away. No doubt they feared another encounter with Hubert the Giant.

Farahilde was glad she left her bladed gauntlet inside the church during this time. While she enjoyed threatening French worms with it, it wouldn't have inspired many volunteers. And, of course, Fräulein would have given her an earful if any violence broke out because of her.

Even she couldn't say if she actually liked Jeanne de Fleur or not. Yes, Farahilde respected her, but she didn't know how she felt about the older French woman as a person. When they had first met, Farahilde had genuinely despised her. The young Austrian had never been able to develop meaningful relationships with other women, aside from her schwester. She just seemed to always come into conflict with members of her own sex.

There was also the problem of what Jeanne de Fleur initially represented. Here was a haughty fräulein trying to rescue her brother who had threatened Austrian sovereignty by invading the Netherlands. Farahilde might have been able to forgive that; it wasn't even the most grievous offense. No, the real reason she had hated Jeanne de Fleur was the latter's refusal to give back her schwester, Marie Antoinette, who was being held prisoner by the Assembly. It was, after all, the right thing to do. If Jeanne was truly dedicated to the safety of Her Majesty, she would have done it. At least, that's what Farahilde used to believe. She had since come to realize things weren't quite that simple. If Jeanne had tried to rescue her schwester against the will of the Assembly, it might have put the queen in even more danger. If Farahilde were in Jeanne's shoes, would she have tried it? Probably; she was that kind of headstrong person. But would it have been a good idea? Maybe not.

Nevertheless, her schwester had been killed anyway, and that fact might prevent them from ever becoming any closer than reluctant partners in crime.

A French teenager approached her and said, "Is this where I sign up to kick Robespierre's ass?" Just wonderful, she thought sarcastically—another boy thinking he's signing up for fun and games.

"This isn't a vacation in the countryside, boy." She said the last word as an insult. "We need *men* for this."

"Tough words coming from a woman," he countered. "Just give me a chance. I want to fight for my country same as all the other guys I've seen come by here."

Farahilde massaged her temple with one hand; she was getting a headache. "Have it your way." She decided to let him join up. *If Fräulein ends up having a problem with it, she can give the kid the boot herself.*

Speaking of which...

The distinct whirring of an airship engine caught their attention. Hubert craned his neck up towards the white peaks of the Alps. "What's that?"

"That, meine large friend, should be our friends coming back."

Sure enough, the unmistakable outline of an airship appeared over the Alps. It descended into town and landed in a nearby patch of dry grass which served as a recreation area for the town's children. Fortunately, there weren't any children playing there at the moment.

***

Farahilde and Hubert rushed over to get a look at the airship. Just as Jeanne had told her, it was of Austrian design, identical to Farahilde's own *Blitzkrieg Rache*. Black and shiny and metallic—that was what military vessels ought to look like!

Before long Jeanne and her officers appeared on deck. They then lowered the ramp and came down. "I hope you've stayed productive," Jeanne bantered to Farahilde.

"We've done all right, fräulein."

"We got lots of people to join us!" Hubert announced jubilantly.

"Good," Jeanne said. She turned to a teenage girl wearing glasses who was standing behind her. "Celeste, I want you to take a couple of the recruits and teach them how to fly the *Minuit Solaire II*."

"Yes, ma'am!"

Jeanne turned back to Farahilde. "It's not easy flying this thing with only three people."

"I can't believe you were able to do it at all."

She shrugged. "We probably wouldn't have if Celeste didn't know airships so well."

"She is your engineer?" Jeanne nodded, and Farahilde was awestruck. This girl must have been quite the *wunderkind* to have maintained the Ordre's two ships through everything they had gone through.

"Nice to meet you," Celeste said nervously. "I've heard... interesting things about you."

"I bet you have," she replied slyly. "And for the record, it's all true."

Jeanne addressed Farahilde. "Anyway, the reason we've returned is because we found out exactly what Robespierre is planning. Let's go inside the ship and we'll tell you everything."

"Why don't you just tell me right here, fräulein?"

"Because I have a pretty good idea of what your reaction is going to be, and I don't want you anywhere where you can hurt any of the townspeople."

Farahilde clenched her fists tightly. She didn't like the tone of Jeanne's voice one bit, and she was certain whatever Jeanne had to report, it was going to be even worse than she let on.

***

"What?" Farahilde roared. "That *arschloch* is going to attack meine Austria? I'll flay him alive!" She flipped over the table in the captain's quarters and smashed several other things before Jeanne could get her to calm down.

She was certainly right about Robespierre being an asshole. "No, he's not—because we're going to stop him. We won't let him carry out his plan." Jeanne had insisted on giving Farahilde the news alone, much to the objections of her officers. She had faced the wrath of the enraged Austrian woman before, and knew she could handle her if she went out of control. Jeanne didn't want anyone else getting caught in the crossfire. She also withheld the fact that the Marquis de Sade was on board; Farahilde was mad enough already.

Farahilde continued to fume. "How much is enough for him? He declares war on meine people, he murders meine schwester..." Her sentence abruptly ended with an anguished howl. She then fell to her knees and proceeded to beat her fists on the deck.

Not for the first time, Jeanne felt sorry for her. However, she had never before seen her former nemesis in such misery. Here was the young woman who had tortured her brother and tried to kill them both... and Jeanne actually wanted to do something to comfort her. "Rest assured, it will all end on May third. You have my word on that. But for the time being, we have to prepare. There is a lot to be done before we attack Paris. I need to know I can count on you." Farahilde stopped assaulting the floor and looked at her hands. They were bloody and raw. She took a deep breath, gathered herself together and looked up at Jeanne. "Yes, you may, fräulein." Her voice was ragged and hoarse, yet determined.

8

12th arrondisement, Paris, France, May 3, 1790 (Infini Calendar), 11:00
     In the southeastern edge of Paris lay the twelfth arrondisement. In the center of the twelfth arrondisement, a dozen members of the French Army stood guard outside one of Robespierre's towers. In truth, it actually looked like an ugly gray obelisk with a metal dish on top. The dish had been carefully aligned so that it pointed directly at the central tower at the Tuileries.
     Last year, this location had been home to the Bastille before it was destroyed in a riot. Some time afterwards, Robespierre ordered a tower to be built from the remains. The tower was built with materials left over, so Robespierre ordered a large wall built around the tower to keep out intruders. Nineteen other such towers ended up being built around the city.
     At this time the guards stationed at the "Bastille Tower" were incredibly bored. They didn't honestly expect anyone to attack one of the towers, and in the unlikely event that someone did, the odds of them attacking this particular tower were unlikely. Therefore, half the guards were sitting down against the tower, resting.
     However, a sound soon grabbed the attention of every single one of them. "What's that noise?" one of them asked.
     "Don't know," another replied. "I'm pretty sure I've heard it before, though."
     "Wait—look!" a third one shouted. Coming in fast from the southeast was a black object.
     "It's an airship!"
     "We don't have any more airships. It must be an enemy!"

They instinctively raised their rifles, and then quickly realized those would be completely useless against an airship. They stood there for a moment, not sure what to do. One of them then ran inside the tower; they had a telegraph machine in there which could be used to alert the Tuileries.

The other members of the French Army waited around, their sense of duty preventing them from abandoning their posts even though there was virtually nothing they could do. The other towers located farther in had steam cannons to protect them, but there weren't enough to go around, and as an outer arrondisement, no more defenses could be spared.

When the airship arrived and hovered one hundred feet above them, then, they stood their ground.

But not for long.

Within minutes people appeared on the deck of the vessel and began dropping what looked like small metal balls on them. These objects looked harmless at first, but when they hit the ground they exploded into bursts of fire and shrapnel.

Some of the men caught in the blasts died instantly— they were the lucky ones. The others ran around on fire, their bodies riddled with burning metal. Those who avoided the initial volley took the cue to run away and run away *fast*.

***

Pierre returned to the bridge of the *Minuit Solaire II* and stood next to the captain's chair. When she noticed him, she said, "Ironic, isn't it? We've come back to where it all began."

"I have to admit, I never expected things to run in a circle like this."

She chuckled lightly. "It's even more ironic that *we're* the ones attacking this site now."

That seemed to remind him of what he came in to tell her. "We finished dropping the explosives. Some of the soldiers below were killed. The others ran away."

"Good," Jeanne said. "I hate the idea of fighting our own people, but this is war. Even though you weren't born in this country, Pierre, I know you think of them as your people, too."

"Anyone who would serve a man like Maximilien Robespierre is no kinsman of mine. I take no pleasure in setting them on fire, but like you said, this is war," he said solemnly. "At any rate, the tower can probably still function if there's anyone left down there to work it."

"That's irrelevant. Like we agreed, knocking them out one by one would take far too much time, and we probably don't even have the resources to do it anyway. We'll stick to the original plan. I think it's time we moved on to the next one." The knights fully expected someone down below to alert Robespierre, and that was part of the plan. However, this would not be the only tower to call for help. Soon, Robespierre would know exactly who he was up against.

***

The knights flew northeast in the airship to attack the eleventh arrondisement's tower. The result was the same: Panicked soldiers ran for their lives, while the tower itself was mostly unharmed.

From there, they flew east to the twentieth arrondisement and attacked its tower. They intentionally flew a seemingly random course, attacking seemingly random towers. This, too, was part of the plan, though not the only part. *Robespierre's about to learn he's not the only one who can rile up the public in secret*, Jeanne thought to herself.

***

Within the central tower, Robespierre oversaw the last-minute adjustments to the Alset Project. Although he didn't want to sound like a cliché, everything was going according to plan. Soon all the towers would be activated, and the entire European continent would bow to French supremacy.

In addition, it wouldn't be long before the Americans got wind of what France would achieve this day. Robespierre was counting on them remembering what the French people had done for them during their war against Great Britain. After all, the Alset Project had nearly drained the country to the point of exhaustion, and the French people would need America's help stabilizing their economy once this was all over. Perhaps the gift of a little technology—just a little— could persuade their friends in the west to lend them assistance. France was far beyond America in terms of technology at this juncture, after all, and the "Yanks" would be open to any deal which would allow them to get their hands on what the French had to offer. How could it fail?

Perhaps in response to that question, the telegraph machine on the wall to his left began uttering a series of klacks and taps as a sheet of paper slowly emerged from the slot. Annoyed that none of the engineers was headed over to pull it out, Robespierre reluctantly did it himself. His annoyance then turned to frustration as he read the paper.

12th tower under attack by black airship stop. Light casualties incurred stop. Request immediate instructions stop.

This was followed by another sheet of paper, which said basically the same thing except it indicated the eleventh tower was under attack. "Someone get over here!" he yelled to no one in particular. "I need to send orders out *now*!" He then yelled to Adrien up on the scaffolding. "Start the tower!"

"But, sir—"

"Do it! We don't have any more time to waste."

Under attack by black airship, the messages said. It could only have been the Ordre de la Tradition. Robespierre had considered the possibility of them returning for revenge, but dismissed it based on the condition they had been in the last time he saw them. He would never forget the look on Jeanne de Fleur's face (nor did he want to); she had been completely broken by the deaths of the king and queen, as well as the sight of her brother rushing to his demise. No one could have recovered from that.

At least, that's what Robespierre had believed. Was he mistaken? Or was someone else leading the group now? He certainly hoped it was the latter. If Jeanne de Fleur was the kind of person who could come back from such a devastating psychological blow, then he might actually have something to fear.

An attendant hurried over and Robespierre instructed him to send orders to the army commanders in the city to send steam cannons to the eleventh and twentieth towers and shoot down the black airship.

***

After having attacked several towers (but not truly disabling any of them), the *Minuit Solaire II* changed course and headed towards the Tuileries, coming in from the northeast. By now Robespierre should have received word of their mischief, and being the inexperienced military leader that he was, he had most likely sent steam cannons out to engage them. But because of the airship's erratic course so far, he would probably send them to the wrong place, rather than making the smart call and waiting for the Ordre to come to him.

When they were above the fourteenth arrondisement, Jeanne turned to Pierre, who was standing next to her chair. "We're only a few kilometers from the Tuileries."

"Yes. No sign of the towers starting up yet. So far this has gone well. Perhaps *too* well."

"You think it might be a trap? Could that Adrien have sold us out?"

"I can't say for cer—"

His words were abruptly cut short when the ship lurched violently. The hull began groaning and shaking in protest to some unknown influence. In front of them, the canopy window crackled with blue energy.

Pierre grabbed hold of the back of Jeanne's chair to steady himself. "So much for the towers staying quiet."

Jeanne grabbed the communications tube next to her chair and said, "Celeste! Report!"

"I think the towers have begun funneling electricity to the Tuileries, and we're caught up in it."

Jeanne got out of her seat and walked awkwardly over to the canopy window, being careful not to lose her footing to the turbulence. Several large arcs of electricity connected the Tuileries up ahead with multiple towers. Furthermore, additional lines of blue energy kept appearing.

It was starting.

Jeanne returned to the captain's chair. "This model of airship was designed to resist electricity, wasn't it?"

Celeste's voice sounded less than confident. "I don't think it was designed to withstand this much, milady."

"Get us out of the way of this electricity!" she ordered Alphonse, the operator.

"It's no good, ma'am; controls aren't responsive. We're losing altitude."

Somehow, she just knew he was going to say that. "You mean... we're going to crash?" *Again?*

He grunted at the controls. "No, ma'am. I think... I think I can get us down safely. It won't be comfortable, but we should be all right."

The *Minuit Solaire II* went down slowly, clumsily on the Rue Saint Honore, a street just north of the Seine. There was another hard lurch as the ship's hull scraped the front of a building, no doubt sending mortar and windows crashing to the ground.

The bridge crew was once again rocked forward as the airship scraped along the ground for a few moments before coming to a complete stop. When things were once again quiet, Jeanne asked everyone on the bridge, "Can I assume you're all okay?"

They each confirmed this. "That was actually fairly benign for one of *our* landings, wouldn't you say, Commander?" Pierre said.

"We certainly don't have the best luck with airships," she agreed. "But I think we got off pretty lucky this time."

***

Everyone assembled topside on the deck of the *Minuit Solaire II*. This included all of the Ordre, Farahilde, Hubert and the two dozen volunteers they had managed to recruit for this mission. The only one left behind was the Marquis de Sade; Jeanne decided he could rot in the brig for a little while longer. That, and she still didn't want Farahilde finding out he was on board.

Jeanne, Pierre and Victor stood at the bow of the ship, looking at the large tower ahead of them to the east. It pulsated and crackled with blue energy coming from the lines of electricity coming in from all directions. In addition, an ominous cloud cover was forming above the city, and the air felt heavy to Jeanne. "The Tuileries is about a kilometer up the street," Pierre said. The Rue Saint Honore ran northwest towards the Tuileries, and eventually curved slightly so that the street ended up being just north of it (or, from their perspective, to the right).

"There's no time to waste," Jeanne said.

The sounds of shouting somewhere behind them caught their attention. "Milady, this is bad!" Celeste called out from the rear of the ship.

The knights maneuvered through the throng of volunteers on the deck and made their way to the stern where Celeste, Farahilde and Hubert were standing. "What is it?" Jeanne asked.

Farahilde pointed to a large group of soldiers—at least three times the number of volunteers the Ordre had—a few blocks down the street who were marching towards them from down the street to the southeast. "It seems not everyone was fooled by our unpredictable flying. It looks like those worms are actually smart enough to come defend the central tower."

Pierre ran back inside the ship and within moments emerged with a pocket spyglass. He extended it and looked towards the advancing soldiers. "I'll be damned. Look who's leading them." He handed the spyglass to Jeanne.

She looked through it for a moment. "Hmph. Lefebvre, that snake. I see by his uniform that he's been promoted."

It was, indeed, François Joseph Lefebvre, the officer of the Maison du Roi who had ambushed them at the Bastille last year and escaped with the Marquis de Launay, the nobleman in charge of the prison. Jeanne later found out de Launay had been killed by the enraged crowd which had attacked the Bastille.

"You know this worm?" Farahilde asked.

Jeanne gave a curt response. "Regrettably."

"What are we going to do about this?" Victor said.

Strangely enough, the solution was presented by Hubert the Giant. "Leave it to me!"

***

Lefebvre led his troops forward towards the downed enemy airship a few blocks away. It didn't take him long to recognize the knights of the Ordre de la Tradition when they came up top after the ship was brought down by the massive amounts of electricity pouring into the central tower. Hell, he knew as soon as the attacks started that it couldn't be anyone but them. Unlike Robespierre, Lefebvre had a soldier's mind, and he knew the Ordre's halfhearted strikes against the other towers was just a ruse, and they would eventually make their way to the Tuileries, so he decided to do the same. And here they were.

Jeanne de Fleur had made a fool of him last year at the Bastille, dispatching his troops like they were school children. He had acted so cool and confident to get her on his side, but she stubbornly refused. Ultimately, he hadn't been able to do a thing against her; escaping with the Marquis de Launay was the only thing he had to show for that skirmish. Fortunately, though, that—along with bringing down the Bastille—had been enough to impress the Assembly and get him a promotion.

King Louis XVI had wanted Lefebvre executed for turning against the monarchy, but the Assembly overruled him, citing Lefebvre's dedication to his country as reason enough for him to remain in the service of France. Of course, the Maison du Roi was disbanded by the Assembly not long after, but Lefebvre was promoted to a higher position within the Gardes Francaises.

Despite what many people believed, Lefebvre knew in his heart that his devotion to the French people was genuine. Everything he had done had been for their welfare. So, what if he himself benefited because of it—that was incidental. Besides, the more power he was granted, the better he could serve them.

He held out his arm and yelled to his men, "Halt!" He wanted to take stock of the situation, so he looked through his spyglass again. Jeanne de Fleur stood on the deck of the airship examining him with one of her own.

Suddenly, the largest man Lefebvre had ever seen emerged from below deck, his arms full of small iron spheres. "What the hell is this?" he muttered to himself.

Without warning, the giant hurled one of the metal balls towards Lefebvre and his men. *There's no way it can fly all the way over here,* he thought. After all, it was a good two blocks between his men and the giant.

But it *did* fly all the way over there.

He didn't know what it was, but he knew if his enemy was throwing it, it was bad news. As soon as he realized it did indeed have enough velocity to reach them, he yelled to his men, "Look out!" He then dived out of the way.

However, his men were in such a tight formation that not all of them were able to dodge the round object. It hit at the feet of one of them, exploding into flame and shrapnel. The poor man was set ablaze, and a few of his compatriots were skewered with metal shards. They cried out, either in pain or surprise, at the unexpected assault. *Explosives! This must be what they hit the towers with.* "Fall back! Take cover!"

***

"Good work, Hubert!" Victor said, patting the giant on the back. Hubert's quick-thinking in grabbing the leftover bombs and hurling them at Lefebvre's forces had bought them some time.

"Yes, but it won't hold them off forever," Jeanne said. "We'll need to act quickly."

Celeste, however, was staring up at the sky. "That army regiment isn't our only problem."

"What do you mean?" Jeanne asked her.

Celeste pointing upwards, explained, "Look at all those clouds gathering above the city. It could very well start raining soon, and with all the electrical currents in the air..."

"What? What are you trying to say?" Jeanne said.

"Water is a major conductor of electricity. If we get a heavy downpour, the electrical currents could travel through the water, electrifying the entire city. Anyone caught outside would be killed!"

Pierre, perhaps sensing what needed to be done, said, "Ma'am, you've got to get to the central tower. The rest of us will hold them off here." There was a cheer of assent from the assembled volunteers, almost all of whom had brought their own firearms. They held their guns in the air and as a group assured Jeanne they would not let the enemy pass. She wasn't crazy about going into the Tuileries alone, but as it turned out, that wouldn't be the case.

A rather confident Farahilde declared, "I'm going with you, fräulein. I won't be able to get revenge on Robespierre by simply butchering his worms out here, and I won't let *you* be the one to save meine Austria from his weapon. He needs to see my face, at least." Jeanne could see Pierre wasn't exactly thrilled with the idea, but he didn't bother to voice any objections. Jeanne was going to need all the help she could get inside the palace; even mentally questionable help from someone like Farahilde Johanna was preferable to Jeanne going it alone.

Jeanne nodded. "All right—let's go. Everyone else, stay here and hold off Lefebvre and his men." They lowered the deck's ramp to the ground and the two women bounded down it and up the street towards the Tuileries.

9

Peeking out from the corner of a building down the street from the Ordre and their downed airship, Lefebre watched as Jeanne de Fleur and a woman he didn't recognize ran off in the direction of the Tuileries. *Dammit! Robespierre may take my head if he finds out I let the commander of the Ordre make it all the way to the palace. If only the other regiments hadn't been stupid enough to obey his orders, running off to chase ghosts while the real enemy was always headed here.*

Knowing he had to move quickly, he raised his hands to signal his troops (most of whom had ducked inside the buildings on this street). But a movement from the corner of his eye alerted him to another explosive ball being lobbed in his direction from the Ordre's giant. He instinctively jumped back around the corner and the bomb hit the wall, scorching it with searing flames.

"Where's that damn steam cannon?" he yelled.

His lieutenant, who had been standing behind him, replied, "It's on its way, sir. But we had to divert it from across the city. It'll take time."

Lefebvre balled his hand into a fist. *As soon as it gets here, we're going to blow those Ordre miscreants off the face of the earth.* He had no doubt about that. As long as he wiped out the bulk of the enemies, he could salvage the situation and earn Robespierre's forgiveness for allowing two of them to get away.

In the mean time, he would divide up his men and move around to outflank the invaders. He was already deciding upon the routes they would take to accomplish that.

***

Jeanne and Farahilde continued to run up the street towards the Tuileries. They had passed the Louvre and were now only a few blocks away from the palace. Various people looked at them from behind windows in the buildings they passed. The Paris citizens looked like they were afraid to come outside and Jeanne couldn't blame them. They probably had no idea what was going on.

"I can see the boxes, fräulein." The Tuileries was basically a series of buildings which together formed the shape of three squares with a large space inside each, hence Farahilde's "boxes" analogy. In the center box was the central tower. The space used to be occupied by an outdoor garden, but clearly Robespierre had seen fit to put it to "better" use.

"As soon as we make it past the Place du Carrousel, we'll be at the palace," Jeanne said.

Suddenly, though, another army regiment appeared a few blocks up ahead. Jeanne quickly ushered Farahilde south into an alley. Together they peered out from behind the wall at the enemy troops. "It doesn't look like they've seen us," Jeanne said.

"So, Robespierre actually *was* smart enough to keep a few worms to protect him. They'll slow us down too much if we stop to fight them."

Jeanne surveyed the alley and said, "Let's see if we can find a way around them."

They began walking south through the alley...

...and the ground abruptly collapsed beneath their feet.

They fell into darkness, both of them landing hard on the rocky, uneven surface below. Farahilde grunted in pain. "Are you all right, fräulein?"

"I will be once you get off me."

"Oh," Farahilde laughed. "Sorry about that. Thank you for breaking meine fall." She rolled off Jeanne and stood up.

"You should be thanking my irodium armor. It protected both of us from these chunks of concrete that used to be the street above."

Jeanne got to her feet and looked around them. They appeared to be in some sort of tunnel fifteen feet below the alley, based on what she could see from the light that shone down from above.

"What is this place? Reminds me of meine fort in the Netherlands. Smells a lot worse, though."

Jeanne shrugged. "It looks like an old sewer network. Seeing how dry it is, though, I'd say it's no longer in use." She picked up a piece of concrete. "The construction may have weakened the ground, allowing us to fall through it."

"It doesn't look like we can climb up out of here. Dammit—what are we doing screwing around here? Robespierre could attack meine Austria at any time."

"Calm down. Let's go through this tunnel and see if we can find another way out of here."

***

The Ordre's volunteers took aim at Lefebvre's troops when the latter utilized alleys and side streets to get around the *Minuit Solaire II* and come at them from both the northwest and the southeast.

Despite the threat of Hubert and his long-range bombs, Lefebvre managed to cajole his men to charge in from both sides. While a few of them were hit by the explosive spheres, there weren't nearly enough to hit them all. It wasn't long before the French Army troops had gotten to within a hundred feet of the airship.

Pierre ran back and forth on the deck from the bow to the stern, positioning the volunteers as needed, making sure too many of them weren't focused on too few of Lefebvre's men, and vice-versa. A few enemy bullets found Pierre's irodium armor, but they were little more than bee stings to the big man.

Most of the volunteers remained prostrate on the deck so as to present as small a target as possible. Pierre thought it was fortunate they had the high ground.

As if to slap that thought across the face, the voice of Lefebvre rang out to his troops from down the street. "Shoot the balloon!" Fresh shots erupted from the rifles of the French Army soldiers. The envelope hovering above the airship—which had come through the rough landing intact—was pierced, multiple holes appearing along its surface. As air left the increasingly lethargic inflatable, Pierre knew they probably less than a minute before it came down on top of them.

"Stay focused on the enemy!" he called out to the volunteers who were getting distracted by the spectacle playing out above their heads. He then removed his broadsword from its sheath at his waist. "Victor!"

"Right!" Victor pulled out his sword and the two of them got ready. A few volunteers, who had brought sabers instead of rifles, saw what the two knights were doing and spread out to assist.

Within moments the envelope came down on their heads, and the men with swords proceeded to slash ferociously at it. This resulted in it being greatly shredded, but that wasn't enough to stop it. They were all engulfed, as if by a hungry monster.

***

"Ha! Look at those fools!" Lefebvre rejoiced as he watched the envelope come down upon the hapless invaders. His plan had worked perfectly; now his men could rush the downed airship with little difficulty.

He was about to give the order when a monstrous hump rose up on the vessel's deck from beneath the deflated envelope. *That can only be...!* The hump rose to its full height and arms stretched out from it. The envelope was unceremoniously ripped apart to reveal the gargantuan man from earlier. The giant then gave a triumphant roar.

Perhaps in response to the battle cry, more shapes—albeit smaller—rose up from the deck. From each of these a sword emerged, cutting its master out of the envelope. The previously trapped men slashed their way out of the dark fabric as if the whole thing was an unholy birthing ceremony.

Not to be outdone, the giant grabbed the bulk of the destroyed envelope with his bare hands, and, with a mighty swing, tossed it to the ground below. *That monster's not human!*

Lefebvre took a deep breath and tried to calm himself. Even if his men ended up being unable to overrun the airship, his steam cannon would soon arrive. When it did, there would be nothing those malcontents could do to win against him.

***

"You pulled us out of the fire again, Hubert!" Victor said, patting the giant on the back for the second time that hour.

Hubert grinned sheepishly and said in his deep voice, "It was nothing. You would have done the same for Hubert."

Victor laughed. "If I had your strength, maybe. There are a lot of things I would do if I had your strength."

"They won't give up that easily," Pierre said as he kicked some remaining cloth off the deck. "Everyone, stay sharp!"

Celeste suddenly poked her head out of the hatch. "Sir," she said, addressing Pierre, "I think I can restore enough energy to the ship to fire off one burst of electricity. You know, the kind that hit us back in the Austrian Netherlands."

Pierre considered this for a moment. "Which of these metal spikes along the hull would it fire out of?"

"I believe the ship would be able to discharge voltage from the spikes on either the bow or the stern. If we fired from the port or starboard sides, it would hit the buildings on either side of us, and the people hiding inside would likely be killed."

"All right. How soon can you get it ready?"

She rubbed her chin as she thought about it. "I would say about ten to fifteen minutes. However, if it starts raining, I would strongly advise against it. It might kill us all."

He thought about what she was saying. It would certainly be dangerous to fire off a barrage of lightning if it began to rain. If the clouds did open up and release a downpour on them, though, he decided they simply wouldn't use it. It was still a good idea to have it ready just in case. "Do it."

"Yes, sir!" With that, she disappeared back down the hatch.

***

Using her armored gauntlet, Jeanne punched through the boarded-up exit at the top of the ladder.

She and Farahilde had groped their way through the darkness of the cramped tunnel underneath the streets of Paris. To Jeanne, it was just like the last time she had blindly traversed an underground passage—namely, her adventure in the Bastille with Pierre and Victor. Fortunately, this time the tunnel wasn't threatening to collapse on top of her.

After walking for a while, they ran into a series of metal rungs which Jeanne realized was a ladder. Wanting to get out of this dark place as soon as possible, they opted to climb up it, which they did... until Jeanne hit her head on something at the top. Whatever it was, she wasn't about to let it halt their progress, and she punched through it.

They emerged in some sort of storage room filled with boxes. There was a light on the floor at the end of the room.

A door.

"It's locked," Jeanne said, trying the handle.

"Then there's only one thing for us to do, fräulein. One... two... three!"

They both kicked the door open, and a flood of light greeted them. Jeanne put her hand over her eyes. "After all that time in the dark..."

"I know what you mean." Once their eyes adjusted to the illumination, they were able to see where they were. "What is this place?"

"I don't believe it. This is the ball room at the Tuileries!" Jeanne said. The large room was exquisitely decorated with expensive paintings on the walls and magnificent crystal chandeliers hanging from the ceiling; it had definitely been furnished for royalty.

In addition, dozens of candles lined the walls, although none of them were lit. The room was instead being lit up by glass bulbs in the chandeliers. Farahilde noticed this. "Electricity?"

"Must be," Jeanne said. "Come on—see those doors at the far end of the room? Those lead directly to the central tower." They began walking towards the doors. With all the chairs stacked up along the walls, they had a clear path.

Clear, but not quiet. A familiar voice unexpectedly called out to them. "That they do. But you won't be walking through them." Up ahead on the right, from behind one of the ball room's two dozen marble columns emerged the man they had come here to stop.

However, it was the two women who stopped. "Robespierre!" Jeanne yelled. "You saved us the trouble of finding you."

Farahilde pointed at the figure in front of them. "That's him?"

"Yes."

He held his hands behind his back in a diplomatic stance. "Hmph. I never expected you to return here, Jeanne de Fleur. But once your airship went down, I knew you would have to come through this room to get to the central tower.

"Allow me to get to the point: There's no way for you to safely shut down the tower without knowing exactly how it works. If you tried it, the result would likely devastate Paris. So instead, why don't you join me in ushering in a new age for France?"

"Please," she said dismissively, "Spare me this speech; I've heard it before. Besides, after all you've done to us, it should come as no surprise to you that we are at this point beyond reason. Our only objective is stopping you, and the most convincing argument in the world isn't going to change our minds."

He rolled his eyes and sighed. "So be it, then. We'll just have to kill you and escort France into the future without you."

"Who's—"

Jeanne was about to say *Who's 'we'?* when Farahilde interrupted her. "Arschloch! You murdered meine schwester!" Without any further warning she charged towards Robespierre, her bladed gauntlet pointing right at him.

However, when she reached the column in front of him, there was a silver and black blur almost too fast for Jeanne's eyes to follow. Farahilde just managed to jump back in time to avoid being cloven by the downward swing of a large scythe.

Jeanne was shocked by how fast it happened. "What was that?"

A figure in a black dress stepped forward from behind the column in front of Robespierre. It was a blond woman with symmetrical pigtails who wore a bizarre white mask with a creepy smiley face painted in red.

"You missed, Marie," Robespierre said, sounding almost bored.

The strange woman said nothing. She simply grabbed the black handle of her scythe, and with an effort picked it up, removing the curved blade from the jagged hole in the floor it had caused. Once it was free, though, she hefted the six-foot weapon like it was nothing.

"Who are you? Get out of meine way!"

"Be careful, Farahilde. Whoever she is, she's no ordinary woman," Jeanne warned.

"You're right about that," Robespierre said, his face lit up by his smirk. "My dear Madame Tussaud has much experience ending lives with her scythe. You'd be surprised at the kind of talent going to waste in prisons everywhere. I dare say Marie is a match for even you, Jeanne de Fleur. However, it looks like she already has a plaything," he said, indicating Farahilde. "Don't worry, though; I have an opponent for you."

From behind the column opposite Madame Tussaud on the other side of the room emerged another familiar figure, drawing his saber. However, this one didn't surprise Jeanne. "I remember you. You fought with my brother at the battle of Mt. Erfunden... before you betrayed him—Napoléon Bonaparte!"

Napoléon stood there with a nonchalant air about him. "You are correct on both counts, Mademoiselle de Fleur. I fought alongside your brother until it no longer suited me, and then I ended our temporary alliance."

"'Temporary alliance'? You scum! Does honor and loyalty mean nothing to you?"

"And whom," he asked condescendingly, "should I be loyal to? A man I barely knew for a day, or the rightful ruler of France? Should I have fought a losing battle for the sake of your naïve sense of honor?"

Robespierre was clearly getting impatient with this discussion. "Enough talk. Marie, Napoléon—kill them."

But at that moment something unexpected happened. While Tussaud readied her scythe, Napoléon casually returned his saber to its scabbard and began walking towards the doors at the other end of the room which led to the rest of the palace.

"Napoléon! What are you doing?" Robespierre said, incredulous.

"You didn't give me a chance to answer Mademoiselle de Fleur's question." His eyes met Jeanne's. "I am loyal to *myself.*"

She was dumbfounded. "You're not going to fight me?"

He walked past her towards the door. "Weren't you listening when I turned against your brother? I see which way the winds blow, and I ride the currents to my ultimate destination."

"Which is?" she asked him.

He stopped, turned his head, and gave her an almost imperceptible grin. "*Emperor,*" he said emphatically. "If you kill Robespierre, I can step in and become the greatest ruler this country has ever seen." He continued towards the door.

Jeanne, however, was conflicted. It would be advantageous if she got through this without having to fight him. But... "You betrayed my brother. For all I know, you're the one who killed him!"

He replied smugly, "You are, of course, free to come at me. But do you really have the time?"

He was right; Jeanne didn't have the time to waste on him. "Go, then. But you'd better hope we never meet again, Monsieur Bonaparte."

Napoléon left without another word. As he walked through the doors behind Jeanne, Robespierre cursed him. "Bonaparte, you turncoat! When this is all over, you're going to wish for exile when I have you flayed alive!"

Unwilling to waste any more time listening to Robespierre's ranting, Jeanne removed her rapier and charged at him. Madame Tussaud tried to intercept her with a swing of her scythe, but Farahilde stepped in to catch its handle between the blades of her gauntlet.

Robespierre chose that moment to run away into the central tower. Struggling to hold back Tussaud, Farahilde yelled to Jeanne, "Go, fräulein! You've got to stop him. Don't let him destroy meine homeland!"

"But—"

"Just go! I'll deal with this one. Just make sure you leave a few breaths in Robespierre for me to extinguish."

"All right. No promises, though."

10

Jeanne ran through the doors and entered the central tower. The whole thing seemed to be one circular room hundreds of feet in diameter and hundreds of feet high. Varied machinery filled the room haphazardly, and thick cables ran the length of the floor in every direction; clearly aesthetics had not been a priority for this area. There weren't any windows in the tower, either. But like the ballroom, it was lit by glass bulbs along the wall.

In the center of the room, and taking up most of the floor, was some sort of bulky metal cylinder rising up about thirty feet. A set of curving stairs led up to the top of the cylinder.

Robespierre stood on top of the cylinder. "Bonaparte's betrayal won't save you, de Fleur! Come up here if you dare; this tower will be your mausoleum." Dozens of metal rods extended from the top of the cylinder to the open roof of the tower, where they supported a massive iron dish which was pointed north. Each rod was frothing with blue energy, and Robespierre gestured to them. "It won't be much longer now. I estimate that you only have about ten minutes before this tower reaches the maximum voltage needed to wipe out Vienna."

Jeanne, however, didn't need any more reason to charge up the stairs after him—she was already doing it. When she reached the top of the cylinder, she got a clearer view of it. It had a level floor, except for what looked like a small pool in the center which was filled with a red liquid. Robespierre was standing mere feet in front of her. "What on earth is that?"

"Why, it's the power source for all of this," Robespierre said.

"Power source?"

He nodded proudly. "Yes. Perhaps you remember your encounter with the Count of Saint-Germaine?"

"So, you admit you were the one who sent him after the royal family."

"It's a little late to be debating guilt now. Surely the Count showed you his special 'talent.'"

"Unfortunately. He used his blood to fuel his alchemy. Wait—you don't mean...!"

Robespierre's smile could have powered the tower by itself. "That's right: blood! My 'Reign of Terror' wasn't just to get rid of my enemies. It was also used to secure the life essence needed to realize my dreams. Airships, steam carriages, propellant, electrical towers; at our current level of technology, none of these can possibly exist without the alchemic techniques devised by the Count. The blood of my enemies runs underneath our feet, powering this tower." His smile abruptly twisted sadistically. "Even your brother's blood is in here."

"You monster!" Jeanne roared. She lunged at him with her rapier. He pulled out his own rapier and parried her attack. They performed a swift exchange of attacks with neither of them getting the immediate upper hand. Jeanne was surprised by his skill.

"You probably thought that as a politician, I'd be easy prey for you without anyone to defend me," he said. "But I have trained extensively to fight my own battles, should the need arise.

"You probably still think you're more than a match for me with your irodium armor. That's where you're wrong." He suddenly began grunting, his face turning red; it looked as if he struggling with some invisible foe.

Jeanne watched in horror as his clothing began to ripple, appearing almost liquid. Within moments it turned a dark gray and solidified into a solid once again. However, this time it was not simple fabric, but some sort of metal armor. Furthermore, it covered every inch of his body. She was fairly certain she knew what it meant. "You learned alchemy from the Count!"

He laughed from beneath the demonic horned mask that now covered his head. Even his voice sounded as if it was being projected by the devil himself. "Not just learned—*improved!* The Count emphasized style over substance. He wanted to terrify his victims, going so far as to use his own blood to turn himself into a monster. But I prefer functionality, which can be achieved without replacing my life essence with a cheap substitute."

"You think you're not a monster?" Jeanne said with absolute contempt. "Monsters are created through actions, and you've committed the most monstrous acts I've ever seen. But no more; I'm putting an end to you today!"

Robespierre laughed some more. "Then come at me, woman... if you think you can!"

***

In the middle of the ball room, Farahilde just barely managed to avoid Tussaud's scythe swings. The blonde woman was much stronger and faster than she looked, coming at Farahilde with a ferocious barrage of attacks. Furthermore, she seamlessly transitioned from a vertical swing to a horizontal one to a diagonal one, and every combination in between. It was as if her large weapon was as light as a dream feather.

Farahilde might have been able to deal with that if it weren't for the scythe's tremendous range. Trying to get in close was almost suicide with her small bladed gauntlet. To think that Farahilde had bragged to Jeanne about the advantage its short length back in the dungeon under her fort. *It has certainly come back to bite me in meine ass. If Fräulein could see me now, she'd probably laugh. I hope she's having better luck with that arschloch Robespierre.*

She was trying to think of a halfway-decent strategy when Tussaud charged in for another volley. Farahilde felt the sting of her curved blade when she failed to fully dodge the attacks. A vertical gash was cut into her left shoulder, along with a horizontal one across her stomach. "Meine clothes! You'll pay for that."

She wasn't expecting a response to her blustering. To her surprise, though, she got one. "Still."

"What was that? Can you actually talk?"

"Stand still," Tussaud said in a lifeless voice completely devoid of emotion. One might as well be ordered around by a steam engine, Farahilde thought.

"Why the hell should I do that?"

"Don't want to... accidentally... ruin your face."

That made absolutely no sense. Still, Farahilde wanted to prolong this break in the fighting. Maybe it would allow her to think of some way to fight this crazy woman. "What do you care about meine face? I know it is quite ravishing, but... Say, are you *that* kind of woman? Do I excite you? You should know that as Austrian royalty, I am probably engaged to some prince or another. I'm not of that persuasion, anyway."

Tussaud shook her head slowly, lethargically. "This one will need to make death mask. Can't be done properly if face is ruined."

"You're a strange one," Farahilde said. "I can't tell if you're a mere dummkopf or a full-blown lunatic. Still—"

But Tussaud was done talking. She rushed at Farahilde, who dove to the nearest wall and grabbed two chairs stacked up against it. Tussaud wasn't the only strong woman in this fight, and the young Austrian proved it (at least to herself) by hurling both chairs at the enigmatic blonde.

Tussaud sliced the first chair clean in half with a horizontal slash, but the second one belted her right in the midsection, causing her to stagger. Seeing that she was temporarily stunned, Farahilde ran at her and slashed at the French woman's throat with her gauntlet.

However, at that moment Tussaud recovered enough to leap back out of reach of Farahilde's attack. The Austrian only managed to break off a portion of the lower area of her mask, exposing the right side of her mouth.

As soon as Tussaud's feet hit the floor she swung her scythe down upon Farahilde's head, parting a bit of her hair. *Damn! That was too close. An inch more and the greatest doctors in Austria wouldn't be able to put meine head back together.*

Back to the proverbial drawing board, then.

***

The Ordre's volunteers were officially out of bullets and bombs. They had dropped dozens of Lefebvre's soldiers, but not all of those had been mortally wounded, and more kept coming. It was times like this that Pierre regretted the Ordre's lack of firearms. Sure, they upheld the romantic ideals of honor and chivalry, but couldn't they do that with guns?

Not that it would have mattered here. They were outnumbered too badly for a few more rifles to make much of a difference.

"They're out of ammunition. Charge!" Lefebvre yelled, safely out of range of any attacks. Pierre really wanted to go crush his windpipe, but that was not an option at the moment; Lefebvre was surrounded by too many armed troops. Pierre might be able to make it through all of them, but he doubted it. Even if he could, he was unwilling to abandon his comrades.

Lefebvre's troops heeded his command and ran to the *Minuit Solaire II.* Once there, they began climbing up the numerous metal spikes jutting out from the hull. Pierre and Victor had pulled up the ramp right after Jeanne and

Farahilde disembarked, but that wasn't going to stop the enemy from boarding them. "Get ready, men! Here they come!" Pierre announced.

At first the volunteers used the butts of their rifles to beat down the first wave of enemy troops. While this was initially successful, the soldiers soon adapted and stationed some of their comrades, who still had bullets left, on the ground to shoot at any man who stuck his head out from the deck.

"Stay back! You'll literally be sticking your neck out!" Victor said to the volunteers. He was standing on the starboard side.

Lefebvre's men were now climbing up the airship from all sides. Pierre was on the port side, hacking at upcoming enemies with his broadsword while using his free hand to shield his head from bullets. He imagined Victor was doing the same on the other side.

Half a dozen of Lefebvre's soldiers managed to climb aboard. They were met by the volunteers, who used their rifles as clubs to attack them. Unfortunately, the volunteers were up against men with military training, and they had to rely on their numbers to hold them off. Pierre knew full well that as more and more enemies boarded the airship's deck, the odds would continue to move in their favor.

As if that wasn't bad enough, movement out of the left corner of his eye alerted him to the reality of what he had feared ever since their forced landing: A steam cannon had now joined Lefebvre. One shot from that could end them all.

Celeste poked her head out from the hatch. "I know this isn't a good time, sir, but the *Minuit Solaire II* is ready to fire."

"Sounds like a damn good time to me," Pierre said as he punched out a member of the Gardes Francaises who tried to outflank him.

"Which direction do you want to fire from?"

For Pierre, that was a very easy decision. "The stern!"

She nodded. "Understood. Just remember that we'll only get one—"

"Just do it!"

"Yes, sir! She disappeared beneath the hatch. Pierre could only hope she launched the attack before Lefebvre's steam cannon fired.

The deck was crowded with bodies both friendly and hostile. There was so little room to maneuver that men kept getting knocked off. Lefebvre's men, as well as the Ordre's volunteers, repeatedly fell with a thud to the hard ground below. However, the former kept coming, and Pierre found himself with increasingly fewer allies in this fight.

A member of the Gardes Francaises suddenly went flying over his head, missing him by mere inches. He didn't have to look far to find the source of the airborne enemy. There was only one person he could see clearly in this melee. "Watch it, Hubert! You almost took my head off with that guy."

The giant stood somewhere between the aft and starboard side. "Sorry!" he said as several enemies tried to gang up on him. Pierre figured that was probably their only chance of beating him.

An explosion of crimson in Hubert's left shoulder, though, gave Pierre cause to regret that thought. They both looked up to see soldiers with rifles on the rooftops. *Damn Lefebvre's smarter than I thought. He's got sharpshooters!*

More bullets penetrated the giant's upper body from the rooftop riflemen. Nevertheless, this only seemed to anger him, and he took out this anger on his most immediate opponents. He thrashed, punched, and slammed heads together in a fury which, up to that point, Pierre had never seen out of him. It seemed nothing on earth could stop him.

That is, until another bullet hit him in the leg. Hubert finally succumbed to the punishment and dropped to his knees, at which point Pierre could no longer see him.

Pierre stole a quick glance back at the steam cannon. Super-heated water was blowing out the back of it, meaning it would be ready to fire at any moment.

The sight caused his resolve to drop as several thoughts raced through his head. Where was Celeste? Was this the end? There were still plenty of Lefebvre's subordinates on board, but somehow Pierre didn't think he was the kind of man who would let common decency stand in the way of victory.

At least we accomplished our mission; we held off the enemy long enough to give the Commander time to complete hers. I just wish... I just wish we could have had a future together. Farewell, Jeanne. Even if I die here, my memories of you will keep me alive wherever I end up.

***

"Status?" Lefebvre asked his subordinate who was manning the steam cannon. As he stood next to the steel carriage which carried the nearly one-ton cannon, he couldn't wait to celebrate his victory.

He could feel the steam emanating from the rear of the carriage. It was incredibly hot, but he didn't care; what he *really* felt was the accolades he would receive from destroying the remnants of the Ordre.

"We can fire any time," the subordinate said.

"Fi—" Lefebvre started to say. His one word was cut short by the sight up the street ahead of them. The strange metal spikes on the rear of the Ordre's airship had begun glowing blue. This reminded him of something he had heard and quickly dismissed because he didn't think it concerned him.

After the Ordre returned from their rescue mission in the Austrian Netherlands, he had heard talk of the Austrian airship they had encountered over there.

Supposedly it had metal spikes along its hull which glowed blue when they were about to fire lightning at the enemy.

Now, he realized, he was dealing with the same model of airship. To make matters worse, it had not been completely crippled as he had assumed. And it was about to unleash an ungodly amount of voltage on him.

These thoughts bombarded him in the space of a mere moment. "Fire!" he frantically screamed with all the urgency he could muster. "Firefirefirefirefirefire!"

The events of the next few moments occurred too quickly for Lefebvre's mind to fully process. With a deafening explosion, the steam cannon rocketed its massive shell towards the Ordre's airship. At that precise instant, a barrage of blue energy erupted from the rear of the vessel. The beams of electricity hurled unrestrained towards Lefebvre, his men and the steam cannon. The onslaught was so intense that it tore large chunks of solid ground from the area directly in front of it, and the sizeable debris went right along with it.

The beams then came into contact with the shell, and, although it was a solid object, it had little effect on the energy currents, and they simply curved around it and kept going.

The shell, too, kept going and within a split-second came into contact with the chunks of the ground that had just been ripped out. The two forces collided, and the shell won, barreling through the debris on its way to the Ordre's airship.

Lefebvre's mind took note of all these things, but did not have time to convey them consciously before the barrage of electricity charred his body beyond recognition.

***

"Everyone, get down! That steam cannon's going to fire!" Pierre yelled as loud as he could to get everyone's attention.

"Don't listen to him!" the enemy soldier nearest Pierre said. "He's just—" But then steam began rising out of the carriage. "No! Lefebvre really is going to fire on us!"

Everyone hit the deck and tried to grab on to something. Pierre grabbed the deck's railing and held on tight. Several of Lefebvre's men actually jumped to the ground below in an attempt to avoid the destruction that was coming, breaking bones in the process.

At that moment he a hum and a faint blue glow emanated from beyond the stern. *Please, God—let that be what I think it is.* The airship was then rocked by the firing of its strange energy system.

At about that same instant, the steam cannon fired. A tremendous explosion sent him flying across the deck. He tried to hang on to the railing—but it came with him!

Moments (or minutes) later, he found himself lying on top of someone, with a crippling ringing in his ears. One of the soldiers had broken his fall, for which he was grateful.

The deck seemed to be mostly intact, only missing sections of railing. Everyone waited a minute to see if there would be another explosion, or if the whole thing would collapse under them. When it didn't, they all got to their feet, friends and enemies alike.

Pierre was now in the deck's center. "Is everyone all right?" He asked, although he was not really sure why since he was mostly surrounded by enemies. By now the ringing had died down for the most part.

"Unh. I think so," Victor said from across the deck. He was rubbing the back of his head which bled slightly.

Lefebvre's men, it seemed, were no longer in the mood to fight. "I can't believe that bastard! He really fired on us—his own men!" one of them said.

"We should have never followed his orders," agreed another.

A third one said to Pierre, "I think... we owe you an apology. We were fighting for the wrong side today."

"I guess we can't really blame you," Pierre said. "We've followed our share of orders over the years. I'm just glad we don't have to fight anymore."

He looked towards the blackened area where Lefebvre had been standing. The steam cannon had exploded, leaving twisted metal and blackened ash all over the place. There were charred pieces of what looked like body parts strewn about, but Pierre couldn't be sure what they were.

Suddenly Victor cried out, "Hubert!" Pierre ran over to the starboard side where Victor was leaning over the edge, looking at something down below. When he got there, the sight of the giant's massive form on the ground bleeding profusely from many wounds greeted him. Hubert's tree trunk-like left leg was bent at an unnatural angle, probably from the fall.

"He must have gotten knocked off when the shell hit us," Victor said.

Pierre and Victor lowered the ramp and went down to check on Hubert. Pierre knew it was pointless; the giant had clearly lost too much blood from injuries made much worse by his fall. Still, they had to do *something* so they could at least say they tried when Jeanne came back and wanted to know what happened.

As they both expected, they found no pulse on the big man. What Jeanne had feared had now come to pass. "He saved all of us up there," Victor said.

"Yeah."

"He's a hero."

"I just wish he could go home and tell everyone that himself."

The two of them carried Hubert's body up to the deck. Everyone up there—even Lefebvre's men—paid their respects to the deceased giant.

Celeste then poked her head out of the hatch. "Is the fighting over?" Her glasses were cracked and one of the lenses was missing.

"For us, at least," Victor replied.

Pierre walked over to her. "That shell should have destroyed us. Why didn't it?"

She shrugged. "The only thing I can think of is that our attack must have slowed it down just enough so it didn't have the velocity."

"Doesn't matter to me how we lived," Victor said.

"Come on, Victor; we have to get over to the Tuileries and help the Commander," Pierre said.

"I wouldn't recommend that," Celeste said.

Pierre spun around to face her, shocked by what she had just said. "'Wouldn't recommend' it? It's the Commander we're talking about! We have to help her."

Celeste shook her head and pointed to the central tower. "With all due respect, sir... I don't think we can."

Pierre turned around and looked at the tower. By now the electrical currents completely covered it; crackling blue energy ran the complete length of the tower and was even striking the ground around the palace.

"If we try to go in there, we'll get electrocuted," Victor realized.

The young engineer's eyes were getting moist. "The Commander is my idol. She's everything I want to be," she said. "But you all are also important. Please don't throw your lives away."

As much as he wanted to, Pierre couldn't argue with her logic. Trying to save Jeanne would be a suicide mission. He could only hope that Farahilde would see her through this.

It was at that moment that a single drop of rain hit his head. "Time's running out," he said, despair creeping into his voice.

11

Tussaud's scythe created sparks as it traced a horizontal slash along the wall where Farahilde's head had been a split second before. Farahilde ducked the attack and slashed at her with her gauntlet. But once again, Tussaud proved to be just a step faster, and sidestepped the attack while simultaneously bringing down her blade in an attempt to split the young Austrian in half. Farahilde barely managed to get out of the way; the scythe gave her collarbone a superficial cut.

This is one fräulein I really cannot stand. Her oversized blade has not yet managed to find its mark, but she keeps getting closer and it's only a matter of time. Meanwhile, I haven't been able to cut her at all. Meine gauntlet simply doesn't have the range to get to her... Wait a minute! I just thought of something.

Farahilde dashed to the opposite wall with Tussaud right behind her. While running, she frantically (and painfully) grappled with one of the blades on her gauntlet.

When she reached the wall, she grabbed another chair with her gauntlet hand and threw it at Tussaud. The blonde woman, however, wasn't about to fall for that again. She easily pirouetted around the piece of furniture and readied her scythe for another swing at Farahilde.

However, for a split second Tussaud was open, and Farahilde wasted absolutely no time taking advantage of this, throwing the blade she had pried from her gauntlet into her enemy's midsection. She didn't have time to aim—she simply let it fly. The razor-like object imbedded itself just below Tussaud's left breast.

Tussaud staggered back, but—true to form—not a sound escaped her lips.

"How did you like that, *weibchen?*" Farahilde crowed. Her right hand bled from having grabbed the sharp implement directly, but she could deal with the discomfort. "Still want to continue?"

Tussaud stared at the blade sticking out of her body for a few moments, then casually grabbed it and ripped it out. Her head flinched slightly at the pain, but otherwise she showed no aversion to the act she just committed.

Dammit. The blade was too slippery from meine own blood for me to throw it with full force. Well... I've still got another blade on meine gauntlet, and this woman should be hurt enough to have lost a step.

Not quite.

Tussaud dropped the small blade and resumed her attack with full force. Farahilde tried to jump out of the way, but it seemed her luck had finally run out. The scythe carved a serious gash down half of her upper body.

She suddenly felt cold, as if Tussaud's curved blade had somehow sucked all the warmth from her body. She fell to the ground at Tussaud's feet, being able only to weakly put out her right hand to break the fall.

"Good. Your face is undamaged," Tussaud said. Her voice still conveyed no feeling.

She gripped the handle of her weapon to pick it up... but found she couldn't. The blade was imbedded in the floor again, and her right hand was wet with blood because she, too, had grabbed the sharp edge of Farahilde's makeshift projectile when she ripped it from her midsection. Thus, she couldn't get a good grip on her own weapon, and it remained stubbornly resting in the floor.

This presented an opportunity—her enemy was presently unarmed—but Tussaud might as well have been on the moon for all the good it did her. Farahilde was shaking from the cold caused by the blood loss, the shock, or both; how could she possibly take advantage of this.

"You will make a good death mask, just like the queen," Tussaud said.

Had she heard that right? "What did you just say?"

"The queen. This one made a death mask from her severed head. It was still bleeding."

The coldness suddenly left Farahilde. There was no longer any pain—only a furious desire to cut flesh. Summoning all the strength she had left (while possibly creating new strength), she began to rise. First to one knee, then to the next. Then to one leg.

"Stay down," Tussaud said. Farahilde ignored her and made it to her feet. However, the young Austrian's energy failed her, and she collapsed onto the handle of the scythe, which Tussaud was still clutching. She held on to it to remain somewhat upright. "Do you see? It is fruitless. This one will kill you in the name of Lord Robespierre."

Upon hearing his name, Farahilde found herself with one last burst of energy. Seizing, it, she roared and plunged her remaining blade into Tussaud's heart. While she couldn't see most of her face behind the mask, she could *feel* the homicidal French woman's surprise.

Tussaud coughed up fresh blood, most of which was blocked by her mask. "No... must get... mask." With that, she fell backwards onto the floor, which was being painted a fresh shade of crimson beneath her.

"*Der Teufel wartet auf dich,*" Farahilde said. *The devil is waiting for you.* She then sat down against the nearest column.

What was she to do now? She had won her battle, but she didn't feel like her work was finished yet. She knew she wouldn't have enough energy to go into the central tower and get her revenge on Robespierre. She'd be lucky to get out of this room alive. *If I ever want to get back to meine Austria, I'd better lay low and try to find someone—a doctor, maybe—to heal me. That might be difficult, but I've gotten through worse situations.*

That would mean forgoing her revenge on Robespierre, but what the hell—Jeanne had just as much right to kill him as she did.

Although there wasn't much time left, part of her hoped Jeanne would kill him slowly.

12

Jeanne struggled to gain the upper hand on Robespierre atop the cylinder in the central tower, but it was a futile effort; he was nearly as skilled as herself, and every inch of his body was covered by armor. At this rate, she didn't see how she could defeat him in the precious few minutes she had left.

"I'm merely playing with you, you know," he said from behind his demonic visage as he lunged at her with his rapier. "I don't even *have* to fight you at this point. It's not like you can even hurt me."

She deftly performed a fencing technique called a *pasatta-sotto*, hitting the floor with her hand and ducking under his attack. She thrust at his torso, but as she expected, her blade could not penetrate his alchemically-created armor.

He laughed at the pointless exercise, and then retreated into *en garde* position. Under other circumstances he would have been a fool to not take advantage of his opponent's mistake, but time was on his side. Jeanne had to defeat him; he did not have to defeat *her*.

She wasn't in the mood to trade words with him at this point. Instead, she initiated an *attaque au fer*, pressing her sword against his. She pretended to try and match him in strength, but in actuality this was a *coulé*, a feint. She slid along his rapier, gaining her leverage which she used to force his blade downwards. She ended this with a savage kick to his armored stomach, sending him reeling backwards into one of the electrified rods which she hoped would find his metal hide a worthy conductor.

He hit the rod, cracking it and causing it to send out a hail of sparks. However, it wasn't the effect she was looking for. While it did send blue energy through his armor, it seemed to only stun him for a moment. "Nice try," he said. "But did you really think I'd fight you in this environment without a means of defending myself from all the voltage in here? My armor is insulated. You may not know that word, but it means I'm hardened against electricity."

Jeanne felt frustration setting in. She knew she had to fight it; frustration would make it impossible to come up with a strategy for beating Robespierre in time. *Looks like I have no choice.*

She reached to her eye patch so she could use her God's Eye. It had been so long since she had needed to do so that she had almost forgotten its usefulness. She received an unpleasant surprise, though, when something wet suddenly hit her on the head.

It was beginning to rain. "Robespierre! You have to shut this thing down now! There's no telling what rain could do if you fire off that dish!"

Robespierre, however, continued to laugh at what he perceived as another of her futile attempts to stop him. "Even if I wanted to, I couldn't. Doing so at this point would cause a catastrophic overload, wiping out a large portion of the city."

"I'll have to take that risk, then." She went to remove her eye patch.

Without warning, though, Robespierre suddenly lunged at her. "I won't let you use your God's Eye!" He unleashed a flurry of strikes that she did her best to parry, but he was employing a technique called *prise de fer*, pressuring her blade to keep her from maintaining control of it.

She was forced backwards towards the center of the cylinder and the blood pool. Completely on the defensive, it was all she could do to keep from being completely overwhelmed.

She soon ended up a few feet from the blood pool. With a final push, Robespierre managed to wrest Jeanne's rapier away from her, sending it sliding across the top of the cylinder, eventually falling off the edge.

He then backhanded her across the face and, to add injury to insult, he ran his rapier through her shoulder. It pierced her irodium armor like it wasn't even there.

She staggered back to the edge of the blood pool. Crimson essence fell from her wound into it, joining with the blood of countless others.

Robespierre laughed again, harder than ever this time. "What do you think of my custom rapier, made impossibly sharp by alchemy?" he boasted. "How ironic! You came to shut down this tower, and now you have just added to its power." The entire tower began to rumble. The electricity flowing up the dozens of rods on top of the cylinder increased dramatically, and the rods themselves started to shake. "We only have a minute or so until Vienna is annihilated. The dish is already pointed towards that city. Would you like me to tell you the secret to how exactly all that blood will make it possible?"

"What do you mean?" The effort to speak caused Jeanne to wince from the pain in her shoulder.

"It's something the Count taught me. There is *power* in blood."

"Power?"

The demonic head nodded. "Yes—power! The blood contains the true essence of a person, and that essence holds their will. Because of that, it can do amazing things."

That didn't make sense to Jeanne. "Then, why is it doing your bidding?"

"Because," he said, "there are so many individual wills in there that it's all become a confusing mass of voices. They have no leader, so they just do what I tell them."

Jeanne thought about it. If what he said was true, there was still a slight chance she could pull this off.

She knelt down and, using the extreme concentration she normally reserved for the God's Eye, she focused all her attention on her will. What she *wanted*, and what she *desired*.

***

"It's no use praying," Robespierre said as he watched Jeanne kneeling beside the blood receptacle. As far as he was concerned, prayer was the last resort of the desperate, of people who had given up. Not that he could blame her for surrendering to the hopelessness of her situation.

At that moment, though, strange things began to happen. First, the blood in the receptacle began to churn. It was only minor at first, but then it began to bubble enough to escape the receptacle in small drops.

Second, the electricity running through the rods abruptly stopped.

"What the hell is this?" he exclaimed, his heartbeat speeding up. He could feel himself starting to sweat underneath his armor.

Jeanne suddenly broke her prayer and locked her eye on him. "*My will.*"

"No—that's impossible! No one is strong enough to—"

He didn't get the chance to finish his expression of disbelief, because at that instant the rods facing him lit back up with blue energy. This was followed by a massive surge in his direction, all the rods in front of him focusing on his demonic form.

He didn't feel anything. He didn't even realize he had been lifted off his feet until he was well in the air.

***

Jeanne watched with supreme satisfaction as the rods' voltage was bent to her will—thanks to the power of all the blood in the pool—and rocketed into Robespierre, lighting him up with a near-blinding brilliance. She savored every moment of seeing him hurled through the air.

He landed on the top of the stairs of the cylinder. His momentum then caused him to roll helplessly down them. She didn't have time to check to see if he was still alive, though, as there was still a job she needed to finish.

Still kneeling, she focused all her willpower on the massive dish looming above. There was only one command she wished to give it: *move.*

She focused on that thought with everything she had, until her head began to hurt. Finally, though, her directive was heeded: The electricity somehow rotated the dish upwards. Away from any country or city.

Now!

With an overwhelming blast the dish released all its electricity into the sky. Jeanne had to cover her eyes because it was far too intense. Not only that, but the entire tower shook from the discharge.

***

"Look at that!" Victor shouted. From the deck of the *Minuit Solaire II*, they all watched as a brilliant flash of light erupted from the dish atop the central tower. Following that, all signs of electricity on the tower immediately disappeared.

"That was supposed to hit Vienna, right?" Celeste asked with hope in her voice. "Milady did it, didn't she?"

"I sure hope so," Pierre said cautiously. He didn't want to start celebrating, just in case it wasn't over yet.

Almost at the same moment he said it, it began to rain in full. It was a complete downpour. If it had come just a minute earlier, there was no telling what kind of damage might have been done.

Everyone on the deck began to cheer. There was no doubt in their minds that disaster had been averted. Pierre didn't have the heart to point out that even if that was the case, what would France do now that so much of the country's resources had been invested in the Alset Project?

For now, he had only one priority. "Let's get in there and find the Commander!"

***

Jeanne reached the bottom of the cylinder's stairs, her shoulder hurting from the wound Robespierre had inflicted on it, and found him gone. Somehow, he must have still had the strength to escape. She wasn't worried; if he went out the way she had come in, then Farahilde would take care of it. Instead of hurrying after him, she went to retrieve her rapier.

But when she went back into the ballroom, she found neither of them. Only the bloody corpse of Madam Tussaud remained.

There was, however, a trail of small metal pieces leading out of the ballroom. Jeanne guessed it was from Robespierre's alchemically-created armor; it was probably falling apart from the voltage it had absorbed. She just needed to follow it to him before he ran out of pieces to drop.

***

Naked, and still largely numb from the blast that damned woman had hit him with, Robespierre limped to the front entrance of the Tuileries.

Despite everything that had happened, he counted himself lucky he had evacuated the palace as soon as the Ordre invaded with their airship. There was no one around to see him in this humiliating state.

I was so close to saving France, he lamented. *Now it's all come to nothing! That chienne has cost me everything. Why, God? Why didn't you stop her? Have you forsaken this once-great country?*

When he reached the front doors, he reached out his one hand that could still move and fumbled with the knob. After several aggravating moments he managed to get the door open, and stepped outside into the large square in front of the palace.

Where everyone was waiting.

He gaped at the huge mob. Despite the rain, it seemed all of Paris had come out to see what was going on. As a result, he stood there in his wet shame.

"It's Robespierre!"

"He doesn't look so tough now!"

"Not only that, he forgot to put on clothes!"

The crowd was wet, and they were cold, but for the first time in ages, the people of Paris shared a laugh. "Why did we ever listen to this guy?" one of them said.

Another one answered, "We were fools."

"He's right. We turned our backs on the Ordre because we believed what this lunatic said."

Robespierre couldn't take the ridicule; he couldn't take them making a mockery of him as if he wasn't even there. "Stop it!" he shouted, while doing his best to keep his manhood covered. "I am your leader! You will show me respect!" To this they erupted in hearty laughter.

A voice behind him then said, in the most condescending tone possible, "It's over, *Monsieur* Robespierre." He turned around to see Jeanne de Fleur standing in the doorway. She had her rapier pointed at him.

The crowd was astonished at her appearance. "Jeanne la Juste!" they shouted, followed by pleas for her to forgive them for betraying her.

He let out a heavy sigh. He was defeated; he could not deny that. With nothing left for him, he dropped to his knees.

***

"Get it over with," Robespierre said. Jeanne had waited what seemed like eons for this moment.

She pointed her blade at his black heart, the tip drawing blood from his exposed flesh. She wanted to kill him. She wanted to kill him so bad she couldn't think about anything else. The thought of taking him down had been the only thing keeping her alive up to this point.

But was that really the way to live one's life?

"Any last words?" she asked him.

He looked up at her with the most pitiful expression she had ever seen. "What I did, I did for the good of France."

She didn't know what to think of that. Perhaps, in his own twisted way, he had truly believed in the path he walked. But there was no possible to way to justify that, no way to make it up to everyone he had butchered to achieve his goals.

So, she stood there gripping the handle of her rapier. Her hand shook, and she found it exceedingly difficult to make the final strike which would end him. Why?

Her thoughts went back to a moment ago. Was living to be an executioner really the right course her life should take? Shouldn't humans be better than that?

It was at that moment in which she realized the answer, why she had been destined to arrive at this point in this situation.

"No," she finally said. "I will let the people of Paris decide your fate."

She sheathed her rapier and walked past him, into the rain. He called after her. "What are you doing? I took everything from you! You should stab me a thousand times over and still not be satisfied!"

She stopped and looked over her shoulder at him. "If you want to die so badly, I'm sure it can be arranged. But know this: The true power of the human spirit is in living when all you want is death." She realized the irony of her statement, but she didn't care. Whether or not it was what God had had in mind for this moment, at least it was what she believed.

With that, she left. The crowd parted to let her through.

13

The London Thames
"French Revolution Comes to Surprising End"
by Robert Westerfield

As many of you know, I have been gone for several months. I was in France observing the country's civil unrest. I have now returned home to London, and for the next several issues I will be sharing my experiences with you.

There are many stories about what happened during France's revolution, but one especially demands to be told to this publication's readers. And as I made a promise, I will tell you that story right now. It is the story of Jeanne de Fleur.

de Fleur, a noblewoman, served King Louis XVI for many years as a soldier. Sadly, that ended when both the king and his wife, France's queen Marie Antoinette, were beheaded during an uprising. Miss de Fleur was heartbroken at the loss of those she served so faithfully. Not only that, but her brother was also killed that same day. As a result, she left to live in solitude for six months.

Then one fateful day this reporter sought her out, and she told me her story. It was terrible; she had absolutely nothing to live for. She was simply living.

I left her shack in the wilds, not knowing if telling her story would help her. I sincerely doubted I would ever see her again.

However, that all changed on May 3. de Fleur reappeared and, with a small band of allies, entered Paris and overthrew France's de facto ruler, Maximilien Robespierre.

I happened to be in the city at the time, and had the most remarkable experience of seeing this firsthand.

When it was over, de Fleur had Robespierre on his knees begging her to finish what she had started. Despite the crowd inciting her to do it, though, she flatly refused. "If you want to die so badly, I'm sure it can be arranged. But know this: The true power of the human spirit is in living when all you want is death," she said as she left the area.

I tried to get a word with her, but was unable to make it through the large crowd, and I do not know where she went. The only trace I found was a purple eye patch which had been dropped on the ground nearby. Mademoiselle de Fleur was known to have worn such an eye patch.

Here is a woman who had everything taken from her, with nothing to live for, yet somehow managed to come back and fight for what she believed in. Not only that, but she declined the opportunity to kill the man who had destroyed her life. Jeanne de Fleur has shown everyone the power of the human spirit.

EPILOGUE

Robespierre sat helpless in his prisoner's clothes, with his arms shackled and his head secured in the guillotine at the Place de Revolution. A large crowd was gathered to watch the spectacle. He didn't need anyone to point out the irony.

Napoléon Bonaparte, that traitorous wretch who had stepped in and taken control after his arrest, stood in front of him. Bonaparte now wore a more ornate blue and white outfit to signify his newfound authority over France. "Maximilien Robespierre, you have been found guilty of treason and mass murder by a tribunal of your peers. You will now be put to death by beheading."

"You think you'll do any better than me, you turncoat?" Robespierre spat.

"That is not the issue here," he replied curtly. To the man working the guillotine, he said, "Do it."

The man pulled the lever, but nothing happened. He tried again and again, with the same result. "It's stuck."

"The people demand his death," Napoléon said impatiently. "If you won't get it done, I'll find someone who will."

Suddenly, a voice behind Robespierre said, "Perhaps I can help you with that."

Napoléon looked at whoever had said that with annoyance. "What do *you* want?"

Someone (presumably the mysterious speaker) put a hand on Robespierre's shoulder. "I just want to repay a debt to meine friend here."

On conclut l'histoire.

What do you think?
Review this book online and help readers to make better purchases.

Also, sign up for my newsletter to receive exclusive content and get news/reveals before anyone else.

www.authorscottkinkade.com

Also by Scott Kinkade

God School (Divine Protector #1)

18-year-old Ev Bannen was just hoping to get admitted to college. He never expected to be recruited to a school for gods, where he'll be spending his days building up his strength, learning to answer prayers and getting an education in religion alongside aspiring god of money Jaysin Marx, the lovely but troubled Maya Brünhart and anger-prone ginger Daryn Anders. But when the world is threatened, Ev must step up to save the day.

Published December 9, 2014.

Amazon US: https://tinyurl.com/y9vy5xsy

Amazon UK: https://tinyurl.com/yaxu6mdq

Amazon CA: https://tinyurl.com/y7htn9ly

Made in the USA
Columbia, SC
14 June 2022

61694333R00163